ROCKSTAR DADDY

WILDER MIND BOOK 1

TARYN QUINN

Rockstar Daddy
© 2017 Taryn Quinn
Cover by LateNite Designs
ISBN: 978-1-940346-46-5

First print edition: Taryn Quinn June 2017
Rainbow Rage Publishing

For those who live in the super snowy places in the world. This is for you.

1

KELLAN

Fucking blizzard.

Again.

Why was I even surprised?

I was the jackass who had grown up on the outskirts of Turnbull, New York, snow capital of the northeast, and had escaped to sunny LA only to return.

Voluntarily.

No one had held a gun to my head or shackled my wrists. Nope, I'd strapped my surfboard to the roof of my SUV and made the trek home to buy property on the very edge of town. Outside of town, truth be told. Because the icy tundra in the city proper—ha ha—wasn't enough for me. Might as well build a damn shack with my own two hands and surround it with pine trees and solitude.

So much freaking solitude.

True, it was just my vacation home. Cue more laughter. My place to escape from the rigors of being a famous rockstar.

At least the rockstar part was right. In my head if nowhere else. The famous? Working on that. Wilder Mind's first single was due to drop just after the holidays, and our manager, Lila Crandall, was prepping us for the big time. A lot of that was smoke and mirrors designed to build us up into being the showmen we weren't quite yet, but under her bluster, there was a kernel of truth.

Wilder Mind was poised to take on the world.

Me? I was poised to chop some wood so I could hole up in my cabin and spend New Year's Eve soaking up the silence.

No other company. No other voices. Especially no incessant interview questions or even the shrill scream of fans. Not that we'd dealt with much of that yet. Only a taste. A hint of things to come if we were lucky enough to make it big.

In the meantime, it would be just me and my old Taylor acoustic, a roaring fire, and a case of Coors.

Hey, I never said I had highbrow tastes. So sue me.

Blowing out a breath, I heaved the ax through the chilly air, savoring the pleasant burn in my muscles. I was chopping way more wood than I'd need for a weekend at the cabin. If I was lucky, I'd make it back to Turnbull a few times over the winter. With the single dropping, we'd be branching out. Spreading out to do shows some distance from LA, which meant all the press that went with that. I'd be talking myself hoarse before I was expected to go up and bleed out onstage for the price of a ticket.

That was my role. My *new* role. The one I'd craved since I was a kid with a cheap thrift store guitar, a joint in my back pocket, and the requisite amount of teenage angst that made me think I could be a great songwriter.

Now I was getting my shot, and the battered composition notebook I'd been lugging around for years—first in backpacks, then in briefcases during my brief stint working at Ripper Records—was definitely getting a workout.

Just like my arms. I slammed the axe into the snowpack and threw back my head. Shit. The chill seared my lungs, yanking out my breath in icy puffs. And I still wasn't smart enough to go inside.

Nope, I kept splitting logs, continuing until the overcast afternoon turned into dusk. The foggy dark hung in ribbons of mist around my forest, and I didn't stop until the distant cry of a lonely coyote made me think maybe it was time for that fire.

We didn't get a lot of coyotes out this way, but we had some. In this much dense forestation, you got quite the range of creatures. Even the occasional black bear. My mom had told stories about one coming up to the back door and rattling the knob of her folks' old ramshackle place, but I had to think that was bullshit.

Maybe I just hoped it. If a frigging bear couldn't just break down a door, fuck the rest of us who rued being so goddamn polite all the time.

Still, much as I lobbied for the rights of bears and coyotes, I wasn't stupid enough to be whaling on logs after dark. Not when I had a twelve-pack and a hot shower waiting for my sore ass.

"Getting soft," I muttered after stowing the axe and piling up the wood to haul inside.

I grunted as I made my way around the side of the cabin in the knee-deep snow, part of a cord of wood in my arms. Obviously, I needed to hit the gym harder before Wilder Mind went out on tour. My body freaking hurt. I was covered in sweat. Probably looked like a frigging maniac with snow sticking to my beardy face.

I jumped around night after night onstage in closet-sized clubs and bars, but I wasn't as hardy as when I'd lived in good old Turnbull full-time. Back when I'd worked on cars and picked up odd construction jobs to get by.

It had been blind luck and a dose of small town friendliness that had even gotten my ass out to LA. Lila's mom and pop ran the local orchard, and my mom had gotten to talking to Lila's mother one day about how I didn't want to be stuck working construction for the rest of my life. One thing led to another and under six months later, I'd been on a plane out to LA to meet with Donovan Lewis, the head of the record label Lila worked for. We hit it off and though I didn't know shit about selling anything that didn't come in a bucket or wrapped in cellophane, I'd ended up as an account rep.

Representing artists. Me. The guy who'd barely graduated high school but could schmooze a quart a milk out of a cow. Or so my mom had claimed to Lila's mother.

Because a way with cows surely meant a way with egotistical, often drugged out musicians. Right.

Somehow it had worked though. Lila said I had a knack. Donovan had given me raises. A bunch of them, in short succession. The mogul some jokingly referred to as Lord Lewis didn't shortchange his talent, and he'd seen something in me. I owed him and Lila a shit-ton of gratitude. First, for hiring me to represent some of their musical acts, and then for trusting me to front a band.

The band part I had more familiarity with. I'd been stroking an acoustic long before I'd stroked my first girl. Let's just say I'd done my share of touching both, and leave it at that.

One more thing about Turnbull? They had some damn fine women, but it was hard to see them clearly under all the layers of outerwear when it snowed for what felt like half the freaking year. I preferred California women anyway. They seemed more good-natured as a rule. Maybe all the sunshine and hot temperatures put them in a better mood.

And goddammit, I loved me a woman in a bikini.

When I reached the front of my property and heard the squeal of tires, I didn't react fast enough. Put the image of a half-naked, tanned woman in the mind of a man who'd nearly frozen his nuts off and who wouldn't miss a car fishtailing off the road?

Right into my ditch.

Tires spun, spewing up snow and dirt and tiny rocks, and a horn went off about sixteen times. And I stared, my wood in my arms. Shocked as hell that anyone had even come down this practically deserted road in the first place, never mind took the curve way too fast and gone ass up in the ditch.

The chick was now attempting to shimmy her way out of the driver's side window. Painfully. With no shortage of groans and screeches and noises no adult female should ever make.

Since she was moving—and frantically at that—I had to figure she couldn't be too badly injured. Still, she could have done harm to herself she'd yet to realize.

With more than a small sigh, I set down the wood on the short set of steps to the cabin, brushed off my hands on the thighs of my sweats, and trudged down the snowy hill to where the squealing damsel's car was lodged.

She turned her neck and gave me the biggest, brightest smile I'd ever seen. I was a little taken aback, since she was half in and half out of a window and her car was fucked up, if not totaled. It appeared to be an older model under the snow and grime, and an accident like hers could screw up the frame. If that happened, the vehicle was shot.

Not that she seemed worried overmuch.

"Hi!" she called over the rushing wind, her voice as cheerful as her expression. "Thank God for you."

I didn't know how to respond to that, so I came around the ditch and eyed her lopsided car. "Yep, well and truly stuck."

She blinked at me from under the pink fringe of a stocking cap. "It's just a little fender bender."

"Oh yeah? Then why are you climbing out of the window?"

She wiggled. "Because the door won't open."

"Seems a bit worse than a fender bender to me." I came around the driver's side, hooked my hands under her armpits in her heavy down coat, and simply plucked her out of the car.

Only afterward did I think of possible internal injuries. Though what possible injury could've allowed her to jump and dance around now that she'd been freed, I did not know.

The other thing I noticed about her right away? She was dressed as if she was in competition with the Michelin man, except her bulk was made out of layers. Many layers. She had earmuffs under her hat to go with her bulky scarf, huge coat, ski pants—likely layered over thermals—and some serious freaking boots with enough snaps and ties to secure a horse.

And yet she was still jumping around, blowing on her gloved fingers, and laughing like a crazy person.

"Whoa, that was nuts. I seriously feared for my life. I saw Jesus and heard angels and all that stuff." She frowned at her car with its likely bent axel. "I paid extra for the best snow tires. I still skidded. That seems like a warranty violation. Don't you think?"

What I thought was this chick was going to talk my head off.

"The forecast predicted two feet today. Typical lake effect. Are you not from around here?" Though it was hard to believe someone from a warmer climate would've been that well-prepared, but maybe. They did tend to have thinner blood than us hardy northern types.

Though what the hell was I saying? I was a California boy now too.

Happily.

I'd never actually heard someone roll their eyes at me before, but her disgust was palpable. "Hello, look at me. Do I seem unprepared for this weather? If anything, I *over*prepared. In my trunk, I have a spare battery kit, a First-Aid kit, a tire repair kit and—"

"Lady, I got it. You're prepared. You just spun out. It happens."

She propped her hands on her hips. Or at least where I figured her hips would be. Hard to tell with her coat.

"Very pragmatic of you, buddy, but now what? I'm stuck and I need to get to Mrs. Pringles' before she goes to New Year's Eve mass. This is her first year without her husband, and she puts on a brave face, but she and Joe were so in love. It was sweet to see, really. And if I can't get there before mass, then I'll have to wait until she gets back, or worse yet, go join her in the church, which would be okay except I kind of got ex-communicated last year."

I wiped away the flakes collecting on my face. I would've hoped my expression coupled with how I looked might've intimidated her—

big, burly, bearded—but if anything fazed this one, it wasn't me glaring at her during her endless monologue.

"I'm sure I'll regret asking this, but why, exactly, do you need to go to grandmother's house?"

She brushed snow off the arms of her coat. It was coming down faster than she could efficiently whisk it away. "Oh, she's not my grandmother—"

"That was a joke, Red." I gestured toward her attire. Red and pink everything, which didn't go together but somehow seemed to suit her. "You also have a car instead of a basket, but let me mix a metaphor or two."

"Ah. Big bad wolf, is it then? Sorry, you don't seem to fit." She marched toward me and grasped the side of my pants. "Wile E. Coyote sweats aren't exactly scary, tough guy."

"Don't touch," I growled and that made her step back and cock her head, much like a puppy. Instead of a floppy ear, she had the bouncy pouf on top of her hat. "I can't just touch you."

She seemed to think about that. It was getting darker, and the snowflakes falling between us were coming faster and harder. But if I wasn't mistaken, she was pondering that comment as if I'd just said the most important thing she'd ever heard.

"No," she said after a moment. "I guess you can't. You shouldn't. Just because Derek ran off with Trini isn't a reason for me to let strange men touch me. Especially ones wearing sweatpants."

"What's wrong with sweatpants?"

The most ridiculous thing about this whole conversation? I didn't *want* to touch her. I was almost sure. So what if it had been a while for me? That was by choice. God knows I had women throwing themselves at me front, back and center, and it only promised to get worse as things took off with the single. I'd backed off the fuck-and-duck game simply because I'd gotten bored.

I was tired of fake women cloaked in pretenses who just wanted me for my fame. As much as I exploited my growing fame to get any damn thing I wanted.

Never said I wasn't a fucked-up bastard, now did I?

"There's nothing wrong with them, per se. They're just not fashionable."

Although my face felt as if it was freezing into place, I cocked a brow. "Oh, and that eye-searing combo you have on is? You practically have on a snowsuit. Like a child."

Her cheeks reddened. I don't know how I could tell the difference considering she'd been awful damn pink from the wind to start with, but somehow, I knew I'd gotten to her. "I'm not a child. I'm a grown woman who likes to be prepared."

"Huh." I crossed my arms and jutted my chin toward her car. "So how's that working out for you?"

She stepped forward, kicking up snow with her gigantic boots. Then she let her gaze wander down the front of me and let out a little *harrumph*. "And you know what else? Statistics say that eighty-eight-point-six of grown men who wear sweatpants are either still living in their mother's basements or they're serial killers."

Deliberately, I moved into her space, dwarfing her with my size. And yet again, she did not back down. "Those are some odds, Red. Are you feeling lucky?"

2

MAGGIE

I WAS SUPPOSED to be afraid of this guy. That was what he wanted me to be anyway. Why else would he be looming over me as if he wanted to do me bodily harm?

But I wasn't buying it. Let's go over the evidence.

Wile E. Coyote sweats.

Enough concern to pluck me out of my car like a wilted vegetable.

Back to the Wile E. Coyote sweats.

Also, possibly the kindest, softest, most intriguing brown eyes I'd ever seen. Surrounded by a frame of inky lashes. Such a heavy fringe that snow kept gathering on them until he grew impatient and blinked it away.

But that was neither here nor there.

"First of all, there are most likely no serial killers in Turnbull or the surrounding towns. That's extremely improbable, given the size of the population."

"So are your dumbass statistics, but I didn't call you on them, did I?"

I wasn't pouting at being called a dumbass. Lord knows I'd been called much worse. As the youngest of six, I'd gotten used to verbal abuse at a young age. I almost enjoyed it.

Just because I looked small and defenseless didn't mean I was. I tended to sneak up on people like a bunny.

Aww, she's so cute and fluffy—CHOMP.

"Then again, you're not making any effort to assist a stranded traveler, so maybe you are planning to Ted Bundy me. Where's your fake cast, huh?" I gave his arms in the sleeves of his surprisingly thin coat a glance before pretending to search the snowbanks around us. "Where's your VW Bug with the passenger seat taken out?"

"What the hell are you talking about?"

"Ted Bundy. One of the most famous serial killers of all time. Don't you people respect the titans in your field?"

"What people is that, exactly?"

His bored tone was making me feel stupid. So much for going toe-to-toe with this giant behemoth. He didn't find me amusing and he obviously had no intention of helping to free my vehicle.

So time for plan B.

"I'll just get my bread." There was no helping my clipped tone as I stomped back toward the ditch. Not that I could even be sure he'd heard me. With the howling wind and the crunch of my boots on the snowy, uneven ground at the side of the road, maybe he hadn't heard a word I'd spoken.

Then his big hands clamped around my upper arms and he hauled me back as if I'd been on the verge of falling into a fire pit. "Hold it. What bread?"

"Kindly unhand me."

He made a low noise in his throat and without looking back at him, I knew he'd done that cocked brow thing again. Pretty hot. I couldn't move one eyebrow independent of the other, so I tended to appreciate skills in others that I did not possess.

"You have no reason to try to get back in that car."

"Yes, I do. I need my bread before it gets cold." I sighed. "Well, any colder than it already is. My hot bag can only do so much."

"Your hot bag? Woman, you make no sense."

"Stop calling me woman, and it's an insulated bag to seal in warmth. I used it to protect Mrs. Pringles' bread. It's her favorite, pumpkin chocolate chip." I craned my neck to look up at him, intending to shove his big paws off me, but his head was tilted and his lips were parted, revealing just a hint of bright white teeth.

And those dark assessing eyes were searing right through every damn layer of my clothing.

"Kindly unhand me," I repeated, not missing the slight chatter of my teeth. I wished I could blame the cold. It was so much worse than that.

I was by the side of the road with a disabled car and a possible Ted Bundy wannabe with soulful eyes, and I didn't even really care that he was keeping me from my bread.

Mrs. Pringles' bread. Same difference.

"You might injure yourself further if you attempt reentry. Let the professionals handle it."

"Further?" I frowned. "I'm not injured."

Was I? Quickly, I took stock. Everything still worked. Arms, legs, mouth. Definitely mouth. Sure, my heart was beating a bit too fast and my thoughts were skidding out of control, but that was normal for me. My dad called me "fanciful," which he partially blamed on my obsession with the macabre. My mama said I spent too much time with my head stuck in a book. My brothers—all three of them— called me some variation of Magpie, my childhood nickname that had stuck like a damn flytrap. Maeve and Regan, my perfect older sisters, just sighed at my supposed antics and went on with their lives.

So yeah, mental babbling was typical for me. And often, actual babbling, though the dude hulking over me was not inspiring to foam at the mouth as I usually might.

I didn't know men like him. The guys I attracted were safe, nice boys. The kind who went to church on Sundays and pulled their elderly neighbor's newspaper out of the bushes and always referred to my parents as "Sir and Ma'am." They didn't have edges. They didn't skimp on their manners. They definitely didn't miss their morning shave.

As far as assisting someone with car trouble, they would've been sweet and helpful and fixed the problem before I could ask. Not brusque and dismissive and now rough as the brute hauled me around and set me a few feet away from my vehicle.

"Stay there." He pointed at me. "I'm going to take care of your problem so you can get on your way."

"About time. Do you have a truck hoist?"

He was already moving toward my car. He studied the door for a moment, then yanked on the handle. It opened for him with only the slightest effort.

Traitorous car.

Fumbling inside, he realized my window was the crank-up kind and shut it so the front seat didn't fill with snow. "Guess the door wasn't so stuck after all," he shouted over the wind.

I rolled my eyes. Sure, if I had the strength of an ox, no problem. "I asked if you had a truck hoist?"

"A truck hoist?" he echoed, clearly not paying attention as he studied my car.

"Yes, to pull me out of the ditch."

"No, I don't have a truck hoist. What I do have should do the trick though." He shut the door without grabbing my bread or any of my belongings, then climbed out of the ditch, pulled a cell phone from his pocket, and hit a button. Smugly, I might add.

This man did not have an air of friendly cooperation, that was for sure. As for neighborly concern? Nope. Nada.

After a minute, his smug expression flattened. His mouth thinned out and he gazed at his phone as if he'd misdialed. He hit a button again, waited, then yanked the phone from his ear. "What the fuck?"

I tried not to blanch. Of course, I'd heard swearing before. I was a college student, wasn't I? But in my family home, we had a tip jar. Anyone who swore put in a five-dollar bill. Forget a one-dollar bill. My parents had wanted us to learn appropriate words swiftly, and parting with five dollars of our allowance had worked fast.

Pretty sure this dude didn't have a jar. If he did, he'd probably smash it with one of his hamhock fists.

"Is there a problem?"

"No. Definitely not. The tow truck place isn't answering. No big."

"It's New Year's Eve."

"You don't say?"

I ignored his sarcasm and lifted my voice to speak over the growing wind. The darker it got, the more frigid it was growing outside. But I'd be damned if I shivered. If he could seem impervious to the weather, so could I. "If you're not using a national company and instead supporting a local business, it's not surprising. This is a holiday. Therefore, holiday hours."

"Thank you, Miss Know-It-All, but I'm well aware of this particular company's hours. It's a family business."

"Your family? Yet you don't own a truck hoist?" I cocked my head. "Seems fishy."

"I said family business, not my business."

"Ah, like your dad? Or your brother?"

"Look, they aren't answering, so we'll have to just wait." He glanced around at the gathering snow as if he planned for us to wait at the edge of the road.

If that was the case, I was definitely going to try to get back into my car. As much as I loved Mrs. Pringle, I knew my stomach was on the verge of roaring. That bread was going to be mine. I'd skipped lunch, and boy oh boy, I knew better than to take shortcuts. They never paid off.

"Okay. Well, thanks." Even if he couldn't be polite, I could. "I appreciate your…" But I wasn't a liar. "Conversation."

I couldn't be certain in the near darkness, but I was almost sure his lips twitched. "Conversation, is it?"

I shrugged.

"Come on," he said, indicating with his chin for me to head up the short incline to a dark, forbidding, *tiny* house.

Immediately, my back went up. And my spidey senses started to tingle.

Or that might have been my extremities due to frostbite setting in.

"No, thank you. I don't think that's a good idea. I'll just stay here and call AAA."

"You have AAA?"

"Of course I do." I bit my lip, vividly picturing the expired notice on my desk at home. I'd paid that, right? It had been at the top of my To Do list, but with the holidays…

Okay, maybe not.

"You seem uncertain."

"Not really."

He gusted out a sigh. "It's freezing out here. Let's go inside and get warm. I'll call the towing company again later."

"If they're not answering now," I shouted over the wind, moving closer when my voice seemed to get sucked away, "what makes you think they will later? It's a holiday. People are out celebrating."

"Are you?" He pointed at himself. "Am I? No. Not everyone is in a fucking party mood. Now come on."

When I didn't budge, he gave me a stern look that made me half expect him to haul me over his shoulder like a sack of Maggie. Then he let out another of those windy breaths. "Please?"

My frozen face cracked into a smile. "Did that hurt?"

"A little. Not as much as my nuts shriveling up into my spine though."

I swallowed. Along with not hearing a ton of swear words on a daily basis, I also wasn't privy to men referring to their nuts as if that counted as ordinary conversation.

Hi, my nuts hurt. Pass the crackers.

"You, um, should definitely go inside then. That sounds painful."

"It is. Come on. I won't bite."

"Are you sure?"

Now he did more than almost smile. He barked out a laugh. "Not unless you want me to, honey, and even then, I'm pretty sure you aren't my type." He tilted his head and lifted his voice above the howling wind. "I'm not into church girls. Even the ex-communicated kind, which does sound interesting."

"It is. No, I'm not telling you." I rubbed my mittened hand over my stinging cheeks. "What happens between a girl and her priest is private."

"Wow. Some *Thorn Birds* shit? Kinky little thing, aren't you?"

Was that actually approval I saw in his midnight eyes? They'd definitely warmed. Speaking of kinky…

"Hardly." I sniffed, and not out of haughtiness.

I had to sneeze, and I had to pee. I was also freezing and starving and desperately in need of a long, hot shower.

Then again, did I dare get naked within the same four walls as this guy? Even if I wasn't his type?

Serial killers had types too. They also didn't kill everyone they met. I couldn't be sure this guy was safe, but if I wasn't in his target victim group, he could be a homicidal lunatic and I wouldn't necessarily be in danger. Plus, I knew some judo.

Oh, the rationalizations a girl who urgently needs a bathroom will make.

"Okay. I'll go inside with you. Briefly. Until we can reach the towing company. Otherwise, I will have many people out looking for me, and they will descend on your place like a swarm of locusts if I'm not home in a matter of hours."

Much to my consternation most of the time. I was well and truly sick of being so overprotected by my family, though I loved them for their concern. It was just hard to have much of a life when you were watched like a rabid animal expected at any moment to go on a rampage through town.

In truth, I just mostly studied and worked, along with spending time with my bestie and my boyf—

Yep, not going there.

"Not if I tie you up and make you call them to say you're okay and not to look for you. Then I might throw your chair in the basement and leave you without food and water."

His voice was entirely too serious, which was how I guessed he was lying. It was a gamble, but I was going to bet that the usual serial killer didn't advertise his intentions so brazenly. "You forgot to add that you'd have your way with me first."

"Hoping, Red?" Before I could stammer out a response, he grabbed my arm and towed me behind him. "Not my type, remember?"

"I didn't say yes," I called.

He promptly ignored me.

After dragging me up a short snowy hill, we made our way up a scarcely shoveled path to a short set of rickety steps. He stopped to pick up some wood, then stomped up the steps and pressed his shoulder into the door. "Come on," he shouted in my general direction before barreling into the dark house.

Hell, I didn't even know if it was truly his. He could be an illegal squatter there for all I knew.

The fact of the matter was that I knew most of the people in Turnbull. This was on the outskirts, true, and the occasional person came or went without stirring my notice, but we lived in a small, self-contained area. We might be surrounded by trees and hills and blocked in by mountains of snow for almost half the year, due to our proximity to Lake Ontario, but we kept track of our own.

Also, it was hard to make quick getaways when a snowpocalypse wasn't a disaster so much as a way of life.

Biting my lip, I cast a quick glance back toward the road. In the time it had taken us to walk up to the house—though calling it that seemed to be an overstatement—my poor car had become even more buried. The snow wasn't coming down in flakes now. More like pellets.

"Red," he growled. "Forget the damn bread."

Something about his irritation made me laugh. I clapped a hand over my mouth, then bent at the waist when more laughter rolled out. I couldn't catch my breath and what breaths I could take were laced with ice. Crappy time to be on the verge of hysteria.

Guess my accident had shook me up more than I'd thought. Or else it was due to the man himself.

So I stood up straight, threw back my shoulders, and strutted inside in my giant boots to my beheading.

At least he'd turned on the lights. As I shut the door behind me and shifted to survey my surroundings, from down the hall came a string of curse words shot off in succession like gunfire.

My eyes widened. If he was trying to ease me into feeling comfortable before he struck, he wasn't too good at it.

"Are you okay?" I asked carefully, darting glances right and left as I crept up the hallway to where his voice was coming from.

And stopped dead at the mouth of the sparse, rustic kitchen.

He was standing at the stove in nothing but a pair of silky black boxers with a spatula in his hand, poking at whatever congealed mess was in his dented pan. It was one like you'd see in a camping kit, meant to be used on nights under the stars and no other time, ever. But that was his home cookware.

Fit him somehow, as did the intricate swirls and lines of dark ink that wrapped around his muscular shoulders and biceps. More ink covered his back and sides. He was a human canvas, tattooed and rippling with muscle.

I didn't find that arousing. That he was the exact opposite of my lanky, inkless ex was merely something I noted.

"Fucking burner is fucking out." He stabbed at the red mass in his pan. Without sparing me a glance, he continued. "Why are you still dressed like a damn polar bear? Get out of those wet clothes. You were standing in a snowbank for a good fifteen minutes or more."

"Polar bears don't need clothing, as they have fur."

That he only growled made me laugh. And cautiously unwind my scarf.

While he continued to fiddle with the non-working stove, I cleared my throat. "You have a microwave. Just heat up the soup." Cautiously, I stepped closer and peered at the gross stuff he kept trying to stir. "That is soup, right?"

"Yes. Tomato. I was going to make grilled cheese to go with it. Can't now, because fucking burner is—"

"Fucking out," I finished, surprised by how liberating it felt to curse. There weren't any tip jars here.

No furnace either apparently, as it was nearly as cold inside as it had been out. Or else I'd caught a serious freaking chill.

"Look at you. Your teeth are chattering." He turned to me and yanked off my fuzzy hat, causing the long hair I'd tucked underneath to come tumbling out. He gazed at it as if he was surprised I had hair at all, then managed to shake off his shock and tugged off my earmuffs too.

Sound rushed into my ears, including the uneven hiss of his breaths through his tightly clenched teeth.

I raised my gaze to his. He was staring at me in a way I wasn't used to from men. When a girl grew up in a small town with three strapping, overprotective brothers, you got used to guys being too afraid to take their shot. As such, I'd grown accustomed to dating the safe, parental-friendly boys. I liked them. They were predictable. No serial killers in the bunch.

None of them made my blood heat the way this one was with merely a heavy-lidded look.

He gripped my hat and earmuffs in his hands, crumpling them. This close to him, without even the buffer of his clothes, he seemed even more huge. Tall, muscled, dangerous.

I didn't know that kind of male. Had never wanted to.

Until now.

"Keep going," I said softly, challenging myself as much as I was him. I gestured to the rest of my outerwear. "Lots more clothes to strip off me, Wolf."

3

KELLAN

I'D KNOWN a lot of women in my day, and the best of them tended to be, shall we say, fickle.

This one, however?

The ficklest in the history of the goddamn vagina.

First, she was all cheerful like a Strawberry Shortcake doll on acid. Then suspicious, as if she suspected I intended to imprison her in a dungeon in my house and use her for sexual favors. She'd barely even come inside, her distrust of me was so thick.

Now? The chick was asking me to undress her.

As in naked.

No fucking clothes. All that silky dark hair spread out around us as I parted her creamy thighs and—

Nope.

I'd go fuck her forgotten loaf of bread first. I had enough problems. The last thing I needed was to get messed up with some local girl who jumped every time I swore.

Local girls were clingy. They were the homespun house and

hearth types who wouldn't understand a guy who made his living on the road. On stage, in front of thousands of screaming female fans.

Okay, that wasn't me yet. But I was on my way. I'd get there, and I'd be damned if I let anything hold me back. Not like my dad had. He'd gotten saddled with a kid and wife way too early, and he'd abandoned his dreams to stay home and pretend to be a doting dad.

He'd split before I turned eight, and I couldn't even completely hold it against him. Some dudes weren't meant for regular relationships. One woman forever sounded like a recipe for heartburn to me.

And this chick? If she ever let a guy in her pants, she probably had *forever* stenciled on her cooch.

"You have two hands, right?" I tossed back her hat and earmuffs, then grabbed my spatula. Better to have something in my hand that didn't smell like whatever sorcery she'd slathered all over her skin. Fuck if it didn't remind me of chocolate.

Who smelled like chocolate other than bakers?

"I surely do," she muttered, and if I didn't know better, I'd say she sounded disappointed. But she swiftly disappeared down the hall, so fast that I wondered if she intended to head out the door and hike back to town.

Don't want what's between my pearly gates? Well, fuck you then! I'll show you by dying in a snowbank before morning!

Though it definitely wasn't a case of not wanting to take the express pass into her drive-through. Without that crazy hat and those stupid earmuffs, she was kind of hot. I'd even gotten a glimpse of her neck as she unwound the scarf of doom. She might even have a pair of breasts under all those layers.

Not that it mattered to me. She could be flat as a board and I'd keep to my plans.

Fire, beer, a night spent relaxing. In that order.

And no fucking soup.

"Put it in the microwave," she called over her shoulder.

I stared at the pan. "For how long?"

"Look at the can." She didn't tack on *dumbass* but it was heavily implied.

"I can't make grilled cheese in a microwave," I yelled back.

"Yes, you can. Cheese sandwiches are great microwaved."

I huffed under my breath. Soup and grilled cheese in a microwave. Whatever.

Most likely, she went to one of those fancy country club-type colleges and was home on her winter break. They probably had sleepovers in her dorm and jumped around in footie PJs while flinging popcorn at each other and chanting the school fight song.

Hmm, that was an oddly arousing image. Clearly I needed to get laid. Fast. And not by Little Red Riding Hood and her basket of bread.

Her ginormous boots clomped over the rough-hewn floorboards. Then I heard her gasp.

I dropped the spatula into the pan of cold gunk and rushed down the hall, stopping short at the carved out entrance to the living room. I'd gone for that exact look, angling the boards and beams to make it seem as if the room itself had been dug out of the forest. Every part of the cabin straddled the line between spartan and primitive. Including the large fireplace that Red was crouching in front of to warm her hands.

Yes, she'd finally removed her mittens. Praise Jesus.

"Go take a shower. You can borrow some clean clothes—"

"My clothes are clean. I changed right before I got in the car." She jerked to her feet and spun toward me, sending those rivulets of dark hair down her back like a waterfall. It was so long and thick that I couldn't keep my mind from very bad thoughts.

Like fisting a handful and pounding into her from behind, working her good and hard just to make her swear with those pretty pink, good girl lips.

"That's not what I meant. I meant you walked through all that snow and you've gotta be all wet."

"Nope." She crossed her arms over her coat-covered chest. Hadn't even loosened a damn button. "I pride myself on choosing outerwear that keeps me dry under all circumstances. Especially a short walk in a little snowstorm."

I snorted. Couldn't help it. "*Little* snowstorm? Born and raised in Turnbull, huh?"

"Maybe." She gnawed on her puffy pink lower lip, and I knew she did it often. That was her tell. Along with those sneaky glances she kept taking of me when she thought I wasn't paying attention. "What difference does it make?"

"Nothing." I turned back toward the hall. "I don't care."

"It's just your clothes would all be too big. If I took a shower," she added, her voice trailing off.

"What do you have on under that snowsuit? Anything resembling a T-shirt?"

"A cardigan and a silk blouse."

With my back to her, I rolled my eyes. "Silk. Of course. Well, you can wear the blouse and tie the sweater around your waist for protection from my roving eyes if you want while you're drying your super pants by the fire. I have a rack in the bedroom."

"I don't know you. It hardly seems proper to take off my clothes and…wash in your home."

"Five minutes ago, you wanted me to strip you in my kitchen. Inconsistent much?"

"My God. I didn't mean naked. You thought I meant naked? No. Not naked. I meant…not naked."

"Oh, so you meant not naked?" I couldn't hold back my smirk. "Just checking," I said an instant before she flung her scarf at me.

Look at that, I'd even spotted a collarbone. Now we were getting somewhere.

"I was referring to my outerwear. In a friendly sort of way."

"Oh right. Gotcha." I nodded. "We've been like best friends this whole time."

Despite her scowl, I could've sworn I glimpsed amusement in her big blue eyes.

Always blue. It was as if the universe knew I was a sucker for them, so I was sent some temptation every few months.

Ah hell, every few weeks. Sometimes every few hours.

I was currently having a dry spell. Or I had been until this one curbed it right into my ditch.

"I'm not sure if you're aware of this, but some girls practice flirting on whichever big brute happens to be around. It's a good way to try out new approaches."

"Huh. Fascinating. Is accusing a guy of being a serial killer one of your approaches as well? If so, maybe retire that one."

She let out a laugh and unzipped her coat. I was so taken aback that she'd revealed her white silk and pink cashmere—had to be cashmere, right?—beneath that I nearly missed the next thing she said.

"No, that's what happens when you're an entirely too street smart criminal justice student. My apologies." She pulled off the coat and tugged her hair over one shoulder.

Luckily she didn't know she'd transfixed me. Just like that.

Maybe it was the firelight dancing over her pale skin. Or the delicate necklace circling her throat. Or her eyes.

Her hair was a consideration too. Fistable, fuckable hair.

But the worst part? That little glimmer of a smile playing around her mouth. As if perhaps she did have an inkling I was more interested than not. She was a woman after all, and they had all their secrets when it came to unmanning the opposite sex.

"Why are you smiling?" I demanded.

"Oh, am I? Sorry. I shouldn't smile without asking first." She attempted to fix her expression into sober lines before letting her gaze drop for a second too long.

And I realized exactly how she knew I was feigning most of my disgust in her direction.

Damn dick, always getting me into trouble. That it was larger than the average tool didn't do me any favors either. At least in situations like this.

Since I didn't have a response, I went back into the kitchen to nuke my damn soup and grilled cheese.

I'd gotten as far as opening the microwave door when she stomped into the room. Her boots always made it sound like she was pissed off, but I didn't check her face to see if I'd somehow offended her with my aroused member.

Fuck it, she'd offended *me* by being smoking hot and interrupting my private New Year's Eve.

"Don't do that," she screeched as I was about to stick the pan into the microwave. I hadn't been sure it would fit, but I was good at angles.

I sent her a sidelong glance as she snatched the pan from me. *Very* good.

"This isn't safe for the microwave. You'll start a fire. We don't need that tonight." She put down the pan on the counter and glanced around the small room before sorting through the cupboards above the broken stove. "Microwave-safe dish?"

"What the fuck all is that?"

She sighed and emerged with a pile of plastic bowls I'd thrown in the cabinet a couple of years ago. Her lips pursed and she blew off the layer of dust before digging one out from the middle of the stack. Then she dumped my soup into the bowl, covered it the bowl with a paper napkin, and slid it into the microwave, programming it for sixty seconds.

"To start," she said. "It'll require stirring and additional heating in thirty-second increments. You'll have to check it."

I grunted something, but it probably wasn't "thank you."

"Any other plastic plates? Flat ones? For the grilled cheese sandwiches," she added as I stared.

"Sandwiches plural? I didn't offer you one."

Her face dropped and for a second, I felt like a dick.

Just a second because she opened her mouth.

"Just like I didn't offer you my underwear, but you assumed. At least I won't be hurting if I don't get your crusty bread." She waggled her brows at my groin. "Can you say the same?"

Then she sashayed out of my kitchen.

A moment later, I heard the shower turn on down the hall, right before the microwave sounded its cheerful little ding. I took out the soup and stirred, then slid the bowl back inside for another thirty seconds. Rinse and repeat one more time after that.

When I finally tasted the results, I was prepared for it to still be cold one layer down. Nope, Little Red Betty Crocker Hood apparently included cooking in her repertoire too.

Fuck it if the damn soup wasn't perfect.

4

MAGGIE

THE BRUTE'S shower was a dream. Like a serious freaking wet dream, set in the middle of a cabin that was more lean-to than HGTV-special.

But now that I'd seen this bathroom, I so did not care. He could've had a fire pit in the kitchen instead of actual appliances, and it so wouldn't have made a bit of difference.

Because he had all *this*.

The tiles were black and white, gleaming as if they'd just been cleaned with a toothbrush. The shower was a combo tub and appeared to be made from some kind of glazed wood. I didn't know anything about fancy bathroom setups or the difference between high-end and simply pretty. All I knew was that the copper fixtures and huge tub and shower stall were calling my name.

So much so that I shut the door and shed my clothes without thinking of a few vital things that only occurred to me once I was under the orgasmically hot spray.

Did I mention the multiple shower heads?

Fuck me. I'd even swear for this one, though in my own head didn't count.

But as amazing as the crisscrossing warm streams of water were, they didn't keep me from realizing I hadn't locked the bathroom door. Or located some towels before I hopped into a stranger's shower and lathered up with—I looked at the large blue-green bottle in my hand —mountain man shampoo, for when you want to bring the wilderness inside you.

Huh. That sounded kind of dirty. And no matter how hard I scrubbed at my hair, I still didn't have a towel.

Head full of suds, eyes stinging from water and shampoo, I tugged back the shower door and gave the bathroom a bleary glance. There weren't even any cabinets in here. Was I just missing them? Where did the dude keep his toilet paper, for God's sake?

My gaze alighted on the roll. That was an idea. I could hop out and dry off with a ton of toilet paper, and he'd never know I was too lame to even think of a towel.

Still, he was really letting down his potential guests by not thinking of their comfort and providing one within easy reach.

I snorted. Yeah, he was definitely Miss Manners in all other ways. He wouldn't even give me a bite of his probably plastic-like cheese.

Screw it. I'd just woman up and ask for a towel. No big. I was a grown woman. He'd open the door—since you know, I'd skipped locking it, some crim justice student I was—and toss in a towel, and I'd finish the best shower I'd ever had in my life in complete peace.

First I would rinse off my hair. No sense in risking blindness.

As soon as I'd finished washing it, I grabbed the long length and pulled it over one shoulder. Time to summon help.

Right.

I took a deep breath. And another. And another, until the already foggy shower door turned seriously steamy.

Just do it.

"Hey—" I yelled out, belatedly realizing that I didn't know his name.

I was naked and wet in his bathroom, but I couldn't even call for him because I didn't know if he was a Bob or a George or a Biff.

Biff would only be fair. He deserved to be a Biff, sourpuss that he was.

"Hey," I yelled again over the roar of the water. I could have turned it off, but then I would freeze. Out there? Super cold. In here? Gloriously hot.

I intended to bask in that heat for another ten minutes or so, until the hot water gave out. Maybe it never would and I could hide in the shower for the rest of the night.

A girl could dream.

The bathroom door creaked open. I jolted, gripping the edge of the shower door as I cautiously inched it open.

This was not good.

A second later, a large tanned hand inched through the narrow opening between the door and the jamb. On the tip of his finger was a fuzzy gray towel.

"Looking for this?" he asked in a singsong voice, and I hated him more than a little.

Alas, I was desperate.

"Oh, thank God. You do have towels."

"A towel, yes."

"Wait. One towel?" I frowned and tried not to fidget. "Is it even clean?"

"It was before I used it for my shower this morning."

"Ugh. *Ew*. Seriously?" As soon as the words were out, I bit my lip. Beggars and all that.

Though there was the TP...

"Sorry, I didn't plan for little Red Riding Hood to deign to use my shower tonight." He started to pull back his hand. "Carry on."

"No, no, wait! How am I supposed to get dry?"

"I have a feeling you spend plenty of time dry, so figure it out."

It took me a second to get his crude double entendre. I chalked up my slowness to the fact that I was standing with one foot on top of the other and swaying as I tried to get some of the hot water on my back while maintaining my grip on the shower door.

"Asshole," I said under my breath.

"Excuse me? What was that? Did the virginal one just swear?" The door swung open and he lifted a hand to his rounded mouth as if he was stunned. "I just can't believe—"

Then he just stopped talking. Stopped breathing too, or maybe that was only me.

I was naked on the other side of the only slightly opaque shower door, and that was discounting my precarious lean around the edge. My breasts weren't tiny. He had to see…everything.

Damn near everything.

He wasn't speaking, and he also wasn't turning around to leave. Nor was I yelling at him to get out.

"Looks like I'm plenty wet right now," I said sweetly, blowing a wet curl out of my eyes.

Dry and virginal, my ass.

When he stepped farther into the room, I realized this was not a man who could be stopped with a smart aleck remark. He'd just toss back something even worse at me.

"You hid a hell of a lot under that snowsuit, Red." His voice was pure gravel.

A more prudent woman wouldn't have darted a glance below his waist. But I'd just been dumped by my long-term boyfriend for a woman who wore feathers and spraypaint for a living, so maybe I needed some reassurance.

That some random oafish man can get hard for your naked body? Nice, Mags. Real nice.

Except he'd been hard for me before, when I'd been more than fully dressed.

As for the current erection situation? All systems go.

Still not throwing him out, are you, Mags?

I cleared my throat and adjusted my grip on the door. I'd left behind wet fingerprints, and only part of the dampness was from the shower. I was that flummoxed by this guy.

By some stupidly hot stranger seeing me naked—and *liking* it.

"Float like a butterfly, sting like a bee," I whispered, the closest thing to a comeback I could summon.

His trance snapped, and his overly generous mouth curved. "You always say the thing I least expect." He followed that up by walking forward and pulling open the shower door while I stood there slack-jawed like a dang guppy. Water sprayed out into the bathroom, hitting his cheeks and chest, and he just took his sweet time eating me up with his eyes.

And I let him.

Almost as if he was moving in slow-motion, he leaned over and turned off the water, then wrapped the towel around me and tucked the end in the front near my breasts. The towel that had been all over his naked body not that long ago.

"I hadn't finished washing," I said weakly. It was a victory that I managed to speak at all.

I'd already gone further with this man than I had with anyone other than Derek, and I didn't even know his name.

"The hot water doesn't last very long." He spoke as nonchalantly as if we were sitting around fully dressed in his living room. "I put in a tank that accommodated my needs, and I take quick showers."

"So you built this place yourself?"

"Yeah. With help, of course."

"It's…nice."

"Glad you approve." He smirked at me, and I fumbled to grip the edge of the towel, making sure it covered me. Not sure why I cared, since he'd already seen everything.

Including that I hadn't shaved or…trimmed up in a few days. I hadn't foreseen a need. My boyfriend and I were through, and I had recently rediscovered my love of flannel pajamas. Besides, what girl goes to town on her lady bits with the shave gel when she's currently hating all men, forever and ever, amen?

Now I'd just been naked with this guy, and I sincerely regretted my life choices. All of them. Including the one that meant I couldn't just mindlessly enjoy carnal pleasures of the flesh with this surprisingly attractive—yet still brutish—man, though I still had a condom left in my purse.

Because we didn't know each other, and I didn't even like his personality all that much. His body, however? The lean muscles and tats that I now had a bird's eye view of wrapping around his shoulders and biceps and right on down his forearms…

I quite enjoyed all of that.

So who said we had to talk to each other? We could just—

Nope. We could not. Ex-communicated from Our Holy Mother Church of The Four Corners or not, I could not do such a thing.

Even if I really wanted to.

"This bathroom is gorgeous," I hastened to add. "It could use just a few more things. Some additional amenities, you could say."

"Oh yeah?" He stepped back and crossed his arms, bracing his thumb against his mouth. "Like what?"

"Storage. You need a linen closet for guest towels."

"I don't have guests here. Next."

"And you need a hamper, to store—"

"I have one towel, and I undress in the other room. Next."

"You just parade around naked through the house?"

The smirk I'd glimpsed briefly a moment ago had now taken up permanent residence on his face. "Who's gonna see? The forest people?"

"You don't have neighbors?"

"Did you see any?"

"I didn't scope out the neighborhood before I steered into the ditch." As soon as I'd said it, I realized my mistake.

His mouth thinned. "You steered into the ditch?"

"Not exactly, I hit an icy patch and—"

"Red." The word was a growl.

I was already growing to like that sound coming from the depths of his chest. It emphasized how much of a male he was. Uncouth, rough around the edges, barely even sociable. Yet still so very male that it made every part of me sit up and take notice.

Including my nipples, which had decided to do the *hey, how you doin'?* salute against his terrycloth towel.

"There was a deer," I mumbled, hearing my father's voice in my head. He'd go up one side of me and down the other if he knew what I'd done.

"You drove off the road to avoid a deer?"

"And her fawn," I added, gripping the front of the towel in one hand and the hem in the other. "I didn't know what to do."

"What you do is not risk your damn life driving off the road when you don't know what you're driving into."

"It would've been fine if my stupid tires hadn't spun out."

"Listen to me, Red." He gripped my shoulders and I went still. Not from fear, but brutal awareness, the kind that I'd always imagined slammed into a person before they were attacked. That one second of utter knowing, complete certainty, that your life would never be exactly the same again. "You don't risk yourself for anyone—or anything—else. You understand me? You are your first priority. Always."

"Survival of the fittest?" Anger brewed in my belly, and I shook off his hold. "I don't live like that. I didn't need to hit that deer and her baby, and I didn't. And I'm fine. Aren't I?" I lifted my arms, which had the unintended effect of causing my towel to dip lower than it should have. But I just hitched it up, climbed out of the stall, and marched with my bare feet and dripping legs out of the bathroom and up the hall.

I wanted the warmth of the fire and to bask in his curiosity in me for a little while longer. He didn't know how to tag me, couldn't quite figure me out, and I liked that. But if I didn't put some distance between us, soon enough he'd have me pegged.

God knows I'd never been anyone else's enigma. I'd always been safe, comfortable, predictable Magpie.

Forcing back a sigh, I rushed into the living room. The space was sparse to the point of almost emptiness, but it helped the house seem bigger than it was. The big fireplace and stone mantel and large flat screen TV mounted on the opposite wall were the main features of the room. Along with them was a long couch perfect for naps and a couple of armchairs, plus a few side tables here and there that looked just rustic enough to possibly have been handmade by him as well.

Guess he was kind of an enigma too. So was the beauty of strangers. The possibilities were endless.

The guitar leaning against the chair next to the fire gave me pause. I ran my fingertips over the cherry wood, shivering again though the warm shower and fire had helped to chase away much of my chill.

Was the brute a guitar player? I tried to imagine him cradling the instrument as he'd cradled the wood and found it wasn't as hard to imagine as I would have thought. I debated asking him about it, then decided obviously it was a hobby. He wasn't the kind of guy to have a prop guitar in the living room to pick up chicks.

I seriously doubted he needed any help.

When he found me staring pensively into the fire a little while later, he didn't speak. Just held out a plate with a misshapen lump of cheese with half a piece of bread on either side.

I laughed. Hard.

"So I didn't have enough bread for sandwiches for two. Didn't expect to need it. The plan was to eat my soup and my sandwich, and get so shit-faced I didn't see midnight."

The gruffness of his tone got to me. I couldn't even say why. Maybe because I knew he was making an effort, and that perhaps he didn't make much of an effort for all that many people. Possibly because people hadn't made much of an effort for him.

There went my college psych classes, rearing their ugly heads again.

I took the plate and picked up the sandwich he'd made me, biting in despite my extreme aversion to melted plastic. It didn't taste so bad after all. I chewed and swallowed before wiping my mouth with the edge of the towel.

His molten dark gaze tracked the movement like a hunter studying his prey. Worse, since I was almost sure he didn't intend to kill me. But what he'd leave behind would be wreckage just the same.

"So where's the alcohol?" I tried to sound casual, as if I got loaded all the time.

I also often went into strange men's houses, and stripped down, and let them see me with a little bit more fluff between my legs than I preferred. Plus, I ate their sandwiches without wondering about possible poison meant to knock me out so they could do bad things to me.

Things that in the case of this guy, I really wanted to be awake for.

"It's Coors. Nothing fruity and pink with little umbrellas."

I frowned. "I drink beer. Girly drinks are for sissies."

"Oh, is that so?" He stepped back and crossed his arms again. I was starting to wonder if he did that intentionally to make all his muscles ripple. Combined with the thick swirls of dark ink that seemed to cover far too much of his golden skin, he seemed dangerous.

Alluring.

And I wasn't even drunk yet. *Yet* being the operative word, since this was New Year's Eve. If tonight was going to be my first night to get even partially wasted, I'd picked an auspicious evening for it.

"Yes. Beer is my favorite." Favorite only if I was dying of thirst and had no other options, but semantics. "Can I have one?"

"Are you of age?"

I threw back my shoulders. "Excuse me?"

"Easy question. Easy answer."

"I'm twenty-three." In February. Close enough.

"Okay. I'll get you a beer and then we'll see about calling the tow truck so you can get on home. Since all your people will be out looking for you soon, I'm sure." He did air quotes around *your people*, and I did not appreciate it.

I did have people. Lots of them. Coming from a family of six kids, it wasn't an exaggeration. Only problem was they were all out partying tonight. I'd been invited to a celebration or two myself, but I'd eschewed the invites to bring bread to Mrs. Pringles. After that, I'd planned to take a long hot shower and curl up with my e-reader.

Alone, but not lonely. I had intended to practice self-love. Self-nurturing, in fact.

But if you could get someone else to love and nurture you tonight…

"You're right. I probably shouldn't take the time to drink with you. I should get dressed and see about getting towed." I took another bite of my sandwich. "I'll just catch a ride home with the tow truck guy."

"Or lady," he said under his breath, grabbing his cell off the table beside the fire.

He swiped a few times, held the phone to his ear, and waited. Frowning, he pulled the phone back and tapped a few times before listening again. "What the hell?"

"Still not answering?" Fussily, I arranged my towel to make sure I wasn't showing too much of my legs. Not that he seemed to be bowled over by desire anyway, but just in case.

Ignoring me, he tapped the phone a couple more times and lifted it to his ear again. After a moment, he turned around and grunted out a message. That, yes, I could still hear though he'd turned his back.

"Hey Beth, been trying to reach you at work. I have a situation with a vehicle that needs transport. Crashed outside my place. Maybe you can give the chick a ride too? If not, I'll deal. Thanks."

My frown grew the longer he spoke in his so-not-hushed tones. Beth. Probably some old girlfriend. Or current girlfriend. I didn't even know his name, so I certainly had no right to be offended that he might not be single.

He'd seen me naked, but so had the doctor at the hospital where I was born. No big deal.

Once he'd ended the call and turned back, I jerked to my feet and set aside the half-eaten sandwich. "I can handle my own transportation home. Don't worry about it. Same with the tow truck. I'll call my Dad and we'll handle it in the morning with AAA, who is never closed."

"No, but you'll be waiting two hours on the morning of a holiday during a big snowstorm. Beth should be here before then." He raked a hand through his shaggy dark hair. "I'm not sure what's going on with her."

"Maybe found a better hot date?" I hadn't meant to be snarky. Normally I was quite pleasant.

He just huffed and strode out of the room.

I picked up the sandwich and took another bite. It really wasn't half-bad. No point in starving myself.

When he returned, he had two bottles of beer and a bowl that I presumed contained his soup. It had to be ice cold by now, or maybe he'd re-nuked it.

He popped the top of my beer and handed it over. I took it, nodding my thanks, and swiftly realized I'd have to actually drink it. Preferably without gagging.

I took a quick hit, then another. Feeling his eyes on me, I kept knocking them back. And lo and behold, after the first few putrid swallows, a nice warmth began to swim through my veins. I started drinking faster just to get more of that pleasant floaty feeling.

"Easy," he admonished. "Don't want you passing out on me."

"Oh, I can hold my liquor." I burped and clapped a hand over my mouth as he grinned.

"I'm sure. What are you, five-feet-nothing and a buck twenty?"

"Five-two and one-thirty-five."

"Wow, a woman who freely discloses her age and her weight."

"I'll also disclose my marital status and my name, if you'd like those too."

He sat on the padded leather ottoman on the other side of the fire and set his beer down. He scooped up soup and hummed under his breath, which might have indicated approval. I couldn't be sure. "Yes. I would."

"Single. Extremely single." Great. Now I sounded desperate and on the make. "And my name is Margaret Kelly."

He choked. "No way. Not the Kelly *virgin*."

5

KELLAN

SHE STARED at me as if I were Satan. Tail, horns, and all.

"I'm not a virgin." She said the word with obvious distaste. "I don't know where you're getting your information, but it's obviously wrong."

"More like outdated." I stirred my lukewarm soup and shoveled in a few spoonfuls before lifting my gaze to hers again. She tended to look like a damn wounded bird, until her shields popped down once again.

I wasn't proud of putting that hurt expression in her eyes even once. Putting her back up was a whole different thing altogether.

She was mouthy and vibrant and I couldn't for the life of me figure out my reaction to her. Was it because it had been a while since I'd been with a woman? Or was there something about Margaret in particular that intrigued me?

"Outdated, huh? What is that supposed to mean?"

"You have an older sister, right? Maeve?"

"Yes." She sighed. "She still thinks I'm a virgin. She probably will until I'm old and gray and have six kids."

"Well, in her defense, I knew her a long time ago." And quite personally, as I recalled groping her more than once under the bleachers at Turnbull High. She'd been a sexy, wild art student who'd done crazy stuff like painting words on her boobs so that when I got her top off, some kind of naughty message would be waiting for me.

Now that I'd seen both sisters' racks, I had to acknowledge that obviously the Kellys had been genetically blessed.

The one thing I hadn't seen on Maeve was her pussy. We'd made out a few times, but we'd never gone that far. I'd wanted to, of course, but she'd claimed to be a good Catholic girl who was saving her "cherry" for a boy who wanted to marry her. I'd suspected that was a load of bull, but then she'd brought up her other sisters, Regan and Magpie, the baby, and she'd insisted they'd all taken a purity pledge.

That had made me hard for a week. Back then, the idea of taking on three virgin sisters had pretty been much my idea of heaven wrapped up in a DD-sized bow.

"How long?"

I counted back in my head. "Probably about a decade, give or take. Fuck me."

She pressed her lips together and stared at her beer. Her probably close-to-empty beer.

"Want another one?" I asked.

I shouldn't be getting her drunk. No matter what she said, I had a feeling she didn't do it often. Especially now that I knew she was the youngest Kelly girl.

In town, she was practically revered as a saint. One of the few young people today who always helped the elderly cross the street and did kind gestures like baking bread for someone when she should've been out living it up like other girls her age.

Though I'd lived in LA for several years, I'd heard enough about Magpie in town from the guys I'd gone to school with. I had the same crew as I always had—including a couple of the dudes in my band, who I'd brought with me out west—and they'd mentioned the Kelly sisters. Hard not to. They were all fucking gorgeous, or at least so I'd heard.

I'd never seen Magpie before, not in the flesh. Now that I'd *really* seen everything, I doubted I'd ever forget.

She nodded quickly, and it took me a second to remember what I'd asked her. Another beer. Right.

Stop thinking about her gorgeous fucking body, jackass. You're never going to touch her.

I set aside my bowl and rose. I'd made it about two steps when her soft voice reached me. "Did you sleep with her?"

"With who?"

"Maeve." She huffed out a breath. "She's beautiful, and she has a lot of fun with guys."

"I didn't sleep with her."

She let out a sigh. Relief?

I should've stopped there. But since I was me, I didn't.

"I wanted to. Would have in a hot second, but she was saving her virginity for marriage."

Margaret let out such a loud laugh that I did a doubletake. "She told you that? Oh God. She must've not liked you then. Or else you have a small penis."

It was stupid to feel affronted. Or to respond with an equally juvenile comment. "Don't think so, since she put it in her mouth a time or five."

She didn't stop laughing. "Yeah, then she must've been trying to let you down gently." She wiped her eyes. "I needed that laugh. Thanks."

"Look at me, Red. Does any part of me seem small?"

Taking a sip of her beer, she let her gaze wander over me. "Not particularly, but some parts of the anatomy aren't built to scale."

"You mean like your huge tits that don't go with the rest of your tiny body?"

I expected her to blanch or stutter or divert her gaze. Instead she nodded. "Exactly like that."

Since I didn't have a reply that wouldn't take us into dangerous territory, I went into the kitchen and got her another beer.

I didn't rush. Nor did I dally. This was my place, for fuck's sake, and I wasn't about to let her drive me into my kitchen. There was a reason I was single. I liked doing my own thing when and where I wanted to without having to check in with someone else. I had friends, of course, and plenty of them, but we all did our own thing and lived and let live.

Even in Wilder Mind, we didn't get in each other's faces. Sure, if someone went way off the rails, either musically or personally, we'd figure out what was going on. Otherwise, nope. No handholding here.

The sound of the TV turning on made me pull my head out of the fridge. I'd been staring into it blindly for a couple of minutes. Like a dumbass.

Not hiding from her, huh? Sure.

Party sounds and music flowed into the kitchen, and at once, I knew what she was watching. That New Year's Fuckin' Eve or whatever it was called. Bunch of boy bands and girls with poufy hair and lots of freezing people standing around Times Square, dancing their asses off.

Great. Now I was supposed to watch that?

I wished I'd brought my cell into the kitchen. Not that I doubted my sister would call me as soon as she got my message. If she wasn't answering the phone at the tow truck shop or calling me back, something must be up. Big time. She always made sure the shop was open on holidays so she had a chance of competing with the big guys like AAA who were open twenty-four/seven. It was hard enough being a female in a male-dominated business without conceding business to the large fish in her small pond to boot. So she went the extra mile whenever she could.

Except tonight. Maybe her babysitter had fallen through. Rainy was three now, and she was touchy with new people. If the regular babysitter couldn't make it, Beth would've stayed home with her.

I couldn't dwell on Beth's whereabouts or it would make me crazy.

Another thing I couldn't do was peer into this nearly empty refrigerator all night long. Just because I had a strange chick in a towel that barely hid her smokin' hot body in my living room wasn't a reason to hide out.

Neither was the fact that I'd messed around with her older sister. Or that I'd seen her naked, and I was pretty sure we'd both wanted to do more seeing. And exploring.

It hadn't much mattered that we didn't know or particularly like each other. If she'd been a groupie, fine. I would've hit that and moved on. We both would've had a great time and that was that.

But she was a good girl. One of the untouchable Kellys. A family of decent, hardworking, *nice* people.

She also had a bunch of burly as fuck older brothers who'd kick my ass if I put a finger on her virginal skin. Especially since I might like a taste of that sweet pussy I'd glimpsed in the shower, but I sure wasn't marrying it. That deal wasn't for me.

No way would I live my dad's life of settling all over again. Much better that I was honest about what I was from day one.

Grabbing another couple beers and a bag of pretzels from the cupboard—likely stale, since I rarely visited the cabin—I headed into the living room. She was curled up in one corner of the couch, singing along to whatever swill was on TV, winding one long strand of dark hair around her finger.

Her towel was about two high notes away from indecency, and bastard that I was, I wasn't going to tell her.

I sat beside her and opened her beer before it passing it to her. I tore into the pretzels, decided they were edible, and passed those over to her too. She sipped and munched, singing along in between swallows. Completely unconcerned that she was letting loose in front of a stranger.

Her voice was better than average. Deep, husky, with a hint of gravel that brought to mind Janis Joplin if you tilted your head just right. She seemed to know the lyrics to everything.

At the first commercial break, she turned to me. "What's your name?"

"Kellan McGuire." The devil on my shoulder was far too curious. "Do you know who I am?"

"Should I?"

That made me smile. "Well, we did grow up in the same town, and I knew of you." A cop-out, but I was allowed a few.

"Yeah, but I'm one of the Kellys. Everyone knows us in Turnbull. We're like the Kardashians, without the bling or the scandals."

I groaned. "You're not like them. Trust me. I've met—" I broke off and cleared my throat. Luckily she was staring at the latest pop star du jour on the TV and not paying attention to me.

Last thing I needed to do was show my hand by admitting I knew one of them. I rather liked that Magpie didn't know I was famous. All right, semi-famous now. I definitely wasn't a household name yet. Maybe I never would be.

But she didn't know me from Adam. I was just anonymous Kellan, a gruff jerk from Turnbull who'd let her into his house and made her a shitty sandwich and gawked at her truly spectacular tits.

Margaret was singing again, and the artist hadn't even started yet. Guess she was warming up. Probably more than the woman in a leather jumpsuit and false eyelashes onstage had bothered to do.

Being on both sides of the stage had taught me how many shortcuts were taken by the talent—and their managers. As many as they could get away with. Not Wilder Mind. We rehearsed the shit out of everything. We had a work ethic, and fame wasn't going to change us.

I hoped.

"You really tell people to call you Margaret?" I blurted, feeling like a jackass as she blinked at me. Her eyes were definitely more out-of-focus than they'd been. Maybe she'd hit her limit.

"No. I just told you that on the off-chance you didn't know my family." She sighed and took a long gulp. "Fat chance."

I stretched my arm along the back of the couch and toyed with the ends of her wet hair. She shot me a glance, lowering her lids until I found myself riveted by her thick dark lashes fluttering against her cheeks. Her pulse was probably just as jumpy. She was unnerved by me, and I liked that. I enjoyed being in control and spending time with a woman who didn't try to mount me like a damn show horse the second she glimpsed the anaconda in my sweats.

Not that most of them really cared about my dick. The part of me they wanted a crack at was in my back pocket and getting fatter with every passing month. Aka my wallet.

"What do you prefer to be called?"

"Let me guess," she said drily. "We've now reached the portion of the evening where you're going to try to feel me up, all casual-like."

I had to grin. This babe let me get away with zero shit. "Who said I'd be casual? Maybe I just intended to haul you on my lap."

She jerked a shoulder. "What would that consist of, exactly?" When I didn't reply, she circled a finger. "The…hauling."

I tried to keep the surprise off my face. I hadn't expected Magpie Kelly to lead me into this kind of conversation. Just proved my initial assessment that she was a pro at keeping me off my game.

"Hmm. Guess I'd start by pulling you on my lap and facing you toward the TV. Since you like to sing and all. Though how you know all these crappy songs is beyond me. Pop's your thing, huh?"

Yet another reason why she wouldn't know me or my band if *this* was the kind of music she preferred. We were a helluva lot harder-edged than the Luscious Lovahboys. Yes, that was the band's actual name.

God save me.

"I listen to a lot of different stuff. Country too. A little R&B."

I grunted. Yep, she wouldn't be hearing Wilder Mind anytime soon.

Not that I cared if she knew my music. After tonight, I wouldn't be talking to her again. It had been a complete accident she'd spun out in front of my house. Since I doubted I'd be getting my sister on the phone tonight, we'd just have to deal with each other until the morning.

From the way she was staring at the side of my face, Margaret was still waiting for my answer regarding the hauling thing.

"So I'm singing and sitting on your lap," she prompted. "Then what?"

A very good question. What kind of answer was Magpie looking for? The truth or something sweet and romanticized?

Not that it mattered. I'd be straight with her and trust she could handle it. If she couldn't, perhaps she'd learn next time not to ask questions she wasn't prepared to hear the answers to.

"Then I'd probably push back your hair so I could kiss your neck." If I wasn't imagining things, she sucked in a breath. "Just light kisses at first, so you didn't stop focusing on the TV."

"Making sure I was distracted while you enacted your devious plan?"

"Making you come until you scream isn't devious. It's a damn charitable act."

She choked on her mouthful of beer, then immediately went back for another hit. For a few moments, she stared at the screen. Not singing. I wasn't even sure she was still breathing.

"So you think you could do that?"

"Kiss your neck?" Knowing full well she didn't mean the neck thing at all. "Sure."

"No. The other."

"Other. Hmm. Coming, you mean?"

"Yes."

She was fiddling with her hair and looking anywhere but at me.

Instead of teasing her, I wanted to know more. To peel back her layers and delve inside—and that wasn't just my way of getting in her pants.

Well, under her towel. *My* towel. Because knowing she was wrapped up in something that smelled like me was sexy as fuck.

"You said you weren't a virgin." I touched her bare knee with the backs of my fingers, expecting her to jolt. She just took a shuddery breath. "Is that true?"

"Yes. Derek and I had sex a lot."

I instantly hated Derek and I had no idea who he was.

"Derek who?"

She bit her lip as she smiled. "You're growling again."

Didn't surprise me. "Answer the question."

"Derek Smiley, my ex-boyfriend. We were going to get married once he'd saved up enough for a proper ring. I didn't care about that. He did. At least that's what he said. He was building his nest egg for us, working three jobs. Lies. All lies." She gripped her beer and rubbed her thumb through the condensation. "He ran off with a stripper," she whispered.

"Excuse me?"

"Yeah. How lame, right? For me, not him. I imagine bagging a stripper was probably the pinnacle of his life. Much more exciting than the famed Kelly virgin. By the way, none of us were virgins past eighteen. So just in case you had some purity fantasy going on, sorry to burst your bubble."

I shifted uncomfortably. "Fantasies aren't to be judged."

She giggled, and I decided it might be the best sound in the universe.

"Really?"

"Absolutely."

"I'm not sure I have any, other than actually coming during sex. I never have. Before or sometimes after, yes, but during? Unicorn." She swigged back more beer then frowned and tipped the bottle upside down. "Aww. It's empty."

I laughed. "Sorry, babe. I think you've hit your limit."

"Why? It's New Year's Eve. I want to get my party on." She licked her lips. "I still have one condom left."

Just like that, my cock stirred. Pathetic. If I was being honest, it had been stirring in her presence all night.

She was still lounging around in only a towel, and I could smell my shampoo on her from where I was sitting. Having my scent on her only made it harder to keep my hand from veering into her silky dark hair to pull her head back. Her full lips would part and she'd inhale deeply, and I wouldn't be able to stop myself.

I'd take, and keep right on taking. And that wasn't fair to do to a girl like her. One who didn't understand the rules.

Fuck and run. No feelings, no strings. Definitely no "I'll call you" afterward.

She was a nice girl who baked bread for neighbors. Bread that was probably a solid brick now. Like the condom that had to be in her purse out in her car, because she sure didn't have any pockets under my towel.

"Is that supposed to entice me? You've got one rubber left from Smiley dude, so I'm supposed to grab you and blow your mind?"

"Sure. That'd be fine."

I had to laugh. She was something else. "I think that's the beer talking, not you. In the morning, you'll be glad cooler heads prevailed. Meaning mine."

"Is it that you don't find me sexy? It's okay if you don't. Maeve is a hard act to live up to. She knows that tie a cherry stem with her tongue trick and everything."

"Maeve was a long time ago. I had different tastes back then."

"Uh oh. You're not one of those Christian Grey-type guys, are you? I don't like to be whipped. I'm kind of pain averse, actually."

"Huh? Who said anything about whipping?"

She shrugged. "I guess I'll have another beer."

"I'm the one being forced to watch this New Year's crap and

you're the one getting loaded."

"Ha. Loaded. Right. Fine, we'll just change the channel." She grabbed the remote from between her thigh and the arm of the couch and flipped channels, stopping at something that was distinctly not PG. Or even R.

Try X.

"Wow." She tilted her head to the side like a puppy. "You pay for this?"

"Better than the stuff you get for free," I tossed back, reaching over her for the remote. "Margaret, give me that."

"You know what they called me."

Halfway leaning across her lap, I stopped and turned my head. Her mouth, puffy and vulnerable, was inches from mine.

"You called me it earlier. Magpie. Because I talk too much and I'm too out there. Always the girl with the crazy ideas. Like wanting to be a district attorney, when Turnbull would have to buy a horse to even be a two-horse town."

Normally I would've laughed, but not when her big eyes were so serious. So intent on mine. "It's just a nickname. Families give those out all the time."

"Do you have one?"

"My mama calls me Kell. My dad calls me son. Bethy—" I stopped.

"Bethy. Before it was Beth. Is she your girlfriend?"

For some reason, it seemed vitally important that I be honest with her. "No, she's my little sister."

"Oh." Her face brightened. "I prefer to be called Maggie, by the way." She reached out to brush the hair away from my forehead, and I swear my damn heart just thudded to a stop.

What the hell was it about this girl?

"I have a request."

All I could do was nod.

"Can you call me Maggie when you kiss me?"

6

MAGGIE

"I'M NOT GOING to kiss you."

I was disappointed, but I did my best not to show it. I might've had two beers in me, but I was still lucid enough to know that I was probably acting out of character.

But I didn't care. I wanted to have fun. To be someone other than myself for one night.

Kellan wasn't a stripper, and I wasn't looking to have revenge sex. Though that screaming orgasm he'd mentioned did sound kind of nice.

For once I wasn't even thinking about Derek. Except to realize I wasn't. I just was thinking about myself, and how I'd missed out on so many things because I was so worried about being safe and good and careful. I didn't want to end up a statistic. Someone who trusted the wrong person and got roofied or something.

Hell, that could've already happened tonight, but for some reason, I wasn't afraid of Kellan. Uneasy at times, but not afraid. He wouldn't hurt me, at least not physically.

He picked up the remote and turned the channel.

Bye-bye porno.

I forced down my dismay. So what if I wasn't a siren? He was a sexy guy and probably had his pick of women. You'd think the surly thing would put females off, but it hadn't put me off so I couldn't talk.

I was partially drunk though and not worthy of being trusted. Plus, I'd dated Derek for four years, hadn't I?

"Four years," I mumbled, staring at the TV.

Kellan had put it back on the New Year's Eve show. Weird, since I knew he didn't like it.

He glanced at me. "Huh?"

"I was with Derek for four years. Do you know he didn't go down on me until year three?" Kellan had been mid-guzzle and choked as I shook my head. "Said it wasn't respectful toward me."

"Tool," he muttered.

"No, his tool wasn't anything to write home about either. Probably seven inches while fully erect." I held out my fingers and tried to think back. "Hmm, maybe six-and-a-half. Flaccid, I think he was like four."

"Wow. You're harsh." Kellan slid me a sideways grin, and I blinked. The expression turned his face from merely attractive to holy-fucking-shit, melt-my-panties.

And yes, I just swore in my head again—twice—and no, I did not care.

"I like it, Maggie," Kellan said, holding out his bottle to clink. Mine was empty but I did it just the same. It felt like a victory, sitting here with this near-stranger on New Year's Eve and telling him about my failed relationship.

I wasn't crying. Didn't even feel misty. I felt…strong. Like I'd already handled the situation with Derek, so now the time had come to stop hiding from life.

But that didn't mean I was going to throw myself at this guy. I was certain Maeve hadn't had to. Short of telling him that I wasn't quite as pure as he believed, I didn't know how else to convince him I could be blasé about a one-night-stand too.

It would help if I convinced myself first.

I shivered, and I wasn't sure if it was from cold or nerves. Turned out walking the talk was harder than it looked. Too bad I couldn't sign up for vixen training at community college along with my regular courseload.

Without saying anything, Kellan reached behind him and grabbed the plaid throw draped on the back of the sofa. He wrapped it around me much as he had the towel, tucking in the edge in the front. Not making eye contact as he hid most of my body from his view.

"Thanks." I swallowed and tugged at the hem of the blanket. "This is big enough for both of us if you get cold. Just boxers aren't exactly enough for this weather."

"Nah. I'm fine. Hot-blooded." He quirked his lips and rose, walking out of the room before I could reply.

He was being a total gentleman, exactly what I'd hoped for when I walked through his door. So I had no right to feel disappointed. It wasn't his fault that I'd decided to shed some of my Derek-related bad memories courtesy of Kellan's rock hard, tattooed body.

I sighed. Oh well. At least looking was free.

Tucking my legs up under me, I focused on the TV. The show would be going for another couple of hours until midnight, so I would just sing my little heart out and laugh at the jokes that weren't all that funny.

Somewhere around eleven, Kellan decided to return with two beers, a bottle of water, and a plate of what appeared to be snacks in hand. The pretzels had sufficed since I'd missed out on finishing my sandwich while it was still edible, but I wasn't at all sure about the irregularly-shaped hunks of cheese and pepperoni.

"I checked dates," he said when I just stared at the plate he held out. "You won't die."

"Promise?"

"Eat, Red." After I took the plate, he opened my beer and passed it to me along with the bottle of water. "Last water I had left. Must've known a sexy brunette would wreck in front of my house while I was here this weekend."

The words *sexy brunette* made a flicker of heat shoot through me. I could tell he had to fight to abide by usual niceties, so he probably wouldn't lie out of kindness either.

"Thank you." I ate a chunk of cheese and a thin slice of pepperoni, washing them down with the beer. That same warmth rolled through my system as before. Thank God.

I was so over being cold.

"Still watching this?" He nodded at the screen. "Anyone decent show up yet?"

"Depends what you consider decent. What kind of music do you like?"

He scratched the hair darkening his chin. It wasn't a full beard, more like a few days' growth. I liked the look on him.

"Harder stuff," he said finally. "Fatal Legend, Oblivion, 30 Seconds to Mars."

"Hmm. None of that here. How do you feel about Madonna?"

His curved lips as he tossed back his beer answered that.

We ate and drank in companionable silence through another few songs, passing the plate back and forth. When a band I'd never heard of came onstage, I glanced at Kellan again. "What do you do?"

"Do?"

"Yes, you know, for a job. I already told you I'm in school, studying criminal justice."

"Not sure you spelled that out in so many words."

"Close enough. I have a couple of part-time jobs too. It took me a while to figure out what I wanted to do."

"Jobs doing what?"

I didn't miss that he'd diverted me from my question, but I let him. Momentarily. "As a secretary in an accounting firm a few days a week, and I also work at Pizza Uno on weekends and the occasional extra shift."

"Full-time in school?"

"Yes. I got started late. I have a lot of ground to cover. Of course, I'll probably move to a bigger town like Syracuse or Albany if I intend to become district attorney someday. Probably Syracuse. That guy's been in office forever. He usually runs unopposed." I shook my head. "Can't imagine no one wanting that job."

"You actually know who the district attorney is in those places?"

"Sure."

"Are you a nerd?"

"I watch *Dr. Who* and *Firefly* on repeat and I've read Harry Potter eight times so far, so what do you think?"

Again, the corner of his mouth lifted.

"Your turn," I said lightly. "What do you do?"

"I work with musicians."

Interesting. Explained his derision of the bands onstage, if that was his business. "You do that in Turnbull? How? Or do you travel down to the city for work?"

The city being New York, but everyone from around Turnbull knew which city I meant. No one called Turnbull anything but a town, and it was barely even that.

"No. I don't live in Turnbull anymore. Haven't for a few years. I live in LA now."

"Oh." And there was no reason at all for me to feel disappointed.

"My family's still here obviously, so I come back."

"How often?" Nope, that didn't sound desperate. Okay, just a little. But shit, the first new friend—sort of friend—I'd made in how long and he didn't even live on the same coast anymore.

Figured.

"Now and then, when I have reason to." His gaze rested on mine for a shade longer than was reasonable before he took another slug from his beer.

"So what's your reason? To see your parents and your sister? Old friends?"

"All the above, plus my niece. Rainy." He smiled a genuine smile, and I found myself doing the same.

"Pretty name. How old is she?"

"Three, and she's a total spitfire just like her mother. Smart as a damn whip. She can count to twenty already and she's reading and everything."

"That's great. Takes after you, maybe?"

"Ha." His shoulders shook with silent laughter. "I sucked in school. Only thing I aced in those days was making out with the cheerleaders. That I was an expert in."

"Are cheerleaders better at sex than the average girl?"

"You would ask that."

"Just wondering."

"You wonder an awful lot. No, they probably aren't. But the uniforms are hot."

"So if I'd worn a cheerleader uniform instead of a snowsuit, we might be rolling around on the rug right now?"

"What rug? I have hardwood floors."

"Just saying. Play along."

"If you were wearing a cheerleading outfit in these temperatures, you'd be blue and suffering from frostbite. And hypothermia isn't sexy. Not much range of motion in frozen limbs."

"True. But some guys don't care if the girl doesn't move, so…"

"Tool," he muttered again.

I smiled and sipped my beer. "So what kind of musicians do you work with? And doing what exactly? Managing them? Set work? I'm afraid I don't know all that goes into putting on shows. I just enjoy them."

"Managing them."

"That must be exciting, being so close to the action."

He shrugged and tipped back his beer. He was drinking a lot more slowly than I was. "It's not all it's cracked up to be."

"No? Why not?"

"Because a lot of music types are egotistical fucks with more attitude than talent. You need ego, but you also need the goods to back it up."

"That's true about everything, isn't it?"

"Music attracts the vain. Some of them just want attention for as little as possible."

I nodded sagely. "Fame whores."

He cocked a brow. "Miss Kelly, I do believe you just said a naughty word."

"I know a few of them," I said before swallowing more beer, smiling around the mouth of my bottle.

"Me too. Maybe we should compare notes."

"I think you just don't want to watch the Luscious Lovahboys' final set."

"You are absolutely correct about that."

Laughing with him felt so natural, as natural as arguing with him outside had. Normally I was shy around new people. Not so with this one. Of course, the way we'd met hadn't been usual in any shape or form.

It was the kind of story meant to tell grandchildren one day. If I was the sort of girl who fancied romantic happy endings, which I so was not.

One-night-stand girl, reporting for booty.

"I think maybe you should share your dirty words first," I said. "So I know how deep we're going here."

"Oh, I always go deep."

Right. I gulped down beer to wet my parched throat. "You go first."

"Tits."

"You said that before. I can handle that." Especially since from the direction of his gaze, he was using his X-ray vision to see mine through the blanket he'd wrapped so carefully around me.

"Making it easy on you. Pussy."

I jerked a shoulder though it was hard to keep my face composed. "I have one. Ain't no big."

"Cock."

It wasn't so much the word itself as the rough growl of his voice. That growl turned me into putty.

I licked my lips. "Good one."

He leaned over and shocked the hell out of me by flicking his tongue along the side of my chin. I didn't jerk back, but it was a close thing. "Missed a drop," he murmured as he eased back.

I rubbed my chin, mainly to hold in the warmth a moment longer. If just his tongue had caused my body to surge to life, what would his lips and hands and all the rest of him do?

I might not survive it, but I was willing to see.

"I thought you weren't going to kiss me."

"You think that was a kiss? Oh Red, you've missed out."

It was probably his smirk that drove me over the edge. That or sheer sexual starvation. I hadn't always been thrilled with Derek's skills in bed, but I'd subscribed to the bread and water theory. Substandard sustenance was still enough to keep body and soul together. Besides, it wasn't like I'd had much to compare him to, other than romance novels and my own remarkably dirty imagination.

Now this living, breathing cranky Adonis of a man was sitting right beside me half naked. Heat pumped from his massive body. He had a smart mouth, a snarky attitude, and mostly sucked at social niceties.

Kellan McGuire was the opposite of my ex in every way.

And he wanted me, no matter what he said. I could see it in his eyes. His gorgeous molten brown eyes. Like hot cocoa set on boil.

I glimpsed more in them than arousal. That was easy, and I'd seen it a few times from men. Not ones like him, but men just the same.

Genuine affection lurked in his gaze, and a hint of fear. Somehow little ol' me, Magpie Kelly, had made this huge, grumpy sex god afraid.

That was the biggest aphrodisiac of all.

Carefully, I set aside the plate of snacks and my nearly empty beer. I dug out the water bottle wedged between my hip and the arm of the couch, taking a quick sip to get rid of the yeasty taste.

I wanted to taste something different altogether.

Before he could counter the move, I shifted onto his lap. His pupils flared wide and he bobbled his beer, grabbing hold of it where it now rested between my breasts. I gasped at the cold even through the layers of fabric, and a muscle in his jaw ticked, a warning I'd be foolish not to heed.

This man unleashed would be more than I could imagine. Possibly more than I could handle and come out whole.

And I did not care.

"You said you wouldn't kiss me," I said, brushing his hair away from his face again as I had before.

The softness was a shock just as it had been the first time. His face and body were all hard angles, but his hair and his eyes and his mouth —oh God, his mouth—appeared so soft.

He gave a minute shake of his head, that muscle in his jaw jumping once more.

Last chance to back out, Magpie. You are seriously out of your depth here.

Exhibit A, the rigid column coming to life between my legs. Straining against me where I was already wet and hot and so needy for more.

"So I'm going to kiss you."

7

KELLAN

WARM, silky lips brushed over mine. Tenderly. As if we were friends who'd met up after years of separation.

Good, *chaste* friends.

Fuck that. She'd ripped the lid off this thing, so now we were going for a dive.

I slid my hand into her hair and molded my lips to hers, tilting her where I wanted her. I didn't press for entrance. Not right away. That was the kind of dick move pulled by guys who didn't care about a woman's pleasure.

I wanted her to open to me of her own volition. Always.

Impatiently, she fisted her hand in my hair and tugged my head where *she* wanted it as our slow, shallow kisses turned into more. Somehow I knew it would always be that way between us. Both of us fighting for dominance until we found our spot.

The spot where her moan poured over me like honey, tearing an answering groan from my throat. I cupped her cheek, spanning her delicate skin with my fingers, opening my eyes as her lips trembled apart for me.

She jerked forward on my lap, her grip becoming restless in my hair at the first brush of our tongues.

One taste was all it took to make me ravenous.

I wasn't fully conscious of wrapping my arms around her and flipping her beneath me on the couch. Even less so of driving into the giving juncture between her legs, thankfully protected by layers of material. Sort of protected. The towel and the throw were all rucked up around her, and good goddamn, I didn't think I could stop. Although I'd never fucked without a condom in my life, I wasn't at all sure I could hold back long enough to suit up.

If I even had a rubber. Which I did not.

"Fuck." I slammed my fist into the arm of the sofa beside her head, and she jumped, the blissed-out expression on her face vanishing in favor of sheer terror.

"I'm sorry." I rubbed my thumb over her lower lip. "I didn't mean to scare you."

She exhaled shakily. "Can we just clarify about what? That it was…like *that*, or that you pinned me down and you're so hard and huge, or that you nearly took five years off my life by shaking the couch with your meaty fist?"

It was such a crappy time to laugh. Then I stopped and stared down at her. Her nearly black hair was spread out over the arm of the sofa, her pale blue eyes blurry, her lips soft and wet from mine.

"What did you mean, like that?"

"Huh?"

"You said it was *like that*. Explain."

Her throat moved as she swallowed, and I wanted to lick it. Wanted to lick her damn everywhere, to explore every secret hollow and crevice of her curvy body. She was slight some places and full in others, and I ached with the need to imprint every inch with my touch. Fuck that Smiley bastard. She was mine now.

Mine for a night. Christ. What the hell was I thinking? Had lust really addled my brain that much?

Evidently so.

"You were there, right?" Her voice quaked. "I don't know how to explain. I just…it's never been like that for me before. Ever. Not even the first time I kissed Derek, and he told me I looked like Snow White."

I threw back my head and laughed. "No fuckin' way. Lines like that work?" As soon as I asked the question, I made the mistake of glancing at her face.

Hurt expression achieved once again. Jesus. I was an asshole.

"I mean, you kind of do…"

The corner of her mouth lifted. "If you're going to lie, I'd rather you say I look like Megan Fox. Snow White is kind of untouchable."

I fisted both hands in her hair and ranged my body over hers, easing into that cradle between her legs as if it had been made for me. Hard to say which of us moaned louder. "You totally look like Megan Fox," I murmured, hovering my lips over hers as I distantly registered the announcer onscreen counting down to midnight.

"Liar." She was smiling as she placed her finger over my mouth, barely holding our faces apart. "But I appreciate the effort."

"Maybe I want in your pants or something."

She arched a delicate dark brow. "Or something? Can you be more specific?"

I shifted my head and spoke against her ear. "I want to slide so deep into your hot, tight pussy that you don't have enough breath to scream."

"Oh." Her chest shuddered against mine. "Is that all?"

The TV announcer shouted that it was midnight. The dawn of a new year. Time to kiss the one you loved, or the one you'd love tonight.

"That's everything." I slid my mouth across her cheek until it covered hers.

She kissed me back with the same fervor that was burning in me.

We didn't take time to ease in. Not this time. This time it was all slashing lips and eager tongues and hungry, wandering hands.

Mine especially. If I didn't touch her naked body, I was going to fucking explode.

I unwrapped the blanket I'd wound around her in the hopes of preventing just this. Just like the big, bulky towel, its purpose was to conceal. If I couldn't see her long as hell legs and her tiny waist and those incredible breasts, maybe I wouldn't throw her down like a damn savage and whisper dirty things into her ear.

Maybe not, but I hadn't counted on her climbing onto my lap. Hadn't counted on her in a million ways.

She wasn't using me for my growing fame. She didn't think I had any. I'd told her a white lie, and she'd accepted it without a blink.

A year ago, even six months ago, it had been more true than not. I hadn't expected to step out from behind the desk. When I'd arrived in LA with a rainbow Mohawk and cockiness and energy to spare, I was solely focused on doing the best for my artists. Back then, I'd had no illusions about stepping onstage myself. I played music on the side, and I'd put that dream aside for reality.

Then my dream had become my life, and I'd soon found it had a dark underbelly. I might get to perform and sing my songs and play guitar for women who couldn't get enough of me, and hell, I might even get a little coin.

But I wouldn't get *this*—a woman who gazed up at me with eyes huge with excitement and wonder, wanting me for me. Not anymore. I'd sold that dream to buy another.

Except for tonight.

Unwrapping her was like peeling the paper off a gift. When I got through one layer, there was still the towel. Pulling that apart and hearing her little hitches of breath had to be the sexiest thing I'd experienced in far too long.

Maybe ever.

She was so wide-eyed, so innocent even if she wasn't a virgin. Did it make me a bastard that I wanted to be the one to show her everything? I craved the chance to teach her every dark, depraved thing scrolling through my head.

Her fingers brushed my scruff and I flicked my gaze up to hers. One more pull of the towel and she'd be fully bared.

A present just for me.

"What're you thinking right now?" she asked softly.

I chuckled. If any other woman had asked me that right before fucking, I would've aimed for the door. Sex wasn't about thinking. It was about letting your actions do the talking.

But she wasn't any other woman. I didn't know why she wasn't, but she was not.

"I'm thinking I don't have any goddamn condoms, and I'm really pissed off about that."

Her face fell and then she grinned. It was like being plunged from darkness into bright, sparkling light. "I do. I told you. It's in the car."

"The car is like ten million miles away right now."

"True." She chewed on her lower lip. "You could always, you know, pull out."

"And come in my hand instead of inside you." Sounded like the worst idea ever.

"You could come on me." Her abused lip disappeared between her teeth again and I had to shut my eyes to keep from grabbing my dick. "Anywhere you want."

"Fuck." I buried my face in her hair, drawing in long, heady draughts of my shampoo. That she smelled like me was another turn-on in an ocean of them.

Swallowing hard, I tugged on the towel and squeezed my eyes tight like a damn kid. If I didn't see her, if I just explored her with my hands, maybe I could hold onto a shred of my sanity.

Her flesh was so soft. Almost like satin. I stroked my fingers down her throat and over her heart, stopping to feel the crazy beat. She was scared too. Overwhelmed.

It wasn't just me.

She rolled her hips impatiently against mine and I cupped one of her breasts, eager to touch every part of her. To learn every inch. Her nipples were harder than diamonds and one flick of my thumb had her arching.

"Legs open," I demanded, and she dropped one foot to the floor, giving me all the room I needed.

I stroked one breast then the other, testing the touches that drew the biggest response. What made her shiver and buck and drag her nails up the back of my neck.

"You won't have to pull my face to your pussy, Red." I had to open my eyes. Just for a second. I was losing it without knowing what she looked like at every step. "I'm trying like fuck not to dive on it like a damn starving man."

She whimpered, tossing her head back and forth on the arm of the sofa.

I clamped my hand over her slit and squeezed.

"Yes, God, yes." She dropped her head back over the side, baring her neck to me. I couldn't stop myself from grazing her pale skin with my teeth, dragging them upward to make her delicate flesh pink. Her eyes flew open, her gaze latching on mine as I slipped a finger into the inferno between her legs she'd kept from me all night.

Like a goddamn fire. So fucking wet. I couldn't believe she could be that ready so fast. Just from a couple of kisses and a few fumbling touches.

"He didn't take care of you, did he? Fucking bastard."

She stared at me silently, watching me as I moved down her body. I didn't need an answer. I had it already, just seeing the dampness waiting for me on the swollen lips of her pussy beneath her trim strip of dark curls.

Time for the thirsty man to take a drink.

Flattening my hand on her lower belly, I closed my mouth over her. She fisted her fingers in my hair, tugging on me from the first lick.

Motionless? Like hell. She was like a live wire beneath me, spreading her thighs before I even had to ask. Splitting them wide open so that every part of her was on display.

I rubbed my thumb over her stiff clit, so slowly that she ground her teeth together. Now I was watching her face. I had to see every response as I discovered her limits and shoved her over them.

Speeding up my thumb made her tug harder. Slowing it down earned me the joy of seeing her raise her shoulders from the couch, thrusting her perfect breasts high. Her ruby nipples were like cherries meant for my mouth. I sucked one while I slipped even lower, using my thumb to wedge inside her entrance. Inching in as she gasped and moaned, gyrating her hips helplessly in her urgency to make me go faster.

I didn't. I slid a finger inside her to go with my thumb, my gaze on her eyes as her pupils blew wide.

"So goddamn tight. Squeeze my fingers."

She did, her throat moving as another moan escaped. The sound seemed to surprise her so I scissored my fingers, stretching her methodically.

I wanted more of her sounds. I wanted them all.

"You're going to strangle my cock," I said against her breast, pressing deeper into her snug channel. "How many orgasms can you give me first?"

"I can't," she whispered, shaking her head.

I withdrew my soaked fingers and pressed them against her mouth. "Suck."

Hesitantly, she drew the tips between her teeth. Moaning softly as I pushed them inside.

"That's what you've given me so far. Gimme more."

I moved back down her body and yanked her leg over my shoulder. And this time I didn't go slow, or ease her in.

Or me for that matter.

Sliding in two fingers, I sealed my mouth around her clit and sucked. The thigh against my ear shook and she bowed off the couch, chasing my erotic kisses as I slipped back then sank in again for more. I flicked my tongue between my drenched knuckles, fingerfucking her pussy with everything I had, half crazed to swallow her down. She was close. Her heart throbbing against my lips, her cries thin and high. The roar in my ears drowning out everything but her. Already I was tuned to her, and the need she couldn't hold back a second longer.

But I could.

At the last second, I shifted and bit her inner thigh. She groaned as I flattened my hand over her quaking pussy, offering enough pressure to keep her revved but not enough to go over.

"Mean," she said, all wounded eyes and pouty lips.

Somehow I laughed through the constriction about to turn my dick inside out. She was worth it.

When her sobbing breaths started to slow, I lowered my head again. I aimed straight for her clit, licking it with short, fast strokes. I slid two fingers inside without hesitation. She was so slick and tight, so ready to come on my hand.

I flexed my hips, driving my aching cock into the cushions. Wasn't enough. When she spasmed against my tongue and her walls quivered around my fingers, I drew her clit between my teeth. I didn't stop sucking through her cries and the frantic throb of her heart against my lips. She yanked at my hair as she flooded my mouth, and I'd never tasted anything sweeter.

Mine. The word wasn't just a passing thought now, but a primal rhythm in my blood.

Gently, I set down her leg and moved up her body to frame her face with hands that shook. I met her mouth with my own, slicking my tongue against hers. Wanting her to taste what I had. Sharing it with her while she coiled her limp arms around my neck and hung on.

"Thank you," she breathed once we finally separated.

I lifted a brow.

"I was taught to always say thanks when I received a gift. I'm pretty sure that's the best one I ever got. Like…by far."

"Jesus." I turned my face into her hair and laughed. "You're something else."

"You too." She skimmed her hand down my back and wiggled her fingers under my waistband. "Can I see your ass now? I bet it's fantastic." She slid her hand lower under the silky fabric and purred like a damn cat as she dug her nails into my flesh. "Oh yes. Fantastic. So tight."

"I think that was my line," I muttered, my ears heating.

She slid her hand around to the front and cupped my cock, her fingers stretching and not coming close to meeting. Just like her lips.

"Holy crap. Should I say thanks again now or later?"

I shoved her shoulder as she giggled and drew me back again for another kiss. A sweet, sloppy one this time, punctuated by more giggles as I traced my fingers up and down her sides. "I have to go outside," I said between kisses.

"No, you don't. It might not fit the first time, but we can keep trying."

My only response was a growl, which made her giggle again.

"Condom," I reminded her.

"Oh."

"Yeah, oh."

She nudged my face back and twirled a finger around her nipple, batting her eyelashes. Because I knew exactly what she meant, I pinched her hip.

"Did I say I thought you were innocent?"

"Yes. I kind of am, in terms of sheer variety of experience. But I read dirty books, so that makes up for a lot."

I grunted and pulled her curious hand out of my boxers. If I didn't get up and go now, I'd never be able to.

"Wait here. Don't get dressed."

She braced her head on her hand and yanked the throw over her breasts. "Nah, those snow pants are restrictive. Why do you think I sat around in a towel all night?"

"To torture me?"

Her lips curved. "Maybe a little. But I tortured myself more. It's freezing in here." Her eyes twinkled. "Luckily the fire and the beer kept me from frostbite. And now…other things."

"The other things weren't on my agenda for tonight, but you can be persuasive when you want to be."

"Mmm-hmm. Are you still in here? Go already."

"Going. Need to grab my pants from the other room. Cold out there, ya know."

"Here. Save yourself a trip." She unwound the throw from around herself and tossed it to me before tugging up the towel to cover her breasts and between her legs. "Are you sure the temperature won't hurt it?"

I shrugged, deliberately misunderstanding her. "Cold doesn't break dicks. A prolonged case of blue balls might cause me some harm though."

"Smarty pants. I mean the condom. Let me look on my phone— hey, I don't have my phone." She patted her hip. "Oh God, it's been out there in the freezing car all night. It's probably broken, and I never called my parents to let them know I wouldn't be home tonight after all." She rubbed her forehead as if it ached. "They probably think I'm at Ken's but—"

"Who the hell is Ken?"

"You're growling again."

I crossed my arms and waited.

"Ken is my best friend. Ken*dra*," she added with extra emphasis on the second syllable. "Why do you care? It's not like you intend to call me tomorrow, Mr. I Live in LA and Hobnob with Musicians."

I did more than 'hobnob' with them, but she didn't need to know that. "I'm not a call tomorrow kind of guy."

"Good." She jerked a shoulder and the towel slipped, revealing the mouth-watering curve of her breast. "I don't want that. I've decided I'm going to be a one-night stand kind of girl. I've spent enough months whining about Derek."

My sore, still not completely deflated dick—thanks to the glimpse I'd gotten of her breast—really wasn't interested in her relationship issues. But I felt bad for her, and she was a nice girl.

Way too nice for the likes of me, so what the fuck was I doing with her?

I scratched the back of my neck. "So, ahh, how long has it been? Since you guys ended."

"Two months since we first called it quits. But we weren't sleeping together at the very end. He was always too tired from working so hard. Truth was he was banging the stripper." She sighed and shifted halfway into a sitting position, somehow missing the fact that both of her nipples were now peeking above the towel and waving hello.

And my eager cock was saluting right back.

"That's unfortunate."

"Not so much. You have a better ass." She grinned at me, and I was frigging dazzled. Like lights blinding me, can't see due to the damn spots in my vision type of shit.

Fuck me.

Time to get outside so we could finish what we'd started. Then I could move on and accept the reality of what this was. Excellent sex with a hot as hell, cute girl who was a little crazy and a lot fun and different from any of the women I'd been with in a long time.

"Keys?"

She flushed and bit her lip. "Think I might've left them in the car. I panicked when I went off the road."

This chick, man.

"I'll be right back." I tossed her the blanket. If she thought I was going out in a damn near blizzard in just that and my boxers, she was nuts. "Keep warm for me."

"Oh, I'm warm. Running hot right now."

"We'll see about that."

"Can you grab my phone too? It's in my purse. Just bring the whole thing in. Please and thank you."

"Uh-huh. Anything else?"

"I wouldn't mind some chocolate. PMS is a bitch."

Ignoring her, I headed to the front door and grabbed the sweats and hoodie I'd thrown on a peg. I tended to strip down the moment I came in the door.

Once I'd pulled them back on, I stuffed my feet into my boots and grabbed my coat. And opened my door to a world of white.

Fucking hell. Her pussy was the only one in the universe worth dealing with that.

"Be careful," she called, her words sucked away by me closing the door.

I stomped my way through drifts that were way higher than they'd been even hours ago. By morning, we'd need to dig our way out of here.

Maybe we could just stay in and fuck all weekend. Scavenge for whatever was left in the cupboards and discover a few new positions.

With one condom? Not likely.

A crazy part of me almost didn't care. I'd never gone bareback before, but she was making me do things tonight that made no sense. I was already so out of my comfort zone with her. Next we'd be cuddling in the afterglow or some shit, and I wasn't even sure I'd mind.

I'd just blame it on the cold currently singeing my eyeballs and focus on getting that treasured piece of latex and back the hell inside.

Trudging through the snow, I made my way to her car, still tilted precariously in the ditch. I tipped my head back and stared at the cloudy sky. A night like this should've been prime weather for Beth to make some good money. Maybe she had more work than she could handle and that was why she wasn't answering the phone. Or calling me back, all these hours later.

Tomorrow I'd get over there as soon as I could shovel my way out of here. I'd give Maggie a ride home and we'd figure out how to get her car towed. Either through Beth or AAA or some other place.

Then I'd get on with having the rest of my relaxing solo weekend before I had to get my ass back to LA in time for the promotional tour for the single. That song release would mark the day my life officially became insane, possibly for good.

If I was lucky, even if living in a fishbowl no longer sounded nearly as incredible as I'd once believed.

I skidded down the side of the ditch and yanked on her car door handle. It took a few tries due to the damage and the cold—amazing how it was harder when I didn't have her nearby to show off for—but I finally pried the door open.

Getting inside wouldn't be nearly as easy.

Angling my body, I twisted and wedged inside, fumbling across the seat for the fluffy thing I figured had to be her purse. It looked like a chia pet made from pink fur. What the hell?

Halfway back out, I spotted a tinfoil-wrapped lump on the floor that had to be her friend's loaf of bread. I snagged that too and bumped my elbow against the bulging glove compartment, attempting to close it, but the contents spilled out everywhere. I could barely make out most of them in the watery moonlight through the windshield. Mostly maps and papers and girl crap it looked like. Hairbrush and tampons and inexplicable female items. I dug through the stuff just in case she'd shoved chocolate in there too for emergencies—which was not a pussy thing to do since I was hoping to get laid—and was about to give up when a miraculous piece of foil practically jumped into my hand.

She kept her condoms in the glove compartment? Damn, girl.

My mind filled with images of her rolling around in the cramped backseat with the Smiley dude and I nearly crushed the foil in my fist. Nope, that wouldn't do.

Picturing me rolling around with her in the back, however, worked just fine. Okay, *her* rolling and bouncing, and me shoving her pale thighs wide before I slid deep into her slick pink pussy—

"Fuck." I pushed my wrist against my twitching cock through my sweats. Just thinking about nailing her had me practically creaming in my damn pants.

You really think you'll have burned that out of your system by tomorrow? Good luck, brother.

I pocketed the condom and tried to pick up as much of the mess on the floor as I could. Impatience was riding me hard, so I pushed things into the glove compartment haphazardly and slammed the door closed. Then I backed out of the car and shut the door.

Shit, her keys.

Fighting the wind, I retrieved them through brute force and extreme desire for sex. And okay, so I wanted to do a nice thing. Turnbull was beyond safe, especially on a night like this, but the keys shouldn't be left outside any longer. Being trusting was one thing. Unsafe another.

Isn't that why she's sleeping with you? Because she's way too trusting and sweet?

Not going there again.

I slitted my eyes against the driving snow and trudged back to the house, clutching her ridiculous purse and her beloved loaf of bread as if they were priceless.

My stomach grumbled as I hunched my shoulders against the howling wind. I was going to enjoy eating that freaking bread almost as much as I'd loved eating her pussy.

Almost. Nothing could compare with that salty sweet perfection.

My cock leaped against the soft material of my sweats and I nearly groaned. I wanted to go down on her again. I'd have to get her off that way one more time before I finally pounded her deep.

So fucking deep.

I clomped across the small stoop, trying to dislodge the snow attached to my boots and slipping inside to soak my sweats and my feet. A hot shower sounded excellent, with my sexy little car wrecker for company. I wouldn't mind washing her back.

Or her front.

Pushing my shoulder against the door, I muscled it open. I juggled purse and bread and checked my pocket to make sure that important piece of foil was still safe and sound. Oh, and her keys. Perfect.

I set down what I'd retrieved and shrugged out of my coat, hanging it and my hoodie on the peg. I kicked off my sodden boots and shed my sweats—and boxers too.

The time for being subtle had passed, as evidenced by the major wood I was sporting as I carted her purse and bread into the living room.

Fussy pink purse, check, old lady's borrowed bread, check. Keys and rubber of glory, check.

Massive cold-proof boner, double check.

"Sorry, no chocolate, unless it's in this crazy thing." I held up her purse by the handle and glanced at the couch.

She was sound asleep.

My chest tightened and my dick wilted, pretty much in succession. Then I smiled, because it matched the rest of the night.

I'd never forget it, that was for damn sure. Or her.

I set down her stuff and went to crouch beside the sofa, intending to adjust her blanket. She'd said she was cold, and she was half uncovered.

She rolled over, her arm dangling, thick lashes fluttering. "Kellan."

Softly, she started to snore.

Somehow that did it. Her murmuring my name while she was unconscious meant she had to sleep in my bed, even if no other woman ever had. Not here in my sanctuary. But she was already different in a matter of hours.

More different than I wanted to consider.

Carefully, I gathered her up in my arms, brushing kisses against her forehead as she stirred. She fell back asleep almost immediately and didn't wake as I carried her down the hall to my bedroom.

I placed her on the center of the bed and tugged up the covers. I'd have to start the fireplace in here too. She wasn't like me and hot despite the weather.

Besides, if she didn't realize I was doing it, this didn't count as taking care of her. I was the only one who would ever know, and for this moment, I could pretend. I could imagine that maybe I wasn't a dickhead rockstar who'd fuck her and roll out of bed to head to the next town and the next conquest.

That I was worthy of a girl like this wanting to marry me like she'd wanted to marry that Smiley dude. And not just for the money that would someday be mine if the fates—and a hell of a lot of hard work—aligned.

A lot of maybes, and no one was in my head to hear them but me.

Once I'd started the fire, I went to grab her stuff from the living room and set it on the nightstand, including the condom and her keys. Then I crawled into bed with her. Close, but not too close. Giving her space.

Until I couldn't any longer and slid my arm around her waist, drawing her against me. She smiled in her sleep and I was sunk. I shut my eyes and let myself pretend once more.

That this beautiful, funny woman was actually mine.

8

MAGGIE

I WOKE IN DARKNESS.

I blinked, trying to figure out why the moonlight was slanting across the bedroom ceiling. It didn't in my bedroom at home, except on rare occasions. I turned my head, my eyes adjusting to the lack of light. No curtains? Mine were lacy and white and billowed in the breeze.

There was another glow on the ceiling, a flicker of orangish-yellow flames. I rose on one elbow, squinting at the fireplace opposite the bed. My gaze darted to the heavy arm pinning me down and my heart leaped into my throat before throbbing between my legs.

I didn't sleep with a man in my parents' house. Not even with Derek, and we'd all believed I would marry him one day. That was just the rules—no sleeping with the opposite sex outside of wedlock under my parents' roof. Since I appreciated being able to live there for low rent while I finished up my courses at the community college, I abided by their wishes. For the last couple of months, I hadn't had a man to invite over anyway.

Now I had one in bed with me—a huge, muscular guy with more

than a little scruff that had abraded my thighs when he'd gone down on me. Something I wanted again, desperately.

He'd put me in his bed. When had I fallen asleep? Had we…

No. I remembered him going out to grab the condom and my purse from the car, but the rest was a blur. It was probably because I'd had sucked down all that beer. I was a total lightweight, so it didn't take much. Add in the orgasm of the ages and no wonder I'd been down for the count.

Now I was just down for more sex. Like pronto. But that didn't mean I had full control of my mouth when Kellan opened a baleful eye and let his gaze drop to my exposed breasts.

"It ain't morning," he rumbled, and I swear my nipples tingled as if he'd sucked on them.

"No. I slept like the dead though." I rubbed my eyes. "You didn't roofie me, did you?"

Yep, that would be the "not in control of my mouth" portion of the program.

He tightened the arm around my waist and hoisted me on top of him so I was straddling his hips with the sheet twisted beneath my breasts. My natural inclination was to cover them, but I'd seen enough approval in his eyes as he gazed at my naked body tonight to brazen my way through. Even in the low light, I could tell he was checking me out and his open perusal emboldened me.

"I gave you three beers and one helluva orgasm before you passed out on me." His fingers dug into my waist. "I don't drug women. When I found you sleeping, I brought you to bed with me. Where we slept."

His tense tone made me want to soothe my thoughtless question. As a criminal justice student, sometimes me and my classmates employed weird ways of alleviating the heaviness of the topics we dealt with. Along with making morgue jokes and inappropriate remarks about serial killers, a few of us also had a fetish for slasher movies. I was guilty of all three.

"I'm sorry," I said quietly, rubbing his bare chest. Touching him freely was a revelation. His skin was rough with hair and so hot, barely seeming to contain the corded muscles beneath. "That was tasteless of me and a side effect of my studies. It's not anything to be kidded about and I apologize."

"Your studies lead you to talking about roofies? Yeah, I guess they would," he said before I could answer.

"I learn all the ways people hurt each other, and the methods we have of classifying them and stopping them."

"You can't."

"No, but we can try. Trying is our only option. Otherwise, every person we don't try to protect is on our watch."

"A crusader." He touched my bare belly and I dropped my head back. "I admire that, even if I think it's a lost cause."

"More or less lost than me getting you inside me tonight?" I asked huskily, well beyond any pride. I knew what I wanted, and I was tired of not getting it.

If this was my chance to show the universe I was willing to claim what I desired most, I intended to start with the very fine specimen of Kellan's cock.

"From accusing me of drugging you to demanding sex. You're an odd one, Magpie Kelly."

I was still running my hands over his chest. Couldn't stop. I dug my nails into his skin and savored his hiss of breath. "When you fuck me, call me Maggie when you call out my name."

Though I'd barely gotten the curse word out, I'd managed it. Definite progress.

He grasped my breast roughly, his touch igniting my senses. Our eyes locked. "When I fuck you, you'll be the only one calling out."

My heartbeat quickened and I leaned back to free his stiffening cock from his boxers. The limited light in the bedroom still allowed me to see the pearl of fluid at the tip. "Are you a betting man, Kellan McGuire?"

Like a damn viper, he moved lightning fast again and rolled me beneath him. He pressed three fingers over my mouth, trapping my words and my breath as he leaned over me to reach the nightstand. "Yes. I'm betting the next thing you do is scream."

I screamed behind his hand just to annoy him and he pushed his fingers between my lips, mimicking the hot shaft he thrust between my legs. Heavy and thick, he pulsed against my aching slit, shutting me up quick.

"Nice to know you have lungs." He pulled out his wet fingers and slid his hand between our tightly wedged bodies, stroking them into me without hesitation. Two opened me up and I gasped, turning my head while he dangled a glorious foil packet over my head. "Think we should try for three."

"Orgasms?"

"Greedy girl." He chuckled darkly. "Fingers. Since you were worried about me fitting. Not a problem, by the way." He spoke against my ear. "You know this snug little pussy would never keep me out."

I writhed against his hand as he made good on his promise. I was pretty sure he was correct. No part of my body was restricted to him. Absolutely none. At least after another beer and some building up first.

Scary as hell and yet I wanted to see how far we could go. How far he would take me.

Willingly.

"Almost there already." He bit my lower lip as he pumped his three huge fingers in and out, stretching me in a way that bordered on pain. It wouldn't be anything compared to his cock, so I wanted the burn. Craved it.

I nodded, whimpering at the angle change when he flexed his hand. He hit some spot inside me that had my eyes flaring wide. All I could see was his intent expression. He was learning me, I realized.

Studying me like I might a textbook, except his method was way more hands-on.

"Oh yeah, you're going to fly for me." His thumb swept over my clit and I jolted off the bed, only held in place by the heft of his body. I liked having him on top of me, forcing me to take more and more. There was no evading him this way—or myself.

His fingers twisted and spread, scissoring inside me until the telltale heat built low in my belly. Too fast for me to try to slow this down. Too fast to do anything but brace my heels on the bed and rock into his dirty thrusts. I could hear what he was doing to me, every lewd bit of it, and that only turned me on more.

I wanted him to put his fingers in my mouth again. So I could taste myself. I wanted to suck on them while his knowing dark eyes drank down every movement.

"Stubborn little thing." He crushed his mouth down on mine, but his tongue was silky soft as he slipped inside. He kept the pressure of our kiss a direct counterpoint to his furious pounding between my legs. He skimmed that secret spot again and again, and I jerked beneath him, helpless.

I had become his instrument, and with just his fingers and mouth, he kept me hovering on the edge.

"I want your screams." He bit my earlobe, and the sharp pain tugged my clit. "Scream for me."

In any other situation, I would've laughed at him and myself for even being tempted. But in this dark, warm bedroom, so far away from the world I'd known before I met him, nothing seemed funny. No request seemed out of bounds.

Then he hooked his fingers inside me, angling just right, and brushed my clit, and I didn't have a choice but to do his bidding. I screamed myself raw, first as the pleasure engulfed me and left me shaking and then again and again as he just kept going.

No cease. No mercy.

The first orgasm was like ripping off a Band-Aid. The second—

and third—were like dropping into an endless rippling pool of warm water. My body floated away from me and my mind followed suit, leaving me at his control. Quaking, moaning, lost to him. Nothing but a mass of sensations as I watched him strip off his boxers.

He knelt between my legs and stroked his hard cock. He was so erect that his shaft stood away from his body, aiming straight at me. He needed the tight warmth that I could provide, and I needed the swift, deep thrusts he'd give me. Vanquishing everything but him and me.

Us, the most beautiful word I'd ever heard.

The sound of the foil packet being opened was loud in the darkness. The fire crackled, the flames highlighting the breadth of his shoulders as he rolled on the latex. He remained silent, staring at me all the while.

I couldn't look away.

He didn't fumble into position. Didn't ask me what I wanted. He just gripped my thighs and hauled me closer, drawing up my legs to hook around his waist. Then he loomed over me and grasped my chin, distracting me with long, slow kisses that belied the jut of his cock against my cleft. His thumb found my clit at the same moment the head of his shaft entered me on a shallow, slippery thrust. He pulled back and surged into me again, deeper now, my body acceding to his invasion.

There was simply no choice. He dominated me. Possessed me. *Owned* me.

My chest hitched on a trapped breath. God, he felt enormous, but I was so aroused there was no discomfort. Only pleasure chased his first pass. And the second, and the third.

So many times I lost track.

He pushed my legs higher, hooking them around his neck so he could pound into me without mercy. I moaned, thrashing beneath him on the mattress. I threw out a hand to grab the sheets and hit the nightstand instead. The pain that sang up my arm barely registered.

There was nothing but him.

The bed springs shrieked. So did my muscles, but I didn't care. I'd never experienced anything like this. Never been taken so ruthlessly. He wasn't showing me any tenderness. If anything, with every thrust, he was rougher, wilder. Grunts burst from his throat and punishing fingers dug into whatever soft skin he could reach. His thumb was relentless on my aching clit.

If I'd had screams left to give as my orgasm built, I would've offered them to him. I was giving him everything else. My eyes, wide open on his. My body, pulsing with need. My heart—

No. That was mine still. I wouldn't give that away again so freely. Not even if I was feeling more than ever before in this furtive moment in the firelit dark.

"There." He grinded into me, so forcefully that I sawed my teeth over my lower lip. "Right there."

I whimpered, nearly delirious. I couldn't breathe, couldn't think. My body was full of him. He was in every pore, every hit of air I took. That alpine shampoo of his, the tang of sweat and sex. Then my own scent as he pressed his damp thumb into my mouth, giving me something to suck on while my core clenched.

I was so close to coming. Just a little more…

"Fuck." He didn't stop, dragging his thumb away and replacing it with his mouth on mine. No matter how crazily he pumped into me, his kisses were always soft and lingering. So confusing. My body didn't get it, and my head definitely didn't.

Tears of frustration popped into my eyes as he drew back and flipped me over on my hands and knees. He clamped a hand on the back of my neck, holding me down while he pushed into me from behind. My eyes blurred so I closed them, biting the pillow at the rush of heat that accompanied his strokes.

I lost track of time. Of myself. All I could do was cry out into the pillow as he ravaged me, stroke by stroke. He finally found his release, his shout breaking against my shoulder. "Maggie."

Just that, over and over. I would've smiled but I had no strength left.

His heaving hips forced me down to the mattress while sweat burned my eyes and my body shook through what seemed like one endless orgasm. I grasped for his hand, for some kind of anchor, and his fingers tangled with mine. Centering me when all I could do was drift.

"Kellan." His name was the only word I could say. The only word I could think.

Before I'd recovered, he rolled me over. He stripped off the condom and disposed of it, then lowered his head to lick my slit. The gesture was so sexy and dirty that I couldn't do anything but part my legs and yank on his hair as he pulled another climax out of my spent body.

There weren't words when he brushed his lips over mine. I was still hungry for his taste. For *my* taste on his tongue. Lifetimes passed while he made love to my mouth and eased me down from my high.

So many highs. So much new.

I scraped my nails down his shoulders, clinging to him like an addict as he tugged the covers over our sweaty bodies.

"Sleep," he said against my forehead, and I couldn't argue. I sought his fingers in the dark, bringing them between my breasts.

Now I could rest.

I dropped into a welcome void of unconsciousness, knowing he guarded me in my sleep. His body so strong and hard as it sheltered mine.

I didn't know how long I slept before a sudden pounding against the wall shook me awake. It sounded like someone was ripping apart the place, board by board. I shot up in bed as the house shook again and again.

Heart in my throat, I fumbled for Kellan, but he shoved me back and murmured, "Stay here."

Someone was knocking. Shouting. More than one voice maybe? I shook my head, trying to clear it, as Kellan pulled on his boxers and grabbed what I assumed was a pair of pants and shirt and quickly dressed in the dark.

"Don't move," he instructed me and I nodded, too out of sorts to argue.

Kellan's footsteps pounded down the hall as I swung my shaky legs out of bed and reached for the glowing phone on the nightstand. But it wasn't mine. It asked for a passcode, and still half asleep, I punched in the most basic one on the off chance he'd taken the easy route.

He had.

The time glowed at me. Six-eleven. Not even daylight. I could hear voices down the hall, hushed, urgent ones. Curiosity and panic warred inside me, but over both was the need to text my own phone. To know he had my number and I had his before we separated.

Because I knew we'd separate, that we'd been headed to this moment since I'd crashed into his ditch.

My phone beeped from within my purse on the nightstand. I had his number. He had mine. If either of us changed our minds, we had options.

If not, it would be only this, and this had been everything.

I gripped a handful of my hair and his phone, holding onto both as I stumbled to my feet. I dropped his cell on the nightstand and swung my gaze around the room. My clothes. Where were they now? Still in the bathroom where I'd shed them before my shower so many hours ago?

Even putting one foot in front of the other took effort. Luckily what was left of the fire lit my way out of Kellan's bedroom and into the bathroom. I flipped on the light and gasped at my appearance.

I'd never looked just fucked before. Or if I had, it had never been like this, of that I was certain.

My skin was reddened from his beard. My chin and cheeks were flushed and bruising skin flared under my jaw and in interesting places along my neck. I turned to look at my back, letting out another gasp at the path of stubble and hickeys that marred my pale skin.

I could feel the burn between my thighs too from his stubble. And his cock. I shuddered and gripped the edge of the sink in boneless fingers, twisting my thighs together as my wonderfully abused clit throbbed.

My nipples beaded as I studied myself, my gaze lingering despite the rising voices coming from down the hall. I couldn't look away from myself and who I'd become in the course of one night.

"Maggie."

My father's shout made me lurch back from the mirror. I frowned and shoved my hair away from my face as I gazed around blearily. My clothes were stacked neatly on the back of the toilet where I'd left them earlier. I pulled them on haphazardly, hating each layer as I piled it back on.

I'd been the next thing to naked for most of the evening and naked all night long. I didn't want to hide in all this material again. More than that, I didn't want to open the door to my worried, frantic father and feel ashamed that I'd been more myself with a stranger than ever before in my life.

But I opened the door anyway, because my dad was concerned due to my careless actions and I loved him. Besides, all fairytales had to come to an end sometime, right?

"Maggie, baby, are you okay? When you didn't come home and didn't call, and we drove the route to Mrs. Pringles' and found your car here, of all places, we didn't know what had happened." He cupped my face in ice cold hands. "Tell me you're all right," he demanded, shooting an accusing glance over his shoulder.

"Daddy," I whispered, pleading for him to understand.

Glancing back at me, he shook his head. My sweet, patient, rule-abiding father took one glance at his baby girl's wild hair and blurry eyes and shut his own.

"Let's go home," he said finally.

I might've argued if I hadn't looked past him and glimpsed Kellan's closed-down face. He was standing with a slight brunette with braided hair and a weary expression. No one was smiling.

I tried to get Kellan to meet my eyes, but he wasn't looking at me. His gaze bounced everywhere else, never landing on any one spot for long.

So much for not calling the next day. He was dismissing me before I'd even made it out the front door.

One-night stand, remember? Now be woman enough not to beg. Time to take your ass back home where you belong.

Swallowing hard, I nodded and gave my father a weak smile. "Just let me get my things."

9

KELLAN

"WHAT THE HELL WERE YOU THINKING?"

My sister Bethy's sharp question hit me between the shoulder blades where I stood at the kitchen window, slamming back black coffee and wishing it were beer.

The amount I had left wasn't nearly enough to get trashed the way I needed to.

Maybe if I had more beer, I wouldn't have to hear Maggie's breathy cries in my head anymore. Maybe I wouldn't remember the feeling of her tightening around me until we both broke.

Eventually I'd get to the point where the memory faded. I hoped.

"Coffee?" I asked.

"No, I don't want coffee."

So she'd said after she returned from towing Maggie's car back to her shop for her techs to get to work on it. She was a mechanic too, though she tended to run the shop more than keep her hand in. I'd hoped she would choose to stay there to work on Maggie's car, not come back and harass me about what I'd been thinking.

I hadn't. End of story.

"You know better than to sleep with a girl like her. She's a townie and you are not. She's not like you, Kell."

"Tell me something I don't know."

"That's not a judgment against you," she said after a moment. "It's just reality."

Like the reality that neither Maggie or I had been paying attention to anything last night. She hadn't called her parents to let them know not to expect her, and I hadn't followed up with my sister to tell her to wait until later in the day to show up with the tow truck.

You know, because wanting more time with Maggie made sense, when I shouldn't have had any with her to begin with.

In the end, it hadn't mattered. Before first light, Maggie's concerned father had driven the route he suspected Maggie would have taken. Upon finding her abandoned car, he'd called the shop for a tow anyway. Bethy had already been on the way.

When she'd arrived, she had tried to convince Maggie's dad I wasn't an axe murderer or a pervert who'd kidnapped his young, impressionable daughter. Of course, the fact that the one and only time the elder Kelly had met me a million years ago, I'd had my mouth on his middle daughter's breast probably hadn't helped things.

Ahh, memories. Ones I hadn't seen fit to mention to Maggie.

No wonder I wanted to get shit-faced.

"The truth is," Bethy continued, "that you break girls. You don't mean to. It's not like you lead them on, or lie to them, but you're good-looking and the asshole personality type is currently in." She held up a hand. "Just more reality."

"What about the reality that Tom wasn't good for you, but you wouldn't listen to any of us?" As soon as the words were out, I regretted them. It wasn't right to slap back at my sister when I was only pissed at myself. "Look, I didn't mean—"

"I paid, didn't I?" she asked quietly. "I'm still paying. So is Rainy. But without him, I wouldn't have her. So sometimes you have to go through some shit to get your goddamn rainbow."

A smile twisted my lips as I glanced at her. She looked exhausted, and she wasn't explaining much about why she hadn't answered her phone last night. I wanted to pry, but at the same time, I was just so fucking grateful she was okay. Strong and whole and untouched.

Tom hadn't hurt her again.

"And sometimes you gotta ride your fucking rainbow for as long as it lasts, knowing the dark is waiting. I won't apologize for it." I tipped back my head. "Fine, maybe I would apologize to someone, but it damn sure isn't you or her father."

"Stuff happens. You were snowed in and bored. Add in some beer and questionable choices…"

What had occurred was so far from that. If only I could categorize it that easily.

"I'm not discussing this with you. All right? We're both adults and that's the end of it."

"You think you can't get bruised up when you're over twenty-one, Kell? And she's barely that. She's a goddamn kid, and you know you're not going to call her. How do you think she'll feel when that single blows up and you're on the cover of every magazine?"

"She'll probably never know. She listens to sweet pop shit, not our stuff. I was just a guy from LA who deals with musicians. Nothing more, nothing less. And I *liked* that."

"It's a lie. You are more than that. You always have been."

I didn't reply.

"What if she gets ideas about you? Romantic ones? Then what? People know you in this town. If she wanted to, she could find a way to contact you, and you'll what, just let her down easy? Crush that poor girl's heart?" I heard Bethy's disappointment loud and clear. "You're the wiser, worldly one. You gotta stop thinking with your dick. Think of someone else for a change, Kell."

I swallowed the last of my coffee and banged the mug on the counter. I'd already had three cups this morning while I waited for my little sister to spit out what was on her mind. Now that she had, I wanted her to leave me the hell alone so I could gear up to deal with my life again.

I'd grown accustomed to weeks spent either seeking or in the spotlight, surrounded by people. Followed by a few days on my own, where I could be myself and actually breathe in my own skin. This weekend wasn't supposed to be about more drama. It was supposed to be where I got to escape it, for fuck's sake.

My phone buzzed in the pocket of my jeans and I tugged it out. "It's my manager, Lila. I gotta take this."

Betty shrugged and grabbed her keys and her newsboy cap. "I have work. Stop by the shop before you roll out of here, all right?"

I grunted an affirmation and waited until she shut the front door behind her before I answered Lila's call.

"You have a radio call coming up Tuesday morning. Additional press for the single," she said after the briefest of niceties.

That was Lila Crandall's way. When I'd met her two days after landing in California, I'd thought she was a stupidly hot blond with a shark's smile and a no-nonsense manner. A couple of years later, I knew her to be whip-smart and intolerant of bullshit. If you couldn't get with the program right away, she wasn't going to wait.

I appreciated Lila's directness, especially today. She reminded me of someone else I'd met who was incapable of telling anything but the truth.

Being with Maggie last night had been refreshing. I'd grown numb to all the plastic and glitz that made up my world until I was confronted by Maggie's honesty. Everything about her was intoxicating.

Christ, I hadn't broken her. I had to believe that. She had no reason to fall for a guy like me.

Just like you have no reason to fall for her?

That was just it. She'd given me a million reasons to fall for her, and I'd given her none. Including not even asking if she was okay after I'd pounded her into the mattress. If I'd hurt her.

That was riding me harder than the rest. If I'd caused her pain or scared her or...Jesus. I wouldn't be able to live with myself. I barely could now.

But it wasn't like I could contact her. I mean, I could. I knew her name and her address, if her family still lived in the same house as they had back a decade ago when I'd been caught indulging in my oral fixation with Maeve. But we hadn't talked about anything beyond sex. We'd practically had a tacit agreement not to speak after last night. I certainly hadn't given her any reason to think otherwise.

Neither had she, so maybe she really had been looking for a one-time thing. She'd just gotten out of a long relationship and a rough breakup. The last thing she needed was me.

Fuck.

"Kellan. Are you still there? I asked you if you still intended to fly back on Tuesday? I'm booking more interviews Wednesday so we need you here and presentable first thing that morning. A limo will pick you up and take you to WKLP."

Presentable meant I had to shave my beard. I could either go for a more "manageable" trimmed look or I could shave it entirely, but either way, my current look didn't match the record company's idea of what Wilder Mind's frontman should look like.

Tomorrow I might even give two shits about that. Maybe.

"I'll see if I can switch my flight to tomorrow. The signal here is crap so it'd be hard to do an interview."

Besides, the sooner I got my ass back to LA, the faster I'd stop wondering if contacting Maggie was a good idea.

It wasn't. On any level. People in my business weren't meant for serious relationships. I'd never been one to try the fidelity thing, but even if I wanted to, there was so much BS in the tabloids that it was almost impossible to keep something going. Sure, some people managed it, and major props to them. But add in the distance and the crazy way we'd met and it didn't make sense. We didn't know each other, and chemistry in bed meant little.

Okay, it meant a damn lot, especially when just the thought of her had me harder than the window frame.

"We can send the jet for you. This media blitz is important." Lila's voice turned into white noise in my ear.

This was actually my life now. Jetting off for press junkets, and formalizing tour schedules, and preparing my look for the public. I wasn't merely the barely middle class son of a sometime roofer and full-time wanderer and a school secretary anymore.

I also wasn't a guy who ignored his gut. That instinct had gotten me out to California and into a business I knew nothing about. At least on the surface. I'd done so well that Lila and her boss Donovan had believed that me and the guys I'd grown up with—with a new addition or two—might just be more than a former high school garage band.

My gut hadn't steered me wrong yet.

"Lila, you're married, right?"

Lila cleared her throat. "Out of left field much?"

"Sorry."

"Yes, I am."

"To a guy in the business. A guitarist, isn't he? In Oblivion?"

"Yes. Why?"

"And you're happy."

"I am, yes. What is this about?"

Hell if I knew. I scraped my hand down my face, buzzing over the beard I needed to shave. My so-called hibernation weekend was ending sooner than I'd planned.

Perhaps that was a good thing. I still hadn't made a move that would create even more chaos, when I had an almost pathological aversion to it.

Since Lila was waiting for a reply, I blew out a breath. "I guess I'm just thinking about a lot of this stuff. How my life is changing. All the things I didn't think were possible suddenly are, and it's just fucking crazy."

"Your single hasn't blown up yet, Kellan." Lila's dry tone made me smile. "Hang on to your mic stand, Axl."

My smile turned into a genuine laugh. "Yeah, yeah, I know. I might die in obscurity or be on one of those *One Hit Wonder* shows in ten years. But what if, you know?"

"Oh, I know. I also know I wouldn't have pegged you as the settling down type of guy. If that's changed, look around you. Examples of making it work are there to be found."

"Yeah, maybe if you're both in the business. If you get how it works. Hell, if you're even on the same coast." I rubbed my temple. "Don't mind me. Just a lot of crap in my head and I'm dumping it on you."

"I often play the role of junior therapist with my artists. I get bonuses when I keep lead singers from running off and quitting the band, usually right before their biggest show. You'd be surprised how often I've had to."

"No, I wouldn't. Remember I sat around that table with you and Donovan and Dex more than a few times, trying to figure out how to keep Luc Moreau from getting arrested during a show."

"He's back in rehab for his sex addiction."

I winced. "Second time?"

"Try third. But he's insanely talented, so we deal with him. Just not sure how much longer that will be true."

"Don't worry. I'm not about to split the band."

"Better not. I vouched for you, you know. Turnbull strong and all that."

I stared out the window at the bright blue sky and the snow shimmering like diamonds in the blinding sunshine. It was as if there had never even been a storm last night.

But there had.

"Turnbull strong," I echoed. "Thanks, Lila. I'll talk to you once I'm back in town." I ended the call and started to slip my phone back in my pocket.

Then I saw an unknown number with a text that I'd somehow missed before. It had been sent this morning. Six-eleven am.

Holy shit.

My heart sped up as I clicked on the message.

In case we need a do-over and there isn't a ditch available. Xo, Red.

10

MAGGIE

Two weeks later

"I'M glad you're not trying to avoid me or anything. Because that would really brass my balls."

The stern voice in line behind me at Starbucks made me turn with a sheepish smile. I glanced up at my best friend Kendra, who was towering over me as she always did. Nothing new there. She also was dressed on point as usual in a red pantsuit that made her appear like the young executive she would soon be rather than a low-rent, harried college student like the rest of us.

What was new was the cocked eyebrow she aimed at me. Typically she saved that expression for one of our professors when they offered up something as fact that was debatable at best. And Ken *did* debate with them. She suffered no fools gladly.

Including me. *Especially* me.

"Why would I avoid you?"

"That's a very good question." Ken tucked her phone in her tiny white, ridiculously chic purse and crossed her arms. "Anytime now, Kelly."

I had to grin as the line moved forward. "I'm not. I've just been busy. Trying to work extra hours before school starts up again in a few days."

"Right. I hear that. Me too. Except I still manage to text my damn best friend every day just the same as I have since, oh, junior high. I still manage to ask her if she wants to meet up for a latte or a movie or a drink if it comes to that. You know what I get in return? Whole lot of nothing. Line's moving, by the way."

I hunched my shoulders and moved forward. She was right and I felt like a complete jerk. Just because I was messed up and I didn't really know what to say to anyone right now wasn't an excuse to shut her out. Anyone but her.

We'd been tight since the day in kindergarten when Sam Broughton pulled my ponytail and made me trip on the playground. Kendra, the new girl who had transferred to the school mid-year, poked him in the chest and demanded he apologize to me. Which he had, stuttering. Then I'd asked Kendra to nap beside me and we'd been together through thick and thin since.

Everything except Kellan McGuire. He'd been the first person who made me need some distance from everyone in my life. Including Kendra.

Not because of them. I was blessed to have amazing people in my life. But because of me.

I'd known Kellan wasn't the type to call the next day. He hadn't made a secret of it. I appreciated that honesty and yet I couldn't help hoping. Couldn't help wondering why I was the kind of girl who might be good for a night or even a few years if worst came to worst. I just wasn't the kind of woman who made a man run away from his life.

And yes, I knew that was nonsense thinking. I couldn't help it.

Mainly because I was pretty sure I'd run away from my life for Kellan, and that scared the hell out of me.

I loved my family so much. Loved my classes and my friends and even my little town that had more snow than residents. I loved being known by name at most of the places I went to on a regular basis. I liked the sense of community that came from growing roots in the same place generations of your family had grown theirs.

Before I crashed in that ditch, if anyone had asked me if I was dissatisfied, I would've said no. A little sad, yes. Definitely lonely. It was hard to go from being in a serious relationship for years to being single again, even if the relationship had soured a long while before your guy split.

But otherwise, I'd been happy. Settled. Now I just wasn't. It was as if a door to a whole other world had popped open for me for an instant and then slammed shut while I still had my toes inside.

I was hurting. Way more than I'd hurt over Derek. I didn't know why. Didn't understand any of this.

And Kendra was still waiting for me to explain that I was unhappy and heartbroken and felt stupid because I knew better. So it was my fault I even cared about a guy who couldn't care about me.

To tell her that though, I'd have to admit what had happened New Year's Eve. I hadn't told her yet. No one knew, including my brothers and sisters. My older brothers would've gone to California and kicked Kellan's ass for hurting me. It didn't matter that I was a grown woman. To them, I was their baby sister and I needed protection. Sometimes even from myself.

My older sisters weren't much better. Maeve and Regan in tandem made a formidable opponent. They'd probably book seats on the same flight with Angus, Lachlan, and Liam. So would Kendra. She'd just tell me to stop wallowing first so I could help her beat Kellan to a pulp.

That wasn't the answer. What, I was supposed to hate on the guy because he didn't love me? I didn't expect him to. We were strangers. Barely more than that. So what if he already knew my body better than I did? It was an accident, just an aberration, like that whole freaking night.

The best night of my entire life.

"Miss, what would you like?"

I stared at the barista as if he'd spoken in a foreign language. Coffee. Right. My order.

"She wants a grande caramel macchiato, soy milk, no whip."

Leave it to Kendra to save the day.

"No, I want whip." I placed a hand on Kendra's arm. "Extra whip, please," I told the barista.

"Since when? You hate whipped cream. I don't understand how, but whatever, girl. Now you want extra?"

Shrugging, I lifted my brows at my best friend in a futile attempt to get her to let it go. I knew she wouldn't. Coupled with being out of touch recently, changing my established drink order was akin to admitting I'd been kidnapped by aliens for medical experiments.

The barista smiled. "You got it. Anything else?"

Kendra let out a long sigh. "I'll take a venti green tea latte and one of those peppermint cake pops." She slid me a sidelong glance. "Want? Or did you decide you hate peppermint now?"

Since I was starving, I practically salivated at the words 'cake pop'. "I'll take two actually. One German chocolate, please. I'll pay you back," I said under my breath to Kendra as she stared.

"Stop it. I'm not worried about two dollars. It's that you never eat two. You barely eat one without fretting about that jackass making some comment about your stomach."

"Your stomach looks great to me," the barista offered helpfully, putting all three of our cake pops into a little cardboard holder.

"She's smokin' hot," Kendra said with a wink. "If I went lesbian, it'd be for her."

The construction guys in line behind us nudged each other and laughed. I flushed so much that I had to fan my face as I stepped aside to let Kendra pay. It was her turn anyway, but after that comment, oh yeah, she was ponying up for my extra cake pop.

"Seriously?" I whispered to her as she joined me at the coffee pickup area, wearing a huge shit-eating grin. "You just cannot help yourself, can you?"

"Not really. Besides, it brought some color to these cheeks. You're hella pale." She pinched my right one as her smile dimmed. "You're not sick, are you?"

I shook my head. Now probably wasn't the time to mention how tired I'd been the last few days. I was working a lot, so I figured that was it. Not being able to sleep when I actually hit the bed without imagining Kellan making love to me didn't help.

Neither did having to slide my hand beneath my cool sheets to take care of business for myself—sometimes two or three times before the ache subsided. I hadn't touched myself as much in my whole life as I had in these past two weeks.

Bastard.

"Not sick, not returning phone calls, look super tired, being all vague and secretive and shit, uh huh." Kendra gripped my shoulders. "Diagnosis: dick. As in you got yourself some."

"Shh!" I looked around, hoping we hadn't been overheard, caught between utter mortification and a laugh. Then she started to laugh and point at me and I knew it was over.

Jig was up. I *had* gotten some dick, and it had basically ruined me for any other dick, ever.

We waited for our drinks and then she carried them to our favorite table in the corner, which we only got after she stared at the couple sitting there until they finally left. Following her, I set down our container of cake pops. And promptly stuffed the peppermint one in my mouth, shrugging and pointing at my face when she pelted me with questions.

"Asshat." She laughed and tossed a balled-up napkin at me before taking a long sip of her latte. "Fine. If you don't tell me, I'm going to assume you went back to Dickless Derek. If that's the case, I may just disown you."

I snorted and pulled what was left of my cake pop out of my mouth. I'd demolished that sucker. "Yeah, right. You threaten that daily. Not gonna happen."

"I can't threaten anything daily since you don't talk to me anymore."

Guilt swamped me and I set down my barren stick. "I'm sorry. I shouldn't have shut you out."

Kendra sipped her latte and waited. She was like Buddha. She'd sit there patiently until the end of time if that was what it took to get me to 'fess up.

It took way less than that, because I'd missed my best friend. Desperately. I needed to confess all to her, even if I knew she'd tell me I was suffering from unrealistic expectations. Again. Though I was the criminal justice—and hopefully soon, pre-law—student, she was the one who always said, "if you can't do the time, don't do the crime."

My crime? Dreaming too much and not realizing that people had flaws that had nothing to do with me.

"So there was a guy."

"I knew it. What level guy are we talking about here? And it's not Derek. Tell me it's not Derek or I will probably go homicidal on your ass."

My lips twitched. "Not Derek. He was…a stranger."

I felt scandalous even saying it. In what universe did I, practically innocent Magpie Kelly, have torrid sex with a stranger? One who I'd practically begged to fuck me? It was almost inconceivable, especially since one of the reasons my ex had given for leaving me was that I didn't have multiple orgasms so sex wasn't "as much fun as it could be." As if that was all my fault. Besides, I'd managed to come right, left, and center with Kellan, so whatever.

There was nothing wrong with me that a talented tongue, fingers, and big dick couldn't solve. My problem was I wanted Kellan to work on my particular puzzle over and over again, and he'd probably already banged a bevy of babes in LA since he'd been back to work.

Me? I'd only banged my hand. *Both* hands. Possibly my cute little button vibrator once or twice.

"No way." Ken sipped her latte, her dark eyes wide. "Seriously?"

"So seriously."

"When?"

This was when it got a little stickier. "New Year's Eve," I said hesitantly, ducking to avoid the flurry of napkins she tossed my way.

"Two frigging weeks ago? You suck. I tell you the minute my dude pulls out, and you're keeping that shit from me for this long?" She sat back and crossed her arms again. She did resting bitch face so well. "Uh uh. Disowned. Read my lips. Dis-owned. Also? I wouldn't go lesbian for you now. Not even."

I giggled and buried my face in the crook of my arm before peeking up at her. From her grin, she wasn't pissed anymore. Much.

Thank God.

"So a stranger, huh? How did it happen? Let me guess. You both reached for the last round of celebratory New Year's Eve pepperoni at the Quikky Mart."

"Why do I like you again?"

"Because I call you on your bullshit and still come back for more? And because I buy you two cookie pops even though you only ever buy me one?"

"Valid points." I nodded and took a sip of my macchiato, shutting my eyes as the delicious hot liquid slid down my throat. It was a chilly day, and boy, was this drink hitting the spot. "So remember I was making bread for the neighbors and Mrs. Pringles?"

"Yes. Former Girl Scout of the year, checking in for duty."

"I was on my way out to Mrs. Pringles' house when I saw a doe and her baby and swerved to avoid them. It was icy and I drove into a ditch. That was the night of the big storm, remember?"

"Oooh." Kendra cupped her hands around her drink and leaned forward. "Hottie tow truck driver helped you with his plow? Literally?"

"Oh my God." I laughed and offered her a bite of my German chocolate cake pop.

While she sampled it, I told the whole, semi-embarrassing story. How I'd accused Kellan of maybe being a serial killer then went all female on him as soon as he saw me naked. It hadn't been like me at all.

By the time I reached the end of the night—after only giving her the briefest of details about the sex—her normally expressive eyes had shuttered. She had thoughts on the matter, I was sure, but she'd gone spookily silent.

"So he just let your daddy drag you home."

"He didn't drag me. I went willingly. Mostly."

"But Wonder Dick didn't stop him or defend your honor or hell, even say call me, sweet cheeks. Am I right?"

I tucked my hair behind my ears and nodded. "Yeah. Though Kellan's not really a sweet cheeks type, which is good. Hello, creepy."

"Okay, listen up. You're wasting good brain cells on this guy. If he was into anything but the pussy, he would've surfaced by now." She held up a hand when I sputtered. "I know, I know, crude. But sometimes you gotta tell it straight. The guy was horny and so were you, so no harm, no foul, right? Right. One-night stand, over and done."

"What if it's not?"

"What's that supposed to mean?"

"It means I can't forget him. He's everywhere. When I go to sleep, when I wake up, he's in my head. In here." I rubbed my fist over my chest as Kendra rolled her eyes. "I know it's crazy. It was one night. Who falls for someone in under twelve hours?"

"You did not fall for him. He just worked you good and you have not been worked good *ever*. That's all it is. Trust me," she said, placing her hands flat on the table. "Find yourself another hot guy and try again. You'll probably be just as into him if he's as great in the sack."

If only it were that easy. How I wished it was.

"What if I'm not? What if, I don't know, we really had a connection and he's just being stupid and pigheaded by not contacting me?"

"If you really thought he just needed a push, you would've contacted him yourself already." She gave me a knowing look. "And you have not."

"No." But all of a sudden, my cell phone was burning a hole in the back pocket of my jeans. I'd left my purse at home, thinking I'd go for a walk while I was out, and instead I'd just beelined straight for coffee. Maybe I'd hoped Kendra would be here, as was her habit before she went to work at her part-time job at Jaxon Industries, an interior design firm.

Maybe I spent too much time hoping and wishing for things, when the answer was I needed to take control of my own destiny. Just as I had the night I'd come on to Kellan. Somehow I'd felt empowered to, as if he made me bolder. I didn't know how or why. None of this made sense to me, but just the idea of texting him lifted some of the heaviness on my chest that I'd been carting around for the last two weeks.

Even if he didn't answer, at least I would have acted. And if he didn't answer, I'd know for a fact he was not for me and it was time to move on. One way or another.

I pulled out my phone.

"You're not going to text him. Tell me you are not."

I didn't answer. Instead I pulled up the text I'd sent myself from his phone and I replied, typing with sure fingers.

Whatever happened, I would live with it. Me and my vibrator, Old Faithful.

Your do-over expiration time is looming. Act now or forever hold your peace. Red.

11

KELLAN

My phone buzzed in the middle of rehearsal. Normally I didn't carry it around in my pocket when we were spending a long day in the studio, but since New Year's, I'd felt the need.

I'd felt lots of needs since New Year's, and I was examining precisely none of them.

I ignored the buzz because we were in the middle of "Felicity," our keyboardist Myles's song about the most important woman in his life. Not his lover, as you'd assume. Felicity was just his closest friend, the one who'd helped him through his darkest days during a bad breakup with an ex and the death of his dog. Myles had never intended for us to cut the song for our first short album. He'd just offered it up for practice fodder, and the next thing we knew, Lila—who'd been sitting in that day—had suggested we record it for the EP.

Myles was still pissed. I was pretty sure Felicity didn't even know he'd written a song for her. Well, the lyrics anyway. The music had mostly been the brainchild of Myles and our two guitarists, AJ and Cooper, with an assist from our bassist, Jake. Bryan, our drummer, had seemed bored with the whole thing.

I guess when a guy came from a gig doing hardcore porn to playing the kit in an up and coming rock band, it was hard to stay, um, engaged.

At any rate, we were on take probably seven of the damn song. If I had to sing about Felicity's "open, giving heart" or "sweet, uncompromising nature" one more time, I'd probably put my boot through my amp. I was seriously starting to dislike the chick and I'd never even met her. I'd known Myles since high school, but he'd met up with the great Felicity back at college in Maryland. He'd been working in a pub there when I called him to come to LA to reform our old band.

Out of all the guys, I'd figured he would be most excited to make our dreams a reality. Instead he'd become more and more quiet with every press gig and photo shoot and rehearsal for the album.

Something was going on with him, and I didn't know what. The hard-partying guy I'd known back home hadn't been one to pine over a chick, supposed best friend or not. But I guess people changed.

Even me. Not that I was ready to admit it.

"Take five," I called as the buzz sounded again, letting me know I'd missed the text. "And Bry, maybe get the lead out before you come back, huh? Have a smoke or something?"

Bryan flipped me the bird and climbed down from the kit. He was always flawless and he knew it. Certainly didn't come from practicing overmuch. He just had an innate sense of rhythm. Maybe it had translated from the "big" screen. God knows he'd been plenty rhythmic on camera.

Not that I'd ever watched his movies. Bad enough I'd had to hear him nail some unsuspecting groupie two nights ago after our show at the Blue Rhino. They hadn't even made it off the damn drum riser. She'd stopped by for his autograph, and he'd ended up bending her back over the cymbals and hitting a high C in a whole new way.

I couldn't decide if I was disgusted or jealous. Possibly both.

"I've gotta make a phone call." Myles rose from behind his

keyboard and shoved a hand though his shaggy dark hair.

He tended to grow it long, and combined with his lean face and woeful eyes, had a poetic look going on that made women nuts. Or so I'd heard. Impossible to tell how women felt about him on a more personal level lately since he kept everyone at arm's length. So I'd gotten closer to Cooper, who still liked to party but kept it lower key than Bryan.

Meaning not humping chicks on stage.

"Sure. Go for it." I started to ask Myles if he was calling his Fee Fee, but the swinging door had already closed behind him. Okay then.

I set aside my old Taylor guitar and made my way over to the leather couch on the opposite side of the room from the mixing booth. We were using the space at Ripper Records, which was where we tended to do our rehearsals most days.

Back in Turnbull, we'd rehearsed at the Gallows, our name for the dank warehouse space beside the town's only bowling alley. On a good night, we'd practiced until our fingers were numb and our shoulders were sore, then we'd gone next door as the high school girls were finishing their games. Of course, back then we'd been in college, so trolling high school girls was only moderately perverted. Some of my buddies still did, but I'd moved on.

I dropped down on the sofa and slid a glance at Coop, who was scribbling frantically in his battered notebook. "Got a new idea, brother?"

"Maybe. Let's just say I don't want songs like 'Fool for You' or 'Felicity' to define our sound."

"Fool for You" was Wilder Mind's first single, and it was hitting radio in a major way just as we'd hoped. We were already in the Top 20, with solid numbers coming in daily. Lila wasn't one of those managers who fed the talent a steady stream of data to keep them pumped—or hid it to prevent depression—but she gave me more leeway than most since I'd started out on the other side of the conference table. I had a damn good idea of the units we were pushing every day and the airplay and how our social media numbers looked. We weren't headed for the stratosphere just yet, but we were definitely building.

"What's wrong with FFY?" I asked mildly, though I already knew our lead guitarist's concerns.

He didn't want to become known as a harder-edged REO Speedwagon for the current set. His desire was to leave the love songs —or songs that could be perceived that way, such as "Felicity"—for later and start off with something more anthemic, like "Welcome to the Jungle" had been for GNR. But times were different and we had our own sound and our own material. FFY was doing just fine on the charts. As for Felicity...

Well, sap had its place. Preferably off my playlist, but who was I to judge?

"Nothing. It's a solid song with a kickass bridge. Just broadening the scope a bit. What do you think of this?"

He ran through some rough lyrics for a new song he'd been working on, one much darker than either our single or Myles' creation. I was already putting the music together in my head, imagining the guitar licks and the build up to the bridge. Figuring out how I'd shred the vocals to produce a different sound than the huskier, romanticized one I'd used on our ballads.

AJ, our rhythm guitarist, leaned over the back of the couch and knocked Coop in the head mid-lyric. "Hey, asshole. I thought you were running out for food."

Coop ignored him and went back to scribbling.

AJ sighed dramatically and turned around, flinging himself over the back of the sofa so that he landed between us with his head dangling toward the floor. "But I'm starving."

"You have a damn car, and I said take five not twenty-five." Shaking my head, I finally gave into curiosity and tugged out my phone to check who had messaged me.

Cooper and AJ's bickering faded away, as did the sound of Jake tuning his bass across the room. The hum of the amps, the too harsh lighting, the vague headache brewing at the base of my skull all vanished.

Maggie.

My throat tightened and I gripped my cell as I fought not to immediately reply. I wasn't this guy. Even women who hated me after a hookup said I had swagger. With Maggie, I had none. Just her words on my screen were enough to make my head light and my heartbeat roar in my ears.

As for my dick, I wasn't going there. Suffice it to say there was more than one reason I hunched over my lap.

I couldn't not answer her. Not twice. Not when every part of me was already hard and aching.

Fingers tense, I typed out a response.

What does a do-over consist of? Exactly.

There. Make it about sex. That kept it in the realm that seemed logical. The one I still understood.

I half expected her not to answer. A good girl probably wouldn't. It wasn't as if I'd left much wiggle room as to the direction of my thoughts. She'd read between the lines and know I was suggesting another hookup.

She didn't need to know it already felt like so much more.

The next buzz vibrated under my thumb, still cupping the screen.

Whatever you can handle, Wolf.

Goddamn. I went as rigid as a damn pike, just like that. Though my buddies were all around me, I was ready to go just from some words on a screen from a woman who was on the other side of the country.

I can't get away right now. Can you?

Get away like what? You mean come to LA?

I'd officially lost my frigging mind. So what else could I do other than to continue playing the hand I'd dealt her?

Yeah. Come to LA.

My classes start on Monday & I'm working til Friday afternoon.

So redeye Fri night. I'll send you a ticket.

She didn't respond for long enough that I was sure she was going to say no. She might've been the one who'd contacted me, but I was the one who sounded desperate.

I was, more than I'd ever expected.

Okay. I'll come to you.

"Hey, Kell, man, are we ever getting back to this rehearsal or are we just going to hold our dicks while you play with your phone?" Jake called, making me glance up from my screen and squint at him as if he were a stranger.

He might as well have been. Maggie was my reality right now. Everything else had just been marking time until I could see her again. Even if I hadn't admitted it to myself.

Christ, I was so fucked.

I held up two fingers to Jake and sent back a quick reply.

Send me your email addy and watch for the ticket tonight. Two days, roundtrip?

Two days where I could do every dark, dirty thing in my head to her and then let her sleep long enough so I could do them all over again.

Yes. Two days, roundtrip. But I'll have people out looking for me if I'm not back on time, so don't get any ideas.

I laughed out loud, well aware that my bandmates were staring. I didn't give a shit.

You're not ready to hear all the ideas I have, Red.

But she would be hearing them. Soon.

12

MAGGIE

"Have I told you that I think this is crazy?"

I leaned my head against the window of the Uber bringing me to the address Kellan had given me in the Hollywood Hills.

Holy crap. I still couldn't believe I was doing this. Correction—I *had* done this. I was here, on the opposite side of the country, staring out the window at palm trees blowing in the breeze instead of leafless branches laden with snow.

First plane ride, first layover at O'Hare, first tropical drink in an airport lounge.

First time I'd ever traveled to meet a man for sex, never mind sex on what might as well have been the other side of the world. Definitely the first time I'd lied to my parents about my whereabouts.

Technically I didn't have to. I was a grown woman. Almost twenty-three, financially stable—ish—and in college. I paid rent, though below the going rate, and I was normally a responsible person.

Just not lately. Maybe I was overdue for a major flake-out. If so, I was going to make this weekend count.

After checking my hair in my compact once more, I sighed. "Yeah, Ken, I think you've weighed in a few times on the subject."

She was my alibi for this weekend. It wasn't as if I could tell my father where I was going. Well, I could have. But did I really want a lecture about going away for a cross-country booty call? Not so much.

It wasn't as if I had many illusions about this weekend. Kellan hadn't asked me how I was or if my car was okay or anything. We'd barely spoken at all. He'd asked if I would come to him, so we could fuck. And I had.

I was okay with that right now. So much.

"Just saying. If you don't call me tomorrow morning, I'll think he killed you and chopped up your body."

"See, this is why you're my best friend. You're as sick and twisted as I am."

"Not hardly. I watch *Dateline*. I've seen this story before. Younger woman gets swept away by charming older—"

"He's barely older than us, Ken. It's not like he's some geezer."

"Is he older than you? Yes. Therefore, older man. Who did not ask you anything except to visit for sex. If that's not skeevy to you, then I can't help you. Clearly Derek the Dickless did more of a trip on your head than I even realized."

"It's not like that. Exactly."

"Right. That's why when you got his text you turned every shade of red and wouldn't even let me read it for like fifteen minutes. This is after shutting me out for two weeks. You never do that."

The hurt in Kendra's voice made me tuck away my compact and stop toying with my hair. "It wasn't because of you. It's because of me."

"Are you going to break up with me next? That sounds like standard relationship-ending BS."

I laughed. "Nah, you're stuck with me. Cradle to the grave, baby."

"Just don't make that grave happen any sooner than it should. I have a shovel, a body bag, and a ready alibi if he screws with you."

"Hopefully he will screw me, and no burial implements will be needed."

The Uber driver winked at me in the rearview mirror. I cleared my throat. Keeping my voice down would be ideal.

"Yeah, well, report back tomorrow. If I don't hear from you by noon, I'm calling the twins and your shenanigans will be up, sister."

The shudder of fear that ran through me was genuine. Liam and Lachlan were both incredible men—strong, loyal, smart. Devoted to family. They also had intense workout regimes and a willingness to hop any number of planes, trains, and automobiles to save their baby sister from the evil clutches of some "LA big shot" as Kendra had referred to him.

I'd told her I didn't think he was all that big. True, he worked at a record label, but there had to be smaller ones. Surely if he had any major artists on his roster, he would've name-dropped. He hadn't mentioned anyone. Most likely he was just trying to make it like the rest of us. Struggling, but on his way.

"I'll call," I promised before hanging up.

Good thing too, since the driver pulled up to the address I'd given him and my chin dropped to my thighs. Right about where the hem of my clingy, deep blue crushed velvet dress ended.

Yeah, so I wasn't the best with casual. I'd gone out and bought some new clothes for this weekend. Sexy things. Including lingerie that I would probably always hide under my sweet pink and purple patterned panties in my underwear drawer. Hopefully they'd have some dirty memories attached, courtesy of one Kellan McGuire.

"Are you sure this is the right address?" I pressed my forehead against the window and bit my lip as I tried to take in the expanse of the property before me. As far as California real estate went, I was sure it wasn't at the top of the range. Not by far. Even a cactus in LA went for more than I could fathom. But still, this wasn't the kind of pad I'd pictured for an up and coming record exec. Maybe he had to keep up a front for the people he worked with to prove he was making it in a cutthroat industry. He might even have wild music parties here for all I knew.

"It's the address you gave me, lady. Guess that man you came to see is doing all right for himself." The driver winked again and tapped his thumbs on the wheel.

Clock was running, and I couldn't stall any longer.

I paid him, adding in my idea of a hefty tip, and waited while he deposited my suitcase from the trunk by my feet. Then as the car pulled away from the circular driveway, I pursed my lips and wondered if it was too late to run back home.

What had made me think I was equipped to handle any of this?

The house was huge and white with tons of windows. They seemed mirrored to reflect the last pink and orange rays from the sunset. Made from privacy glass, probably. I took the stairs that wound up the side, climbing to a large veranda with a killer view of the city.

I stood at the ornate iron railing, hauling in deep draughts of the ocean-tinged warm breeze. The water probably wasn't that close, but my imagination always filled in the blanks. I tugged my short jacket tighter around my body and let my gaze soak up the lights coming on in the high rises that seemed to stretch in every direction in the distance.

This place held so many possibilities. I swore I could feel them in the air. Or maybe that was just anticipation.

The door opened behind me and I braced, not even getting a chance to turn before that familiar presence loomed behind me. I didn't need to look to know it was him. I smelled his alpine shampoo and the clean scent of his basic, utilitarian soap, and my entire body clenched in reaction.

His big hands came up to bracelet my wrists on the railing and he brushed his mouth over my hair. "You came."

My voice was going to shake. I just knew it.

"I said I would, didn't I?" Through some miracle, I managed to sound relaxed. Even a little snarky. I hadn't had to summon my bravado for most of the first night I'd spent with him, but now that I knew what being with him entailed, I was practically a vibrating wire of need.

He slid his nose through my hair, inhaling deeply, and I gripped the railing. It took so little from him to make my system rev. He tapped the pulse in my wrist and I shut my eyes.

I could play blasé all I wanted, but he already knew I was throbbing all over for him. Inside and out. Even my skin felt as if it had shrunk in the warm air.

"Is your father going to show up here to drag you home?" His warm breath skimmed over my neck, as erotic as the edge of a feather.

"No. They think I'm spending the weekend with Ken." He growled and spun me around, and the sight of him again after the last three weeks was a punch to the chest. His hair was different. Shorter but somehow wilder, the top gelled up into a faux hawk. "My best friend, Kendra," I reminded him.

I didn't get a chance to say anything else or even to continue my perusal past his eyes before he dragged me against him and threaded his fingers through my loose hair. I'd left it down, hoping this very thing might happen.

He gave me *that* look, heavy and intense, an instant before his mouth came down on mine. Every time I expected rough, punishing kisses that matched his firm grip on my hair, and every time his lips were soft and gentle. They molded to mine, and he learned my shape again for several frantic heartbeats until his tongue slashed between them. Slick and hot, his kisses left no confusion about where his thoughts—and the stiff length digging into my belly—were headed.

"I have more than one condom this time," he said between kisses, his free hand grasping my waist so he could haul me even closer.

It was never close enough. The clothes between us—hell, even the air—were simply too much.

"Me too." I reached up, eyes still closed, and caressed his jaw. He groaned, but it wasn't enough to cover my sound of distress. "You shaved."

"You like the beard?"

"I did." It was hard to get the rest out. "I liked the way it felt between my legs."

"Christ."

I didn't have time to say anything else before he plucked me up into his arms. He bent us precipitously to pick up my suitcase and carted me inside, kicking the door shut. He set me down long enough to drop the suitcase and to press buttons on a seemingly complicated alarm system. I frowned as it beeped and numbers scrolled past on the screen.

What the heck was all this? He hadn't even locked the cabin in Turnbull, but out here, he'd opted for mega security. Perhaps it just came part and parcel with living in such an expensive area.

"Where's the armed guard?" I asked, only half kidding.

He grunted and picked me up again, this time in a fireman's style carry over his burly shoulder. When I shrieked, he smacked my ass and I fell silent.

So much for a house tour. Apparently we were headed right to the bedroom. I might've protested about that if I wasn't at the perfect angle to check out his ass.

Cradled in worn denim, his buns were spectacular. If I stretched just a bit more, I could bite one.

He toted me up a spiral staircase flanked by walls covered in huge paintings. Of the sea. And fire. And a lone snow-covered tree in the forest, shuddering in the wind. I didn't get a good look at them despite my twisting and gyrating, which seriously pissed me off.

I enjoyed romance as much as the next person, but this didn't feel like a sweet gesture. That wasn't Kellan's way of doing things. Actually I liked that he was more straightforward.

But this? *This* felt like he was trying to keep me from seeing his place.

Halfway up the endless staircase, I slapped his back to make him put me down. He finally obliged, saying nothing as I pointed. "Who painted those?"

"Does it matter?"

I touched his cheek and made him look at me. He was very good at not meeting my eyes, and I wasn't going to allow that this time. "Was it you?"

That muscle I remembered flared in his jaw, giving him away. "Just a hobby," he said under his breath.

"They're incredible. That tree gave you away." Driven to keep touching him, I brushed a stray lock of hair out of his chocolate eyes. I didn't like the product in his hair or the style or his new clean-shaven look.

I wanted the same Kellan back I'd had at the cabin. Rude, crude, uncouth. Raw in all the best ways. Not this slick, polished version who carried me around in a pseudo expression of romance.

"I'm the same man," he muttered, resuming the climb. At the top of the stairs, he took a left and just kept going.

I rushed after him. Had I spoken aloud?

Knowing me, probably. But I wasn't going to hide my feelings. At least not about this.

"You're even dressed different." I pulled at the sleeve of his white button-down shirt and took in the rest of his attire. He had on a black belt studded with spikes, probably store-manufactured bleached and slashed jeans, and trendy boots with a heel that had clanged on each rung of the stairs. That wasn't all. Unless I was mistaken, he was wearing eyeliner.

Genuine panic seized my throat. "Why are you dressed like this?"

He just kept walking. Since I wasn't going to continue to yank on his clothes like a petulant child, I stopped and crossed my arms.

When he realized I wasn't following, he paused and pinched the bridge of his nose. "I told you I work with artists. You gotta play the game."

"That involves eye makeup and glitzy houses and belts that look like they were modeled on a dog's choke collar."

He walked away and left me standing there.

Eventually I gave in and followed him. What choice did I have? I'd flown to the other side of the country like an idiot, so I wasn't leaving without some sex.

Good sex. Tear the freaking roof off and set that shit on fire sex.

It wasn't my problem what he chose to do with his life. He hadn't even asked about mine. Forget that, he hadn't even asked me how I was. Or if I'd had a good flight. He'd just kissed my fool head off and manhandled me, just in case I had any doubts about what he had planned this weekend.

I didn't, but that didn't mean I was going to let him dominate me. In bed was one thing. Out? Nope. Not happening. Not with him or any other male again. Or female for that matter.

Talking to you, Ken, even if it's only in my head.

I marched down the long hallway and did my best not to notice the vaulted ceilings or the off-white walls with fancy crown moulding. This was not my suburban home where paint had been slapped on so many times that the baseboards were covered in a rainbow of hatch marks from all the different colors used over the years. The floor beneath my heels was glossy and black, mirrored just like the windows. If I dared to look, I'd probably see my reflection.

This place didn't fit the Kellan I'd come to know at all.

He leaned against the door jamb of a room at the end of the hall, arms crossed, watching me in a predatory way that made every part of me stand at attention. But I wasn't about to let attraction silence my voice. Not again.

I came to a stop in front of him. "I think we need to get a few things straight, McGuire."

His eyebrow lifted. "That so?"

"That's so. I don't want you to misunderstand me. I might have come here for sex, but that doesn't mean you can ignore my questions and dismiss me. If you don't want me to ask anything, I understand. It's your life. Your business."

His lips quirked. "Glad you see reason." I let him drag me closer and brush his lips along my jaw. "I'm also glad you came here for sex, because I've been devising new ways to fuck you all goddamn week." I shivered as he slid his large hand down my back to cup my ass through my short dress. He stayed above the fabric for a second before dipping his hand beneath to palm one bare cheek. "Shit, a thong?" He eased back to stare at me. "You?"

I shrugged.

"Since when do you wear thongs?"

"Since I meet random men for sex."

"You better be using the plural incidentally."

Again, I shrugged.

"Playing that game, are we? I don't tell you what you want, you shut me down."

"It's not a game. I'm offering you the same thing you're offering me." I wet my lips, lingering on the gesture until his gaze dropped to them. "Your rules, but I'm going to make sure we adhere to them."

He spun me around and pressed my spine against the doorframe so fast that I didn't have a chance to counter the move. "My rules are you fuck me and only me while we're doing this. Non-negotiable. That includes any dalliances with your ex."

"Oh, you're so lucky I don't clean your clock for that one." I jutted out my chin. "Besides, two-way street. You better give back what you ask for."

"You think I've touched anyone else since you?" He braced his arm above my head and cupped my throat with his other hand, his thumb tracing my pulse. "You think I even could?"

I said nothing. While he was away from me, I had no clue how he lived his life. I knew so little about him. By his choice, it seemed.

God, I was so out of my depth here. True, I thought I was semi-holding my own, but it was like a goldfish trying to hang with a shark. At any time he could lean over and swallow me whole.

I wasn't even entirely sure I would mind.

"Three fucking weeks I've ached for you. Then you come in here and Christ, I can't even breathe from wanting you and you're asking me questions. Like I can think. Like I can imagine anything but getting this dress off you and your pussy in my mouth."

He tugged my short jacket down my arms and tossed it on a chair just inside what appeared to be the master bedroom. The room was light and airy, bigger than my mind could comprehend. Giant bed, huge windows, and heavy, expensive furniture everywhere.

Not right now. Worry about that later.

His hungry gaze latched on my face as he licked the inside of his lower lip. That predatory expression made my thighs quiver.

I couldn't wait any longer. Right, wrong, good, bad—I needed this.

Him.

Slowly, I slid my arms up and gripped the door jamb. Not knowing what the hell I was doing or if I should be standing my ground. All I knew was Kellan's jaw clenched as he raked his gaze over me. Without a word, he reached behind me to drag down my zipper. The sleeveless dress slipped down my body, revealing my white strapless bra and sheer lacy thong.

I'd never worn a thong before. Definitely hadn't owned one. I wasn't sure I was a fan of the whole butt floss thing, but I was on board with Kellan's low groan as he devoured me with his eyes.

Still watching me, he crouched and closed his mouth over the wet spot on my panties, sucking me through the material. His tongue flicked hungrily while he pulled the narrow strip of fabric aside to rub my slick folds with his callused fingertips. Then he licked me without even the shield of my panties between us and I dropped my head back against the wood, seeing stars for more than one reason.

Stars? I saw a whole constellation of them at the feel of him sliding one long finger inside me where I was already soaked and clenching for him. Desperately craving what only he could give.

Even without a ton of experience, I understood that this guy was somehow the key in my lock. How I knew that with such certainty defied logic or explanation. I wasn't going to try to make sense of it, even to myself.

He gripped my leg and pulled it over his shoulder. That would have scandalized me enough, but he wasn't done. He grabbed the other one and did the same. I was held up against the wall, supported only by his broad shoulders, his face inches from my slit.

"Stay still," he murmured, and dove in.

Right. As if I could be still while he ate me as if he was dying for my taste. Fingers pumping—two now—lips and tongue working my clit, teeth grazing my swollen flesh. His groans rumbled against my skin, inflaming me even more. I arched, gripping the door frame for purchase, fighting not to panic that he'd drop me. I couldn't stop moving. Hips flailing, thighs trembling, heels beating against his back.

All the while, his mouth and fingers never stopped their sweet torment.

"I'm going to—"

"Yes," he growled against me, and I shattered, letting out a cry as my body fisted and released. I grasped his fingers deep, bending forward to clutch at his hair with one hand while my nails scrabbled at the wood. I was losing my balance, sliding down the wall, so close to falling. Just slipping away.

He wouldn't let me. Even as I lost track of myself, I knew he'd be there to catch me. It didn't make sense, the trust I had in him. It was dangerous. But I couldn't turn off my feelings in his direction.

Any of them.

I was still shaking from the aftershocks when he rose and enfolded me in his arms. "Shh," he said against my hair while I struggled to hold on to him. My limbs weren't functioning properly. My brain was a haze.

Orgasms weren't supposed to leave you broken afterward, were they?

"Only the best ones, Red."

My spine hit the bed an instant later, and he followed me down to the mattress. I hadn't even been fully aware that he'd carried me.

"Some potent shit," I mumbled, and he laughed, pressing his face into my hair.

I wasn't even capable of fretting that I was saying what was in my head. So be it. He wanted the part between my legs, he'd just have to deal with the rest. As would I if I wanted that hard length pressing against my stomach.

And oh, I did.

He kneeled beside me and stripped off his button-down, each opened button revealing the tanned, muscled, inked chest beneath. My heart picked up speed at the sight of that meandering happy trail of hair that led down beneath his belly button to his unbuttoned jeans. Unzipped too. They gaped open, the outline of his stiff cock clearly visible against his dark boxers. He stood to kick off his boots and haul down his jeans and boxers and I stared, my mouth watering.

Without conscious thought, I sat up and undid my bra, letting the cups fall away from my breasts. He swallowed audibly, raking a hand through his hair. Messing it up further than I'd already done with my hands.

Before he got out of this bed, he'd be back to the Kellan I remembered. Scruff growing back in, hair wild, no part of him slick and savvy and meant to be palatable for the masses.

Mine.

Slowly, I kicked off my heels and slid the panties down my hips that he'd just shoved out of his way. His gulp for air was probably the sexiest thing I'd ever heard.

No, I was wrong. When he yanked open a bedside drawer and withdrew a strip of condoms, then tore open the first, *that* was the best sound ever.

He braced his knee on the bed and rolled on the latex, his gaze intent on mine. The expression in his eyes was so much softer than the rigid planes of his face. As if he was studying my reaction, wanting to make sure I was still with him.

I reclined on the bed and reached back to grip the spindles of the headboard. Ones meant to hold during a wild fuck.

He's had other women here. You're not the first. Definitely won't be the last.

But that I managed not to say aloud. Somehow. Probably because some truths were too painful to deserve breath.

He grabbed my calf and yanked me toward him, spreading me open like a wishbone so he could settle between my legs. Without prelude, he captured one eager nipple, drawing it between his sharp teeth while he focused on my face. Always so careful to make sure I was right with him. The pleasure was too keen, pulling a moan from my throat. He switched to the other breast and offered it the same attention, tonguing the tip to a rigid peak. Alternating the pressure from rough to gentle. Watching me, he pinched both nipples. Again and again.

Already half crazed, I circled my hips in a vain attempt to alleviate the ache. I could feel myself readying for him again. Slickness saturated my inner thighs. I needed so much more than fingers this time. Soon I'd beg for his cock.

"So greedy," he breathed against my breast. "So am I."

He rolled me on my side and moved up behind me, cradling me close. His palm covered my breasts, trying to contain them. His hand wasn't large enough. Not even close. He grunted against the side of my neck and squeezed them with almost painful force as I threw my leg over both of his. Opening up my pussy so he was right there, the heat of his erection a whisper away.

"Now," I pleaded, beyond embarrassment.

Kellan lined up his dick with my slit, taunting me with shallow thrusts that heightened my arousal without giving me any relief. He inched inside me enough to make my walls clutch at him, shifting me half on my belly so the friction of the sheets teased my swollen clit. His lips skimmed my ear as he stopped trying to cup my breasts and strummed his thumb between my legs.

"Want to come again?"

I nodded, incapable of words. He chuckled and bore down harder with both his thumb and his cock, causing me to shake and strain for what loomed so close.

Still. Again.

"First deep stroke," he said, his thumb moving faster now. Sliding audibly in the wetness he'd created. "You're gonna cream on my dick."

I shut my eyes and rocked back against him, gaining another inch of his length. My sigh of relief made him push me harder against the mattress. I was half on my belly, half on my side, completely beneath him. At his mercy. Under his control.

Never had anything felt so damn good.

"First deep stroke," he said again, and it sounded like a promise.

Then he pulled back on the trigger and slammed into me, so full and hard, hitting that spot only he seemed to know how to find. And I exploded around him.

"Fuck, yes. Fuck." He rolled on his back and drew me with him, still embedded inside me, his large hands guiding my hips as he lifted me up and down. Using my body for his enjoyment while my climax spun out and went on and on.

I couldn't do anything but loll against him, squeezing him on each thrust. But then I started to push back against him, my hands bracing against his tensed abdomen as I raised and lowered myself on his thick dick. He might be using me but I was using him too, nearly drunk on the power of destroying his will.

He might have decimated me, but I intended to do the same right back.

He swore ripely against my shoulder and fumbled between my thighs to play with my clit, his caresses no longer sure. I was so slippery and he was shaking too, his big body tense and straining beneath mine. He thickened inside me and I moaned, throwing back my head as the pinprick lights in the ceiling multiplied and swam.

"Hell yes. So goddamn tight. Work me with that sweet pussy." He shoved my legs apart and surged up into me, so roughly I feared I'd break.

I loved it. I craved it. Just like this.

Poised on the brink of another orgasm, I reached down to grasp his cock, seating it more firmly inside of me. I whimpered at the hot, hard feel of him drenched with my arousal. I'd never been so wet in my life.

He reached up to grab a handful of my hair, yanking my head back so I stretched out flat on top of him. And he finished us both off, rearing up and pushing into me at just the right angle for me to come again. That shoved him over too, his cock jerking as he spilled himself into the condom and he roared out his pleasure into my hair.

"Maggie. Goddammit, Maggie."

Coming with him shouting my name—and sounding so absolutely pissed about it—made me contract around him again. I couldn't stop coming.

I might be screwed, but so was he.

Half blind, nearly deaf, I slumped on top of him. His arms came around me, banding tight. "You're not leaving this time," he said gruffly, and I nodded without even being fully aware of what I was agreeing to.

I didn't know how I'd ever leave again.

13

KELLAN

I'D NEVER HAD a woman in my bed. Not in my house. Not here.

It was probably not much of a triumph, considering I'd only been renting this place for about six months. But I'd always been careful to keep the lines separate.

Women were for backstage hallways and green rooms. Add in the occasional hotel room, bar bathroom or club VIP area. I wasn't a saint, and didn't pretend otherwise.

Now there was Maggie, who'd blown every rule I'd ever set for myself to hell.

I'd also never been balls deep in a woman one minute and dreaming about her the next. Her hair clinging to my mouth, her soft breasts pillowed against my chest. Evidently that wasn't close enough. She had to be inside my head too, so I woke up with her name on my tongue.

I opened my eyes to find her asleep in my arms, her long dark hair spread all over me. Owning me just as her body did.

What the hell was happening to me?

I couldn't remember getting up to turn out the lights, but the room was now dark. A thin path of moonlight highlighted her delicate features. Her inky lashes, her freckled nose, and her soft mouth, swollen from mine. Her pearlescent skin glowed against the navy sheets, and I stroked her arm just to see the stark difference between our flesh.

She was the light to my dark in every goddamn way.

The contrast between her pale skin, bright blue eyes, and near-black hair would be gorgeous on canvas. In the picture I wanted to paint, her ruby red nipples would peek past the barely closed lapels of the silk robe I'd purchased on a whim yesterday. I'd found myself at the counter of a fancy department store, the satiny fabric clutched in my hands. I'd wanted her in clothes I'd bought and smelling like me again.

Now she did. Our combined scents mingled in the room, dirty and lewd. But her hair still smelled of strawberries, fresh and sweet.

She stirred in her sleep and I fought the urge to roll out of bed. The need to move, to escape, was nearly stifling.

I slept alone. Always.

Once was an accident. Twice was a plan.

Three times would be setting us both up for a fall.

I sat up in bed and rested my head in my hands. I had to get out of here. Just get in my car and go. She had her roundtrip ticket. If I didn't come back, didn't call or contact her, she'd get the message and leave. Go back to her family where she belonged.

She didn't belong with me. I didn't know how to be faithful, just like good ol' Dad. Sleeping with her twice in a row was the longest streak I'd been on since high school.

And if that wasn't pathetic, I didn't know what was.

The sheets whispered behind me and I braced. I still wasn't capable of steeling myself so that the hesitant brush of her lips against my shoulder didn't affect me. I knew she was uneasy, that she'd never experienced any of this before.

Only a bastard would leave her in the dark without any

comforting words. Even something as simple as telling her she meant more to me than a good fuck.

Instead I told her about my father.

"My dad didn't stay with us," I said, somehow shocked to hear my voice break the stillness. She must've been surprised too, because I felt her body jolt. "Having a family wasn't in his plans. So he pretended to do the right thing. But it was just going through the motions."

She didn't respond right away. "Some people aren't suited for family life, I suppose. Or they won't let themselves be. Which is pretty much the same thing."

"Your world was the exact opposite of mine." I let out a brittle laugh. "I'm not saying I had it rough, just that I didn't grow up with the same wide-eyed innocence toward life. It changes you. Hardens you."

Even as I tried to explain, I didn't want her to understand. I didn't want her to be harder. I wanted her exactly how she was.

I owed her those simple, sweet words about what she meant to me. Something more substantial than a random tidbit about my father that didn't matter jack shit. What mattered was how I treated her when it was just the two of us. Without the excuses and the bullshit that I thought justified me acting like an asshole.

She didn't deserve anything but the best.

But I was a bastard, and I'd come by it naturally. So I turned to her and pushed her back against the pillows, gripping her wrists in one hand over her head. My hard dick nestled between her damp thighs. In the dark, her huge eyes tracked mine.

My hips snapped back and I sank into her, one punishing thrust that ripped a breath from her throat.

Immediately, I knew my mistake. I was inside her bare, and she was like heaven gloving my dick. Slick, hot, so giving. Her pussy opening up to me the deeper I went. I drew back and slammed home again, even harder before.

I was taking her raw and I didn't even care. It didn't matter.

She yanked her wrists free and shoved at my shoulders. I thought she was trying to stop me—as she should—so I started to pull back. Both of us scarily silent except for our tortured breaths, as if even speaking required too much effort.

Then she rolled me on my back and climbed on top, her grip on my rock-hard cock so certain as she guided it back inside her. Where it belonged.

Where *I* belonged.

She rocked her hips, taking me deeper as one hand skimmed her belly and breasts. The other clutched her own hair as she rode me, her instinctual moves the most beautiful thing I'd ever witnessed. Her sexy body soaked in moonlight, her witchy dark hair tumbling over her shoulders and back.

I had to stop her. Stop this. With every flex of her pussy, my balls grew tighter, the need spiraling higher. This couldn't last forever. If she kept on fucking me, her eyes closed, her hands exploring her own curves as if they were all new to her, I'd spill myself inside her and not give a goddamn.

"Maggie." Her name tore from my lips like a curse. "We can't."

But she didn't open her eyes. Maybe she didn't even hear me.

She slid her hand down to delve between her thighs, her tentative explorations making her cry out. Making me more rigid than a damn steel beam. I couldn't stop myself from seizing her hips and driving into her. Her eyes flew open as she frantically rubbed her clit and grasped me so tightly inside I never wanted to leave. Every time I pulled out, fighting the grip of her swollen, soaked pussy, I swore and plunged in again. I couldn't get enough.

"Get me wet," I demanded, and she nodded, her fingers a blur between her legs. Her walls rippled around me and I threw back my head, powerless to stop the shout of completion that roared through me along with my release.

I came and came, filling her up until she was dripping with me. And then I flipped her over on her back and lifted her leg in the air, bending it toward her chest as I moved down to taste what we'd made.

Goddamn, she tasted sweet. Sweeter when her tight little pussy was saturated from what we'd done.

After a couple minutes, she whimpered and pushed my head away. I moved back up her body and gripped her chin, sealing my mouth over hers. She moaned at the flavor of our kisses, leaning up to chase my mouth and wind her fingers through my hair.

Sweaty, spent, we rolled across the bed, her hair tangling around us. I cupped her face and kissed her again, slower this time, my lips rubbing against hers. "Full of you," she whispered, her eyes bright in the night.

My gut twisted.

She wasn't just kind and smart and curious and beautiful. She was naughty as hell and eager to learn everything I wanted to teach.

Fuck if she wasn't my perfect woman, wrapped up in a smart-assed bow.

I skimmed my hand down her damp back. "I should feed you."

The corner of her mouth lifted and she ran her hand down my torso to grip my length, making me laugh. "Hungry," she said breathlessly, licking her lips, and I jerked in her hand.

"Dirty girl," I said, outlining her mouth with the tip of my finger.

She nodded. "Dirty for you."

"Which we'll get back to later." Lightly, I popped her on the ass. Her giggle was like frigging music. "Now you're going to let me feed you."

"Grilled cheese and tomato soup?" The hope in her voice made me grin.

Especially because I'd made a grocery run for exactly that, along with a few other necessary items.

"You want that at," I craned my neck to see the glowing lights of the clock on my nightstand, "three-eleven am?"

"Yeah." Her belly rumbled and she glanced down at it, laughing at herself while her hair fell forward to frame her gorgeous face. She glanced up at me and my chest tightened, so painfully that I couldn't breathe.

This couldn't be happening. Not here, not now. Not when she didn't even know who I really was.

She scrambled off me and shoved her hands through her tousled hair. "What I want most right now is a shower." She rubbed her throat and gave me a sheepish smile. "It was a long trip and—"

"And I got you dirty for real." I sat up and moved to the side of the bed, then drew her between my legs, cupping her ass in both hands. "En suite's that door over there."

"En suite too. Fancy schmancy."

Though she was only teasing, her words reminded me of the dangerous game I was playing. One we both couldn't win. As soon as she found out I'd lied to her, she'd be on a plane to New York. Exactly where she belonged. She didn't like this side of me, and this was who I was when I was in California. This had been my dream, and I had to deal with everything that came with it.

Including shielding her from a life I knew she'd have no interest in being involved with.

Hell, my lie was probably the best thing for her. Since I hadn't made a clean break the way I should have, the truth would do it for me.

She climbed off the bed, and even without seeing it, I could tell she was standing with one foot over the other. Her nervous stance, the way I'd caught her standing at the cabin more than once. "You're not going to shower too?"

That was a road to perdition. At least I could feed her and act like I wasn't a complete lech without any redeeming qualities. One who had summoned her across the country for sex without any intention of anything more.

Well, I was that guy. But I could pretend while she was here that it wasn't a complete joke that a decent woman like Maggie Kelly might find me worthy of anything but dark, delicious fucking.

"Nah, I'll shower later. I'm hungry too."

"Okay." She started to search for her clothes and I stilled her with a hand on her arm. I rose to go to my closet, grabbing the robe I'd bought off a hook.

"Here." I held it out to her, stifling my urge to help her put it on. I had to kill those tendencies, because all they would do was confuse her and muddy the waters.

She said she understood I'd invited her here for sex. If she could keep those boundary lines in her head, she was a better person than I was because I could not.

More and more with every passing moment.

Even in the pale moonlight, I glimpsed her wrinkled nose. "Another woman's?"

"No." I started to tell her that no other woman had been in this room and stopped. Not necessary information. "It's just for guests."

She arched a brow. "You, the guy who didn't even have a spare towel at the cabin, stocks robes for guests."

I shrugged.

"I never thought I'd say this, but I miss cabin Kellan." She pulled on the robe and let out a purr as the silky material settled against her skin. "Oh God. This feels glorious." She tugged on the belt, tightening it around her waist, and frowned. "This seems like it was made for me. My size exactly."

Yes, because I'd described her as best as I could to the woman at the store. I'd gone over her measurements painstakingly, trying my hardest to come as close as possible without knowing her proportions. There might have been hand gestures involved.

I shrugged again.

"It's so soft." She rubbed her cheek against the fabric, her eyes narrowing. I couldn't see that in the dim light, but already I knew her reactions. The way she'd study me when she thought I wasn't aware, her busy brain spinning as she tried to fit puzzle pieces into one cohesive whole. "Thank you," she said, her voice barely a whisper.

"Yeah." I cleared my throat and snatched my jeans off the floor. "I'll go make us some food," I said before I escaped.

I waited at the top of the stairs until I heard the water come on in the bathroom. I could just imagine her looking at the mirrored tiles in wonder, her eyes getting wider as she took everything in. She was so unspoiled, untouched by all the excesses I saw daily.

Who could blame me for wanting some of that purity for myself? I missed life being that simple. Black and white, right or wrong.

Back in the day, I'd been that way too. So long ago. I'd criticized my father for his fickle ways. I hadn't understood why my mother and me and Bethy hadn't been enough. Bethy, who'd just been an accident one night when my father breezed through town. My parents had argued like they always had and then spent the night together, and I'd ended up with the brightest, toughest little sister I'd never known to wish for. For all the years afterward when my mother found her solace in one man after another, Bethy and I been each other's. And all along, I'd cursed my father, never guessing that I was doomed to repeat the same pattern.

Branch from the tree and all that. Maybe I'd been a fool to ever believe I could break the streak. In time, I'd stopped trying.

Not everyone was built to be faithful. Or else it was like Maggie had said. Some guys weren't meant for family life or they believed they weren't, which amounted to the same thing.

At least I never lied. That was the morality I clung to. It was okay that I didn't know how to build a relationship, because I never led anyone on. I was always honest, a lot more than my father could say. But honesty could be a crutch too.

And I needed to get the food started before Red found me brooding and asked me what was wrong.

Only everything.

I jogged downstairs and checked the security system again out of habit. All was secure, each of the different sectors glowing green. On second thought, I grabbed her suitcase and ran back upstairs to leave it for her in the bedroom. As I stepped back inside, I heard her singing in the shower. I smiled, unsurprised at the tightness in my chest this time.

I'd missed her singing. All it had taken was one night for her to burrow into me in so many ways.

I was still finding new marks, little slashes I'd never expected. She'd touched me deeper than anyone. Even her preference for boy bands amused me more than pissed me off.

Feeling like an idiot, I stood near the closed bathroom door while she sang the latest hit by the Luscious Lovahboys. I only recognized it because of that stupid New Year's Eve show that had started so much.

When she shifted into another song of the pop variety, I went back downstairs to the kitchen and took out the fixings for the sandwich and soup. Her husky voice echoed in my head as I buttered bread and heated up the skillet, then dumped soup in another pan. The image of her curvy body twisting under the spray hijacked my thoughts until I was straining against the denim.

Again. Still. I was a perpetual walking hard-on around that woman.

She came down into the kitchen, humming under her breath, her long wet hair in thick ropes. Water gleamed on what showed of her legs before they disappeared under the white robe. "Your bathroom is...whoa." She blew out a breath and stopped just over the threshold. "Just like this kitchen. Oh my God. Are you filthy rich and forgot to tell me?"

I stirred the soup and adjusted the burner. With one whiff of my scent on her, my spine locked. "You used my shampoo again."

Fuck, I loved it when she smelled like me.

In every damn way.

"Was I not supposed to? I brought some in my bag, but I didn't realize you'd brought it upstairs. Next time I'll use my own."

"No." The growl left my chest and I saw her smile before she ducked her head. "Use mine."

"If you insist. You might not like mine anyway. It's strawberry banana like my body wash." She moved toward the stove and stopped, frowning. "Ugh. Why does that smell like that?"

I checked the grilled cheese sandwiches on the skillet to make sure they weren't burning. Nope, all looked good. "You bitchin' about my cooking, Red?"

"No. It was surprisingly good last time. It just smells off." She moved up against my side and took over stirring the soup, though I could tell she was taking shallow breaths so as not to inhale too much.

I was doing enough inhaling for the both of us. Hell, in a second I'd be burying my face in her hair.

"My best friend thought I was crazy to come out here."

"You are."

She shot me a look under her lashes. I was sure she hadn't touched up her makeup since she hadn't even realized right away that I'd brought up her bag, but her lashes were so thick, framing all that blue. "And yet."

"And yet. Damn Turnbull girls, so wild." I couldn't keep the amusement from my tone. "Must be fun for your dad, trying to harness all three of you."

She snorted. "Yeah, right. We're past the age of harnessing. At least Maeve and Regan are. He's given up on them to focus all his parental excesses on me. My mom tries to reign him in but it's basically a lost cause." She sighed and stirred. "You'd think after six, you'd loosen the strings a little."

"I'd think after three, I'd be getting snipped."

"Three, huh? Is that the magic number?"

"No." I didn't know why I'd even said that. I should've said before any, I'd get snipped. Why take any chances?

But I was the guy who'd just fucked a girl I barely knew raw. And she'd let me. Hell, she'd even encouraged me. That seemed about as much like the Maggie I'd met three weeks ago as buying her a robe fit me.

Screwing each other and screwed up.

"So you didn't, ah, ask."

"How you can afford this house? I hinted at that question, slyly, through compliments. But you didn't take the bait." She turned off the burner under the soup.

"Not that. I mean, before. Upstairs. I'm clean."

It was her turn not to look at me, and I found it vaguely disconcerting to be the one trying to get her to meet my gaze. "I'd hope so."

That was it?

"You're not going to volunteer the same?"

"I'm figuring you assumed that already or you wouldn't have risked it." She flashed a sunny smile. "Damn near to a virgin in your mind, aren't I? Besides, if I could risk it with you, not like you're in a place to judge."

"I'll have you know I've never done that before. Not even once."

"Mmm-hmm. Let me guess. You also like long walks on the beach, making love in the rain, and drinking pina coladas too?"

"Huh?"

"Before you ask your next question, I'm on the Pill. I went off after the ex then back on after the cabin. So we're good."

I grunted. That was excellent news. I should've known better.

Maggie would never risk a baby with the likes of me. Her father would probably disown her.

Not that I could blame the guy.

"Really, I don't need your lines," she continued. "They're tiresome. Not to mention Derek got there before—"

I let go of the skillet and closed my fingers around her wrist, jerking her against me as her pupils flared wide. "Don't ever compare me to him. I know he was important to you and you were together for a long time, but I'm not that asshole. I'm not feeding you lines."

"Oh no?" She yanked her wrist back and gave my chest a hard shove. "Don't think you can use your strength against me. If you don't like what I'm saying, that doesn't give you the right to try to shut me up."

I swallowed. "You're right. I'm sorry."

"And you know what else? I know exactly what I'm doing. I might not make the same choices everyone else does, but that doesn't mean that I'm stupid and uninformed. I know coming here is a risk. I get that. I know what happened upstairs was another one. But I had my eyes wide open. If trusting you is a mistake, at least I made it myself. I'll deal with the consequences that way too."

"You trust me?" I swallowed again over the grit in my throat. "How?"

"I don't know. Okay? I don't get any of this. But that doesn't mean I'm not adult enough to handle whatever comes my way. I might be headed for a cliff but at least I see it coming. At least I have my hands on the wheel. I didn't do the right thing, the safe thing, and still somehow put my belief in a man who ended up treating me like trash."

"Because I treated you that way from the start," I said hollowly.

"You did not. You pulled me out of my car and you took me into your home when you didn't want me there. You fed me your dinner and listened to my music and dealt with me in your space even though you were itchy to be alone. And you made me feel—" She looked away and I cupped her cheek, desperate to bring her eyes back to mine. "You just made me feel," she whispered. "I wanted to see if it could be like that one more time. Not thinking it really could."

A tremor went through my hand and I curled my fingers against her soft skin. "And?" I asked, voice hoarse.

"You very well know, because you feel it too. You asked me to come here because you feel it. And it scares you every bit as much as it frightens me." She rose on her tiptoes and pressed her forehead against my chin. "You're not like him, Kellan. You couldn't be. Just like I can't be the me I was with him either. This is all different."

I gripped a handful of her robe. "I bought this for you." She lifted her chin and nailed me with her all too perceptive gaze. "Just for you."

"Mmm-hmm," she said again, but her lips curved this time.

The pan sizzled beside me and she made a face. "Ugh. Burning."

I grabbed the pan and flipped the sandwiches, hiding the burned side from view. "Just a little charred. Adds flavor."

"We'll see about that. Want me to set the table?"

"Sure." I pointed out cabinets and drawers and grinned at her expression upon discovering my plates and bowls were yet again the disposable variety. "Hey, when I find something that works, I go with it."

She opened a drawer and slung plastic knives on the table to go with the paper plates. "So I see."

"I always enjoyed picnics."

"Me too, in Bailey Park. But my mom always brought her china and best silverware. No reason not to use the nice stuff even if we were eating on a blanket."

Her smile settled inside me as I used the spatula to dish out the sandwiches. "So you lied to your parents about coming here."

Like a cloud moving over the sun, her smile dimmed. "I shouldn't have, but I'm still at the fledgling stages of being a badass."

I laughed so hard that I nearly bobbled the pan of soup I'd just picked up. I turned around to find her grinning at me, her dark hair curving over her cheek.

It took everything I possessed to pour the soup into the plastic bowls she'd set out and sit down beside her to eat. All I wanted to do was to tug her into my lap and kiss her until that worry that had flitted through her expression was vanquished forever.

Worry I'd caused. Selfishly.

"Good?" I asked after she took the first bite of her sandwich. "A little crispy," I acknowledged, grating off the burnt parts with my crappy plastic fork.

"Adds flavor."

"Smart ass." Once I was done with my sandwich, I grabbed her plate and shaved off the darkened parts on her bread as well. I knew she was watching me, but I didn't glance up from my task.

Turned out I liked the heavy warmth of her stare on my skin. Liked way too much about her.

"Better?" I asked once she'd sampled the sandwich I'd returned to her.

She nodded. "Almost perfect." Licking cheese off her fingers, she rose and went to my fridge, yanking open the door and bending over to peer inside.

I nearly choked on the hunk of bread and cheese I'd just popped in my mouth.

Damn. That ass.

She rooted around for a second, then came back out with a jar of pickles. I held out my hand so I could open it for her as requested by every woman I knew, save my little sister. Maggie didn't even look up, dispatching the lid with an efficiency that made me shift on my chair.

Damn, she was hot.

She sat back down and pried apart her sandwich. Neatly, she placed five pickles on each side of the torn bread. Then she smashed both halves back together and took a big bite, her eyes practically rolling back in her head. "Oh yes. Yes."

I cocked a brow. "Need a moment alone?"

"Try it." She pushed the jar at me, waiting until I'd fixed my sandwich the same way.

I took a bite and nodded. Not half bad.

We talked about everything and nothing while we polished off the rest of our meal. Her flight, her work, her classes starting on Monday. She didn't ask me about myself anymore, and I found myself missing her sneaky little questions that weren't so sneaky at all.

Your choice, remember? You wanted to keep your distance.

Yeah, too bad I hadn't been able to do that with her since the first time I'd seen her hanging out of her car window.

"Don't like the soup?" I asked after she took a couple of mouthfuls, her forehead wrinkling every time. She was too polite to say it wasn't good, but if she wasn't a fan, I wouldn't make it next time.

Right. The next time that wasn't going to happen. I'd just remember that.

"Normally I do. It's just the smell." She pushed the bowl away. "Sorry."

"It wasn't expired. I don't think." I hadn't exactly checked.

She grinned. "Such confidence in your cooking."

"Well, not my best skill."

"No?" She braced her chin on her hand. "What is your best skill?"

"Probably playing guitar."

She blinked and I realized she'd been playing around. Great. I should've said eating pussy or fucking. Those were the kinds of answers that fit the level of intimacy I wanted to exist between us outside of bed.

Leave it to me to mess up my own rules.

"Guitar? Really?" The interest in her expression made me grip the edge of my plate until it crumpled. She glanced at my hand then back at my face before she averted her focus to anywhere but me. "Is that a deck out there?" she asked, gesturing toward the French doors. A couple of floodlights illuminated the wide, iron-railing flanked space.

I nodded, the tension in my shoulders easing. It wasn't as if I could tell her about my music without mentioning the rest. I'd lied and lies were forever. I couldn't just magically take them back.

No matter how much I wished I could.

"Overlooks the pool," I said tightly.

She hopped to her feet and moved to the glass doors, then stepped out into the night. It wasn't quite morning yet, but the sky was already beginning to lighten. Her hair blew behind her in the wind as she leaned over the railing to check out the pool. As she climbed up on the bottom rung, my gut lurched.

I was striding toward the doors and out to her before sanity descended. Just like I gripped her hips and pressed my mouth to the top of her head before I was even aware of doing it.

Somewhere along the way, my instincts had gotten all wrapped up in her. The instinct to keep her close, to try to make her happy, to protect her from any threat—including me.

Especially me.

"Kellan, it's beautiful."

I nodded against her hair, saying nothing.

"I bet you could climb up on this railing and jump right in—"

"No," I growled, making her laugh and turn to face me. "Not on your life."

"Spoilsport."

"Maybe, but you're not jumping. It's not safe from this height."

"I wasn't really going to." She reached up to feather her fingers along my jaw. "Your scruff's growing back in," she murmured.

"Is that an invitation?" I asked, recalling her earlier words.

I had no problem at all with living between her thighs.

Cocking her head, she pulled the tie on her robe, letting it fall open so that her sexy body was on display. Her perfect breasts, the slight rise of her belly, her mound with its arousing dark strip of curls. "Depends on if you've had enough time to recover."

"Red, I was recovered before I finished licking up what I left inside you." When she shuddered, I lowered my head to nuzzle her nipple. "Let's see if you can say the same."

14

MAGGIE

I WAS HAVING the best dream.

My co-star was a grouchy man who made love to me with so much hunger that I never doubted his desire.

I wasn't his first, and I probably wouldn't be his last. I might not even have been his first this week, despite what he'd indicated. But when he touched me, I knew he was all in.

We both were.

The days spun out, the hours stacking like dominoes that fell too quickly. I reached for the cell to call Kendra more than once and laughed as Kellan held my phone high above my head, just out of reach.

I understood. I didn't want to deal with the outside world either, and maybe I liked that he wanted to protect our happy bubble for just a little longer.

Ken would keep my secret. She was my best friend, and she knew I'd have to come home soon enough.

Too soon.

Even the best dreams had to end.

The pluck of guitar strings made me shift against the sheets. I didn't know the song. Didn't recognize the lyrics he sang in a low, sexy voice. That voice that skimmed over my skin as if it were a silky caress, arousing impulses I couldn't satisfy alone.

The only respite was when he was inside me. His mouth on mine, our bodies moving together.

The pinch of his fingers, the heat of his lips. The buzz of his scruff on sensitive flesh. His groans, broken and raw. As if I was laying him bare.

What I wouldn't give for just that, again and again?

I whimpered, rocking my hips, and he moved against my back, cradling me close. "Shh," he murmured, his talented hands sliding over me to quench all the needs that he'd created.

The music was gone, but I didn't need it anymore. He was singing to me, so softly I had to strain to hear the words. Catching them in mid-air like a dream as he parted my slick thighs and dipped inside me, already knowing just how to soothe the ache. His fingers slipping in and out, oh so slow. Filling me, chasing away all the cold. Replacing it with so much heat. And then before I could ask, he was pushing his thickness inside me, widening me for him the way it should be. Open and wet, my body throbbing. Offering him all of me so I could take so much more.

Going so deep that my spine arched to give him everything.

Pleasure rippled through me, starting way down low in my belly and fanning out like bubbles in the pool we'd sat beside for hours. Singing along to the radio and reading some of Kellan's many books until my skin burned. Then he'd smoothed lotion over my skin so patiently. Replacing the pain with something sweet.

He groaned against my neck, his body going still before his hips jerked. That precious liquid heat spurted inside me, making me moan. So dirty. I clenched to keep it all inside—to keep him inside—not wanting to waste a single drop.

Another groan, fractured this time as his mouth found mine. Together, we tumbled back into sleep.

The pattern repeated so many times I lost track of time. In between, we got up long enough to eat and cuddle on the couch in front of the giant TV in the living room. Laughing as he intentionally selected the video channels and teased me about my taste in music with our feet tangled together and our hands wandering everywhere.

Showering in cool water with his broad, hard body behind me, holding me up as he gave me orgasm after orgasm. With his fingers, his mouth, his cock. Using all three in tandem to destroy me and fit me together again.

"Don't go."

Imagining the words, wondering if I'd said them myself. I must've, because my grumbly guy didn't ask me for anything. Not unless I asked first.

I looped my arms around his neck and climbed up his wet, corded body as if he were my own personal cliff. Maybe he was. "I wish I could stay," I said between kisses, not really caring if he'd actually verbalized the statement. If I had to be the brave one, I would.

I would be the one who said the words and made the plans and put my heart on the line until he was right there with me. For me.

For *us*.

"Tomorrow." He slanted his mouth over mine and cupped my ass to lift it higher, his grip sure and true. "That's soon enough."

I blinked back the water starring my lashes, pushing my soaked hair back until we were nose to nose. Dark eyes bored into mine, and everything I needed to see was right there. No shields, no pretenses.

"One more day together," he said, and I nodded, not caring about classes or work or anything but hanging on to *this* for one more day before our lives ripped us apart again.

"Yes?"

I grinned. "Yes."

He kissed me, then furrowed his brow as we eased apart. "Red, we need to talk."

Panic filled my chest, pressing against that perfect bubble of joy we'd created. I couldn't let it pop. Not yet.

We needed more time. Just a little more.

"Later," I whispered, using my finger under his chin to bring his dark eyes back to mine. Waiting until he nodded.

Until the ropes around my chest eased enough again that I could breathe.

Wrapped in thick towels—he had one for me this time—we stood at the kitchen counter and ate pickles out of the jar. We'd blown through most of the groceries he'd picked up for the weekend, and if I was staying one more day, we'd need more sustenance.

"Mr. Wong?" he asked, holding up a menu by the corner.

I laughed and snatched it out of his hand. My stomach was growling again. "Chinese sounds heavenly. I could eat a pint of pork fried rice all by myself. And like three egg rolls. And…Kendra."

"Cannibalism is a little extreme."

"No, I need to call her. I should have called her before." I gave him a hard stare, though he was giving me his best innocent expression.

Yeah, right.

"She would've told you to come home." He held up a hand. "Yeah, where you belong. I was being selfish—"

I gripped his towel and yanked him against me. "I like it when you're selfish." I leaned up on my tiptoes and nipped his chin. "I also like when you're beardy for me."

He grabbed me around the waist and lifted me up on the granite counter as if I were made of air. "Beardy and no makeup and hair all crazy." He ducked his head so I could push my fingers through his hair as I had all weekend, taking every opportunity to muss it up. "Anything else you like?"

"I like when you touch me with these." I picked up one of his hands, running my fingertips over the ridges of calluses that rubbed my skin just right. "How does a pencil pusher get such rough hands?" I teased, remembering his guitar comment and the fragments of music that had wafted over me in the night when I was too disoriented to make them out.

He started to speak, then cleared his throat and begun again. "I told you I worked construction before."

A fact he'd volunteered without prompting during our long afternoon by the pool. "Mmm. I remember you hauling around wood that day at the cabin. Being all super manly." When he ducked his head again, from embarrassment this time, I decided to make it worse by reaching down to stroke his cock through his towel. "Though you carry around a pretty sizable piece of wood every day…"

"Nymphomaniac." But he grinned as he tilted his hips toward me, jutting his eager dick into my hand.

"Maybe. Only for you." I wound my legs around him, drawing him close. I brushed a kiss over his bare, damp shoulder, spying the forgotten piece of paper on the floor. "Oh, the food! Let's order."

He let out a deep laugh as he pinched my hip through the towel. "Love a woman with priorities," he said, laughing again at my rumbling stomach.

"You order the food, I'll call Ken."

"Go for it. Just be prepared that she'll want you to come home today like you planned."

"She doesn't tell me what to do. I want dumplings too."

"Anything else?"

I found my purse and tugged out my phone. I wasn't sure when he'd tucked it back inside. He might have added a few extra obstacles to calling her, but the truth was I'd been the one who turned off my phone and avoided reality. I didn't want to hear her lecture. When it came right down to it, I knew she'd be pissed at me, but she also loved me. Better to ask for forgiveness than permission, right? Besides, I'd given her the address where I was staying for safety's sake. I was almost twenty-three. Just a couple more weeks.

It was time I started living my life for me and no one else.

A million messages were waiting for me. Deliberately, I didn't read them, except Ken's last cryptic one sent just four hours ago. What the hell? She'd been up early on a Sunday. It was only early afternoon in California and three hours ahead on the East coast, and my bestie normally loved to sleep in.

Guilt and concern battled inside me, and I bit my lip as I read her last text.

I warned u. I hope u're okay & u know we <3 u. That's why we're doing this.

Doing what? My mind reeled and I typed as fast as I could.

Ken, I'm fine. I'm HAPPY. I'm sorry I didn't call, but we've been having fun. We're in love.

I stopped there, hitting send before I could erase and retype. It was insane. I'd taken months to fall in love with Derek, and he'd taken almost that long to fall for me. At least to tell me he had. This had to be infatuation. Extreme lust combined with forced proximity a couple of times, and the excitement of the whole clandestine, secretive thing we had going.

The good girl and the wild boy. It was like a Lifetime movie waiting to happen.

Of course, I'd think I was in love, and that he might be in love with me even if he'd never, ever admit it in one hundred years. Somehow that made me believe it more.

I was certifiably nuts.

Kendra replied immediately.

Love? C'mon. U don't even know who he is. Do u?

I frowned, sliding a glance at Kellan while he repeated our order to the person on the phone. There was some confusion about egg rolls and combinations, but he didn't speak harshly or cop an attitude with the restaurant. His voice stayed even, polite, and patient. My grouchy guy wasn't that way all the time. Sometimes he was downright sweet.

Instead of answering her, I shut off my phone and set it down on the counter.

Was I just being crazy? It wasn't possible to fall in love so fast. My dad and mom had, but they were unusual. Maybe I'd just heard the story of how they'd met one weekend and been engaged by the next so many times that it had infiltrated my brain.

So how come you didn't fall for Derek that fast then, huh?

It could be a rebound thing. Stuff like that happened all the time. Maeve went through guys like tissues, so she probably got over one guy by getting under the next. Maybe I was just using Kellan.

Sure, and maybe the Pope lived in Beijing.

"Hey." Kellan touched my shoulder and I jumped, hitting my hip on the counter. Before I even said, "ow," he was rubbing my leg to ease the hurt.

Yeah, he was so badass. Such a horrible person I didn't know and couldn't love, because hey, if a person isn't a ray of sunshine and doesn't immediately tell you their life story, better run the other way.

"McGuire," I mumbled, clutching his hand at my hip. "Your mother works at Bailey High. Mrs. McGuire with the son who always skateboarded and got hurt."

He frowned. "Yeah. You knew my mom?"

"I didn't make the connection until now. You mentioned she was a school secretary." Only when I'd traded his access to my body for some details about his family, but whatever. I hadn't been trying to pry or learn all his secrets. I just wanted to get a sense of who he was when he was away from me.

Breaking his cardinal rule, probably. But he'd broken plenty of mine too.

Like the one where I didn't fall for a guy before I knew his family. I'd always been a girl who believed family gave the strongest clues to a person's personality, and without knowing them, you missed a vital piece of the whole.

"I was teased in school," I continued quietly, staring down at the black and gold granite floor. "I wasn't good at sports and I didn't have a ton of friends. Just Kendra. I didn't fit in."

"No one does at that age. Doesn't mean a damn thing."

The vehemence in his tone made me smile. "I stopped going to lunch because when Ken was working on extra credit projects, I didn't have anyone to sit with. So I ended up helping your mom with filing. Eventually we ate lunch together. She didn't think I was a weirdo." I laughed softly and dashed at the stupid tears I didn't know why I was crying. "Well, I am a weirdo. But she was nice to me." Swallowing hard, I glanced up at him and lifted my hand to his cheek. "You have her eyes. I didn't realize until now."

He closed his hand around mine on his face and didn't say anything. Just brushed away my tears with his other hand.

It was all I needed. More than I'd dared to want.

"I should probably tell you I met your dad back in the day too." He cleared his throat. "It may have happened when I was, ahem, massaging Maeve's breast."

I raised a brow. "You met my dad when you were massaging my sister's breast?" That bore repeating.

"Yes. With my mouth."

I laughed, tipping back my head while my tears changed to ones from mirth. Didn't it just figure?

"So that explains why he thought you were the devil."

"Well, the ramshackle cabin in the woods probably didn't hurt."

"Least you didn't have the heads of your enemies on posts beside the door."

"Hmm, might be a design aspect I should look into."

I hooked a finger in the towel around his waist. "Perhaps save it until after you meet my parents. Both of them this time, not just my dad. You know, like a family dinner."

Just like that, his open expression shuttered. If I hadn't been so intimately involved with the situation, I might've even found it humorous.

Look at poor Maggie Kelly. She believes in family and settling down, yet she's mixed up with a commitment-phobe who claims to hate those things. Isn't that hilarious?

Except it was my life, and it was harder to be amused while the tears were still drying on my cheeks.

The doorbell chimed, and he couldn't move fast enough to get away from me. I didn't follow. Suddenly my appetite for Chinese had dimmed.

You can't blame him for this. He never lied to you or led you on. If he had, it would be different.

The door opened, and the voices that boomed through the house had me jerking away from the counter and down the hall before I fully knew what I was doing.

Kendra stood in the doorway, her hair a mass of braids that clacked as she spoke. Low, angry words that were probably laced with threats, if I had to guess. Beside her, my older brother Liam, one of the twins, glared at Kellan as if his stare alone could kill. He might have normally friendly blue-green eyes and an easy smile, but right now his expression was pure ice.

Shock rooted me in place.

As did Liam's reaction upon seeing me. Relief came first, then joy, then resignation, each emotion scrolling across his face. He dropped his gaze to my attire, and I remembered all at once that I wore only a towel.

A towel that matched Kellan's.

I didn't have a chance to react. To insert myself between them before Liam spun back to Kellan and decided words weren't necessary since he had two perfectly good fists. He plowed one of them into Kellan's face, snapping his head back so hard that I cried out and rushed not to him, but my older brother.

Who I punched soundly in the chest, hammering at him until he stumbled back and Kendra waded into the fray.

"Enough," Kellan roared, cupping his bleeding mouth. The sight of the red liquid squeezing out between his fingers was enough to make me rear back, nauseated, but he still wasn't done.

"You came to take her home. That's probably for the best." He raised his hands and stepped back. "I'm not going to fight with you or make a scene."

Because I'm not worth it.

I swallowed the bile rising in my throat and forced myself to glance at Kendra instead of the man I'd spent the weekend with. She was already watching me, her careful attention all the proof I needed that I must look like hell.

"No," Liam said, shaking out the fist he'd used to hit Kellan as if I hadn't pummeled him. "Why would you? There's more where she came from, I'm sure."

I didn't know what he was referring to, but all I wanted to do was leave.

This gorgeous sanctuary we'd spent the weekend in now felt like a prison, the walls closing in to trap me.

"I said to just go," Kellan snapped, his jaw flexing. "I'm not doing this with you."

Kendra laid a hand on Liam's arm, and for a second, surprise at how close together they stood replaced my own shock and heartbreak. Since when were they getting along? They'd been like oil and gasoline since high school. Before then, probably. If she'd gone to anyone, I would've figured she would have picked Angus, who was no-nonsense and didn't say much but was the guy you'd want by your side in a crisis.

Just as I'd believed Kellan was. Forget a crisis. He couldn't even stay by my side to face my family. Guess it took a couple times to beat that into my thick skull, since he hadn't exactly stood firm to my father either.

"You didn't need to come here to collect me," I said, pleased my voice didn't tremble. I didn't even sound particularly affected. "I had a ticket back tonight, and I'll use it. Alone. Thank you for coming, but I'm fine to get back on my own. I'm also old enough to take care of myself. One of these days, maybe you'll realize that." I looked between my brother and my best friend. "*Both* of you."

Liam drilled me with his gaze. "You don't even know who he is, do you? Ken said you didn't, but I thought she was shitting me. You come to a place like this and you think you're just dealing with Joe Nobody? C'mon, sis, there's being naive and there's just being stupid."

Kellan reached out, whip-fast, and shoved Liam back. "You're not going to speak to her like that. Say what you want to me, but not to her."

"Oh, that's sweet. Chivalry from the lying cheat. Now I'm touched."

"Liam, stop it," Kendra demanded, glancing from him to me and back again, her eyes full of an apology I didn't understand. "This isn't the way to do this."

I didn't want to ask. Didn't want to ask *them* especially. I'd already asked Kellan so many things, only to get evasions and small truths. Nothing big. I had attributed his behavior to a personality quirk rather than an attempt at genuine secrecy, but maybe he had good reason.

Some criminal justice student you are, Magpie. Can't even read the clues right in front of your face.

Pushing back my shoulders, I stepped forward and gripped

Kellan's forearm. "I'm going to ask you what they're talking about. Not them. You don't have to tell me. You haven't had to tell me anything. But I'm asking you."

For the longest moment, he didn't look at me. As usual. His jaw twitched as he turned his head, pinning me in place with his stare. "I'm in a band."

Liam choked out a laugh, but I didn't spare my brother a glance. "A band."

Kellan nodded.

That explained the guitar comment, and the calluses, and the music while I was sleeping. Probably also explained why he'd been hiding out in a nondescript cabin in the woods in Turnbull, but his home was…this.

"You don't manage bands then."

"I did," Kellan said, eyes narrowing at Liam before he returned his focus to me. "For several years. That's how I got this gig. My manager Lila gave me a chance to get the band back together I fronted in high school. A spot on the roster opened up, and she saw something in me."

"Was that before or after you slept with her?" Liam questioned.

Neither of us spared my brother a glance. "You're a singer then. A guitarist."

It made sense, even down to the pictures he'd admitted to painting on the wall. He was artistic, though he hid it under a layer of gruff. Just like the talent he buried down deep, only taking it out for those with the price of a ticket.

He'd offered it to me for free, but I hadn't known what it was. Or what it meant.

Rather than replying, he took out a crumpled piece of paper from his back pocket, smoothing it against his arm. His jaw working all the while. "Your brother and Kendra wanted you to see this, to know the kind of man I am. But you already know me, Red, better than anyone ever has." He held out the paper. "Remember that."

I stared at it, torn between wanting to see and not wanting to know. Did he really believe that I knew him that well? That what we'd experienced this weekend wasn't just a mirage?

Or worse, that I'd experienced it alone.

Been there, done that.

Regardless of what he meant, I couldn't deny that it *felt* true. I got him on some fundamental level, and even if he hadn't come clean with me, that truth remained.

He'd never said anything that was an outright fabrication. He didn't have to. He deflected by changing the subject or looking away or sharing things that once had been reality, so they weren't technically lies if you didn't care about little things like timelines.

Except I did. I cared about timelines, and being straightforward, and understanding what I'd dived into headfirst.

Swallowing hard, I took the piece of paper and let the headline soak in before I studied the pictures.

New band Wilder Mind explodes on the scene in more ways than one.

The first picture wasn't of Kellan at all. It was of a guy with crazy hair bent over a woman spread out beside a drum kit, her bare breasts and the area between her legs blurred out. Probably since crazy hair guy's hips were between them. His bare flexing butt wasn't blurred out though. Guess crack action was okay for a tabloid.

Good to know.

"My drummer, Bryan," Kellan said tightly without being prompted.

"Classy dude," Liam offered, holding up his hands at Kendra's sharp look.

The inset picture contained Kellan in a leather vest, no shirt. Hair spiked up like it had been on Friday, eyes heavy with makeup. He was smiling down at a tiny blonde who'd wrapped her leg around his thigh and flattened her hands against his chest. His name was clearly visible in black Sharpie on the cleavage revealed by her brief top.

"When was this taken?" I asked once I was certain my voice would be steady.

"A couple nights before you texted me."

"Busy weekend for you then." I folded the paper and handed it back to him. He shook his head and jutted his chin toward my brother and best friend.

Of course. The only reason he was telling me now was to get me to leave.

Because good girls don't hook up with rockstars. We head home to lick our wounds and think about our steady, secure ex-boyfriend, who had just happened to run off with a stripper.

Hell, I was starting to see the appeal of those in the entertainment arts, since I'd certainly done some running of my own.

I secured my towel, unable to meet his eyes. Or Kendra's. Or Liam's. "I'd better pack so I make my flight."

"So you're going then." Kellan's voice was even. Measured.

"What else do you propose I do? Maybe you'd rather I let you sign my breasts before I go?"

He said nothing.

"Mags." Kendra stepped forward, her voice contrite. "I'll help you pack."

"I'm good. Really. I appreciate the time you took to come here. Thank you, even if the effort was misguided. I hope that someday you'll learn to trust my choices," I said, encompassing my brother in my statement.

He rubbed the back of his neck, his brow furrowed.

"Not this time though," I added brightly. "Since anyone can see the colossal mess this is. But hey, lesson learned. I got a nice trip out of it, right?"

"Mags," Ken said, gripping my hand. "Let's go upstairs and talk for a few minutes. Alone."

"No, thank you." If I didn't keep this shield of politeness in place,

I would shatter like china. Just break apart in Kellan's foyer like the fragile doll he hadn't trusted with the truth.

Why would he? I was the sweet, innocent girl from Turnbull he'd had lark sex with. You know, something different and easily tossed aside.

Flavor of the week. Or weekend, since I hadn't even gotten that.

"Maggie," Kellan said, and that single word was nearly my undoing. So low and raw, as if it physically pained him to say my name.

I let go of Kendra's hand and walked to the spiral staircase. I climbed to the third step, then stopped and turned. "Just tell me this. Did you lie to me intentionally? Or was it an accident?"

I didn't see how it could have been. The truth was the truth. You didn't forget it if you were tired or unprepared.

Honesty didn't happen on a whim. Either you were forthright or you weren't.

No do-overs.

Kellan held my gaze for so long I thought that was his answer. I turned to continue to climb, but his response stopped me.

Stopped everything, including the warmth in my chest that hadn't even really had a chance to take root.

"I lied to you on purpose. Over and over again."

I tore my gaze from his and ran upstairs, my only thought to escape. Until I reached the bedroom I'd shared with him and glimpsed the tangled sheets hanging off the mattress. We'd fucked like animals in that bed. I patted my ass, realizing I didn't have on my jeans. My phone was down in the kitchen.

But his was sitting right there on the nightstand, and I was willing to bet he hadn't changed the passcode from the easy one he'd had the last time I'd broken into it. And I didn't feel the slightest bit guilty for breaking in again either.

I snatched his cell and tried the passcode that had worked before. *Bingo.* I didn't go to his mail app or his messages. Instead I went straight to YouTube and typed in Wilder Mind. I had to see. Had to know.

The first clips that came up were grainy without great sound. I didn't care. I just wanted to watch Kellan at work. To see the man I'd fallen for making thousands of women fall for him onstage.

Within seconds, I found what I was looking for.

He gripped the boxy mic and gazed straight into the audience, his hips moving as if they had a mind of their own. Truly, he had to be double or triple jointed.

Warmth scalded my cheeks. I'd thought much the same this weekend.

But there he was, seducing the crowd with that honey and gravel voice that had made me wet so many times. I wasn't the only one. Girls were screaming and crying and pulling at their clothes as if they couldn't stand the constriction. He didn't do the crazy moves some singers did, just gave his all to the song. He threw back his head, making the cords of his neck stand out in sharp relief, and he slid his hand down the mic stand as if he was caressing a lover.

Even angry and ashamed—since yet again I'd made another stupid mistake in who to trust—I couldn't help shifting on the bed. Pressing my thighs together didn't stem the ache. My nipples tightened and I sucked in a breath, holding it as Kellan onstage opened his eyes and seemed to stare right at me through the screen.

I had no defense against that look. Not on the video, and not when footsteps in the hall alerted me to his presence. Defiantly, I turned to glare at him without shutting off the video.

Barefoot and bare-chested, still clad in only his towel, he stopped in the doorway. His jaw was tighter than I'd ever seen it.

"You baited me about the music I liked. Did it bother you I didn't know yours?"

Nothing. Not even that muscle tic in his face that was his usual tell.

"No, of course it didn't." Though it was surprisingly difficult, I stopped the clip and tossed his cell on the bed, then I rose to look for my shoes. I hadn't had much use for my heels the last couple of days.

He remained silent. Just watching me.

I dragged them out from under the sheets dangling on the floor and slipped them on. Now what? I had to go in the bathroom to get dressed or else I'd have to do it right here.

Screw it. He'd seen me naked plenty, and I was tired of hiding.

I unwound the towel and walked over to root through my suitcase in just my heels. His rough intake of breath gratified me immensely.

At least I could take comfort in the fact that his lust for me hadn't waned. As many times as we'd had sex, that was probably a feat.

"Red."

His nickname for me was my undoing. Hot tears sprung into my eyes, but I battled them back and unzipped my suitcase.

I'd be damned if another man saw me cry anytime this century. Especially when *he* was the cause.

If only he had told me the truth. I wished like hell he hadn't hidden his true identity from me for some reason I couldn't quite comprehend. I didn't understand the whole rockstar thing, but I would have tried to. For him, I would have fought to deal with it even though that lifestyle couldn't have been further removed from my own.

He was worth it to me. *We* were worth it. Too bad those feelings didn't run both ways. To him, I must've just been a lark. Clearly he hadn't seen anything serious happening between us—even after this crazy weekend—so what did it hurt to lie? I was just his latest hookup. It wasn't as if I'd be a permanent fixture in his life or anything.

Message received loud and clear.

"You know me," he said again, his tone strangely hollow.

Just like I felt inside. Hulled out and empty.

Somehow those three words sliced me deeper than all the rest. Then he turned away from the door and left me alone to pack.

15

KELLAN

Two weeks later

"FROM THE TOP," Cooper said, shooting me his fiftieth odd glance of the night.

I wasn't leading the rehearsal. Shit, I was barely participating in it. Considering I'd nearly called out ten times before I'd dragged myself into the car and to the record studio, without showering and in yesterday's dirty clothes—hell, the same dirty clothes I'd worn all week —it wasn't much of a surprise.

Naturally Lila had decided to sit in on this rehearsal so she could report our progress to Donovan. We'd be recording another song for the EP next week if Cooper's new piece came together the way it had during the first week we'd rehearsed it.

That was the week before Maggie visited, when I'd been horny as fuck and full of aggression I'd poured into the song. Anticipation too. I'd been raring to go in a million ways where Maggie was concerned.

Now? I was operating on a flatline. Just doing the bare minimum to get through each day.

I tried to lose myself in the music—the pounding drums, the shrieking guitars, and Jake's steady, rhythmic bass. Myles came into the song with a slam of the keys, rising off his bench the way he often did during shows. That they were all so into the song helped me to dig down deep and find the growl that was my signature. I cupped the microphone and bowed my head, rumbling the words that were etched into my brain from brutal repetition. I'd probably dream about "I Can't Sleep" tonight.

You break me apart, rip me to shreds
Ask me if it's forever
Only to do it again
One night with you has me on the edge
I can't sleep
Oh, I can't sleep
One hour away and I'm ready to beg
Tell you to come back
Before I ask you to go
Our last night together
And I can't sleep
I can't eat
One more night, give it to me
Before I learn
Before you learn
Before we learn
What goodbye really means

At the bridge, Cooper and AJ went into their epic solos, both competing to prove who could climb up and down the frets faster. Cooper went to his knees, throwing his head back so his long dark hair skimmed the floor. AJ was just as crazed beside him, his fingers flying as he added some unmistakable flourishes of his own. Bryan hit the skins behind us, and Jake closed his eyes while he went into his own trance on the bass. He didn't go for the tricks that AJ and Cooper did, just provided a backbone for the song so they had space for their theatrics. Myles was still jamming on the keys, hitting them with the skill and sly grin that had made me so sure he'd be the perfect fit for the band. For him, nothing mattered as much as the music.

That had been me too. Nothing had ever come close...until now.

I came back into the song with a low vibrato that grew into a roar. I yanked the microphone stand to the side, nearly dragging it down to the floor as I worked for those last notes. Pulling them out of me as if each one was formed from my blood, sweat, and tears.

And my memories, because I sure as fuck understood not being able to sleep. Or eat. Or do anything but wonder where the hell I'd gone so goddamn wrong.

The song ended with the vibration of the amps as Cooper brought the strings down from scream to mournful cry. I jerked my head up as someone started to clap.

"Finally. That's what I've been waiting to see in these rehearsals." Lila Crandall walked forward, her long blond hair restrained in a clip, her blue eyes shrewd and assessing. Her pumps clicked on the floor with every step she took toward us, her gaze sweeping over each member of the band in turn. "If I see more of that, you'll be booking outside of California soon. Possibly even beyond the west coast."

A cheer went up from the other guys. Bryan stomped his feet, and I rolled my eyes. Right. He was excited to sample other varieties of pussy. Midwest pussy, East coast pussy, and definitely couldn't forget Southern pussy, which AJ claimed was the sweetest of all.

"It's a little early to cheer, but you're getting there. The recent press you've received from some of your, ahem, exploits hasn't hurt either." Lila held her ubiquitous iPad against her chest. "Donovan is ready to capitalize."

"First we gotta get the EP out. Ride FFY for a while longer—" Jake said, always the pragmatic one.

"FFY is on its last gasp. We're barely hanging on to top 50. Time to get 'Felicity' out there so you can keep the momentum going. Hopefully 'I Can't Sleep' will be a single too. With some of the summer festivals already getting close to capacity, having that in your arsenal would be a big shot in the arm. Donovan may even recommend pushing ICS out first. It's a more natural fit for the summer concert season at the venues we have in mind."

"Hell yeah." Cooper pumped his fist, going quiet as he realized Myles was giving him some serious side-eye. "But of course, 'Felicity' would make a great single too."

"As a filler between this EP and a full-length album, yes. We always planned on Wilder Mind bringing a more harder edge to the market, and ICS delivers on that promise. So we'll see." Lila shifted her laser-like focus to me. "You've been drinking that tea and honey I recommended?"

I gripped the mic and cleared my throat. Her stare only got sharper. Even clearing the throat could be rough on the vocal cords, and that I was doing it so much meant I hadn't been taking care of my voice the way I should have been. "Not as consistently as I should."

"Get the honey drops too. You sounded amazing, but your voice was fraying at the end. It shouldn't be. We want you to work with a coach."

"What?" I gazed at her, dumbfounded. "Since when? You said you liked that my voice was raw. That the imperfections made it unique."

"This isn't about imperfections. It's about treating your instrument with care, and you are not." She gave the others a dismissive glance. "Great set today, everyone. You're all free to go. Except Kellan," she added, making me tip my head back with a groan.

Myles gave me a sympathetic glance as he filed out, and Coop patted me on the back. Jake and AJ both called out goodbyes.

Bryan was already on his phone, probably to some chick he'd picked up outside the record studio. We were starting to have clusters of fans show up now and then due to our openness on social media—something that had worked well for Lila's other bands—and Bry wasn't wasting any opportunities to get laid.

I sprawled on the couch, sagging back until the cool leather cushioned my aching head and neck. The lack of sleep was getting to me. I hadn't been working out either and not having that outlet didn't help.

As far as sex, I wasn't going there. I'd been on an abstinence streak before she who would not be named had entered my life. I could deal.

Lila sat at the other end of the couch. "What's going on with you?"

I crossed one booted foot across the other leg. "I didn't realize you cared."

"I do, and you know better than that. Is something going on with the band?"

"No, Lila. Your investment in us isn't in danger."

"It is if you don't start taking your vocal care more seriously. You sounded crispy today."

"Fuck that. I nailed that song."

"Which would be wonderful if you were performing at a school chorale concert and didn't have to do a ninety-minute set."

Even as Lila spoke, I was thinking about Maggie. The way she touched me so gently and intently listened to everything I said. I knew if she had been here for the meeting, she'd be riding my ass about making sure I protected my voice.

If she even still cared about me. I wouldn't blame her if she didn't. I'd pretty much ground her feelings to dust with my cruelty, and I didn't even know if she had any in my direction. At least beyond what I knew instinctively when we were together, which made no sense.

None of this made sense, including the fact that I'd been like a dead man walking since she left my place with her best friend and her brother. She hadn't cried in my presence, but her disappointment had rung out loud and clear. That I deserved it didn't make it any easier to take.

"You're right," I said hollowly. "I need to be more careful. Got it."

"You think it won't have consequences. I've seen what happens to a guy with a blown out vocal cord. It isn't pretty. We're talking likely surgery and months of—"

"I said I got it, all right?" I snapped. "I'm not your usual strung out junkie lead singer. I'm fully lucid and well aware of what you're saying. Your concern is duly noted. And unnecessary."

"It's not unnecessary until you show me I don't need to be concerned any longer." She crossed her legs and gripped her iPad in her lap. "We're friends, are we not? Come from common stock and all that."

It made my lips twitch. "Common Turnbull stock, you mean?"

"Yes."

"You think that makes a difference?"

"You'd be surprised. I've found there's a different sensibility out here." She shifted toward me on the sofa. "Just putting it out there that if you wanted to talk, I could listen. Or pretend to ignore you. Whatever makes it easier to spill your guts."

"I'm good." I heaved out a breath and stared up at the ceiling. "I'm not, but I can't talk about it. Not work-related though, I promise."

Lila nodded and stood. "I understand. If that changes, let me know." She walked to the door and paused with her hand on the handle. "Maybe there's someone else you should talk to instead."

"Playing shrink, Lila?"

"No. Taking guesses as a friend. By the way, you won't piss me off with your patented routine. You forget I am married to the poster child for bad attitudes and not only dealt with him but married him. Mostly voluntarily."

"Does he cheat on you?"

I hadn't meant to ask the question, but Lila didn't miss a beat. "If he did, he'd be missing some vital equipment and I'd be halfway to Mexico."

Shaking my head, I chuckled. "Sorry. Inappropriate question."

"A little, so I'll give another inappropriate answer. No. If I truly believed he would, I wouldn't have fallen in love with him. Granted, my judgment has been skewed before, but I'm confident in my choice this time."

"Even though he's in a rock band and has access to—"

"Every flavor of pussy he could ever dream of and twice on Sunday. Yes. I'm well aware."

She didn't blink, but I sure did. Lila was not one for that sort of language, ever.

"Yet you're cool with it. Not worried he'll slip."

"He's an adult male, not a confused toddler. Sliding between a woman's thighs is not the same as sliding in some juice on the kitchen floor. No, I don't believe he'll slip, just as he doesn't believe I will."

"Profession aside."

"I'm around plenty of supposed temptation too. If rockstars are so hot, well, hello, rainbow of varieties to choose from. But I don't go there." She held up her hand, tapping her wedding ring.

"But what if the situation was different? What if you were, let's say, a stay-at-home mom. Or a lawyer," I said, remembering Maggie's biggest ambition. "Surrounded by lawyers instead of rockstars day in and day out. Would you still feel the same?"

"It doesn't matter who either of us is surrounded by. It comes down to who we are and what we value. I could be in a crowd of David Gandys and still not be tempted because I want that jerk, and he's mine. And vice versa." She frowned. "All right, so there would be a little temptation. Infinitesimal. But I wouldn't act on it, no matter what."

I laughed and locked my hands behind my neck. "Thanks for answering my strange questions and being cool about it."

"Who is she?"

I started to say no one. There wasn't a she. From the status of my head right now, that was more than obvious. I'd had Maggie—at least in the flesh—and I'd lost her. Big time. But she didn't have to be physically present to be a factor in my life. "She's from Turnbull."

"Good choice. Now I have to know who. I might be able to share juicy gossip about her if you give me a name. You know my parents talk to everyone who comes through Happy Acres."

Happy Acres was her parents' apple orchard, and yes, she was one hundred percent correct. They talked to everyone and knew everything that went on in Turnbull. "Maggie Kelly." I held up a finger. "If you so much as breathe a word to anyone—"

"Maggie? She's the sweetest. She used to paint faces on kids during the fall festival. I taught her myself. Passed on the baton, as it were." Lila cocked her head. "How did you meet? Did you two have one of those clandestine romances from childhood? Though you'd be robbing the cradle a bit there." She tapped her chin. "Hmm."

"Only about five years between us. Not even that. But it feels like light years, man." I scratched the back of my neck. "She crashed into my ditch on New Year's Eve."

"Now that sounds romantic."

Quickly, I told her what had happened. I left out the details, but I didn't skimp on my own assholedom. I had royally fucked up this whole situation, and I wouldn't shirk the responsibility for it, even while talking to a friend. Who just happened to be my manager.

She didn't say anything, just listened. When I finished, she tapped her nails on her iPad. "So you told her you lied to let her down easy?"

I frowned. "There wasn't a lot of easy involved. Mainly just to make a clean break. I knew it was best for her."

"What's best for you?"

I didn't answer.

"Perhaps it isn't best for her. Ever think of that? She's a smart woman who knows her own mind. If she's interested in you, she probably has reason to be. You're a good guy, Kellan. You just don't give yourself much credit for it." Lila turned the door handle. "And for what it's worth? I don't think you'd ever slip. I bet Maggie would trust you not to as well."

The door closed behind her and I reached for my phone before I could kill the impulse. My mom answered on the second ring.

"Kell?"

"Yeah. It's me. How are you?"

"Good. Everything okay?"

I turned on the speaker and set aside my phone, then reached for the guitar I'd left leaning against the sofa. I strummed through the beginning of "Turn the Page" before blowing out a breath and tapping out the beat against the body of my old Taylor. "Yeah. Everything's good. You?"

"Good. Just as it was two minutes ago." There was a smile in her voice I'd missed hearing. We didn't talk much anymore. She was actively dating and she was busy at school, and I was on the opposite coast most of the time. Bethy usually seemed to be our go-between other than on holidays.

We definitely weren't the Kellys or anything close.

"Sorry. I'm a little scattered today."

"That's all right. I'm just glad to hear your voice."

"How's school going?" I asked, deliberately picking a topic I knew would keep her talking. Once she finished, maybe I'd have summoned enough nerve to say the reason behind my call.

Cheerfully, she told me about some of her favorite students. As I listened, I rubbed my knee through the hole in my jeans. Even that gesture reminded me of Maggie and how she'd disliked my rockstar look. *Hated* might've been a more accurate assessment. She liked me better bearded and in sweats and rough around the edges. No hair gel or eye makeup or glitz.

Me fucking too. Her preferred version of me was my true self, not the prettied-up version that sold albums. The stage look was my uniform, just a crazier one than most people had to wear on a daily basis. But when I was home, I could be me again. The me Maggie appreciated.

The pseudo rockstar was the version she had no use for, and God, I loved her for that. Just loved her period, and it scared the shit out of me.

I'd tried to talk myself out of it. Tried to ignore my feelings and bury them and pretend what I was experiencing was just lust. Except lust wouldn't make me ache like this to see her again. I wanted inside her sweet pussy, but that wasn't all I wanted. I craved hearing her laughter, her teasing, the way she laid her hand against my cheek and studied me so carefully while she tried to figure me out.

In other women, that might annoy me. Not with her. She didn't have an agenda and she wasn't looking to change me. She wanted me as I was. God only knew why.

Or at least she had, before.

"You knew Maggie Kelly," I said during a break in the conversation, unsurprised by her silence. "Years ago."

"Yes." Her voice softened. Warmed. "I remember Maggie. Such a kind girl. Easily wounded, but she hid it well if you didn't know how to read her."

I did. Somehow I did already, and knowing I'd hurt her—even though I'd tried to convince myself it was for her own benefit—was killing me.

"She told me about you." I cleared my throat and decided I'd work on not doing that another day. I could only fix so many flaws in one goddamn week.

This week, I was working on the reason why I'd driven away the best person I'd ever known. Because I wasn't good enough for her. Because I didn't want to possibly harm her down the road. Because I might turn out to be just like my fucking father.

Instead I'd hurt her right from the start.

"I didn't realize you knew Maggie," my mom said, her pleasure evident.

"It's a new thing. We met on New Year's Eve. I'm probably in love with her."

Yeah, that was me. Subtle all the way.

My mom laughed. "Wow. Well then. Are you calling to tell me you're thinking about getting married?"

I didn't have a reply for that one. My vocal cords had glued themselves together in sheer terror.

Married? Was that the way this had to end?

Probably. Just not right now. A guy needed some time to ease in, even if he had basically fallen in love in the course of a night.

Christ, I was so fucked.

"If so, I can't wait to help her pick out a dress," my mom continued. "Maggie was such a tiny thing. Big family. Big strapping brothers who grunted if anyone so much as looked sideways at her. I always thought she was a bit stifled, if you want to know the truth. Overprotected in the extreme. Why, she was practically treated like a doll in the window."

"Yeah, just what I want to deal with. Barreling through a football squad to get to her. Oh, and the wedding thing? No. Not now. Not yet." Any more qualifiers and I might as well cancel the whole statement.

"Oh."

"Don't sound like your dog just died. I just met the girl." I shook my head, amused rather than irritated. My mother hadn't hidden her desire for more grandchildren. She just usually harassed Bethy, not me. I wasn't likely to produce one this century.

"Just met her and already love her. Marriage is next," she proclaimed. "Marriage and babies, just you watch and see."

I was not going down that road. First I had to win her back. Or at least talk to her and see if she hated me. Hate and love were supposedly flip sides of the same coin, so maybe I hadn't been booted completely out of the arena.

"Yeah, well, don't count your eggs yet, of the human or chicken variety," I muttered, smiling despite myself at her delighted laugh. "I called because I need your help."

"What can I do? Tell me."

"Can you go check on her without letting on that you're checking? She works at Pizza Uno on Franklin on weekends so she should be there tomorrow night if she isn't tonight."

"Sure, sure, I can do that. I love their pizza so it's no hardship. I've been dieting for the past few months, so that's probably why I haven't seen her in there. I've been trying to limit splurges. Down twenty-two pounds so far," she said proudly, and I felt like a jackass for not calling more often.

One more item for my self-improvement list. If I kept this up, I wouldn't even recognize my own asshole face in the mirror anymore.

Maybe that wasn't a bad thing.

"That's great, Mom," I said, meaning it. "I should do the same."

"I could send you my diet plan—"

"Nah, I'd rather just hit it harder in the gym."

"Really, it's all about cutting out carbs. It's not so difficult once you formulate the habit."

What I was hoping when it came to not being a fuckhead regarding Maggie and relationships in general. I might suck now, but with repeated practice…

"You'll go down to see her, right? Just make sure she's okay. That's all."

"Sure. I'll do that. I can get a slice of veggie. You know, I've missed that girl. So much. I should've contacted her before now. We see each other around town sometimes, but it's so easy to let time get away from you. I can't keep doing that anymore."

"Me either," I murmured. "Thank you. It means a lot to me."

"No problem, sweetie. I'll call you after I see her."

"Thanks." I ended the call and took the phone off speaker, then stared at the screen. Now that I'd opened the can, I wasn't quite ready to close the lid.

Sending my mother to check up on Maggie wasn't even close to enough. I needed to see her myself, in person, so we could talk. Openly and honestly. No holds barred.

What I needed was a plan. It wouldn't be easy to get time off right now, but I had to try to make things right, whatever it took.

I wasn't my father, and I was sick and tired of letting his past determine *my* future.

Before I could stop myself, I texted the number I'd done my best to forget these past two weeks. There was just one thing that mattered right now. Well, only two things. Soon enough I'd be saying those three words to Maggie too, God willing.

I'm sorry.

16

MAGGIE

I'm sorry.

Those two words replayed on a constant loop in my mind, alternating with five other, albeit more urgent ones.

Please no more throwing up.

The throwing up was a new thing. It had just started a few days ago. Before that I'd been nauseated for a week. It was either the slowest moving flu bug in the history of the world, my misery had a strange new physical component, or I was knocked up.

Considering the state of my life since December thirty-first, I was going with door number three.

I still held out hope I wasn't toting around a tiny human. *Small* hope. The smell of tomato sauce making me want to hurl wasn't an awesome sign, especially since I worked at a pizza shop.

The pizza shop I was currently throwing up in.

My life sucked. Hardcore.

Someone knocked on the door to the cramped one-person bathroom, and I covered my mouth with one hand while sticking my foot out to the side to brace it against the door. The stupid lock kept breaking. "Just a second, please," I called between dry heaves.

At least they weren't wet any longer.

The knock came again. "Hello?" A woman. Her voice was familiar but I couldn't quite place it. "Is that you in there, Maggie?"

I was so shocked to be addressed by name that I stopped heaving long enough to listen more closely. Nice to know my baby wasn't a complete ruiner. "Yes?"

"Maggie, it's Mrs. McGuire. Can I come in?"

Sagging against the wall, I stared up at the ceiling. This could not be happening. It was just a bad dream. Had to be.

I hadn't seen Mrs. McGuire in forever, probably not since last summer. We rarely got a chance to say much beyond *hello, how are you* as we rushed past each other. She hadn't stopped in Pizza Uno the entire time I worked there. Now she had to use the bathroom at the exact same time I was puking from being preggo with her son's baby.

Seriously, who had I pissed off in a past life? Maybe I needed an exorcism. What did one do to remove a curse?

I shut my eyes and prayed to pass out. The floor was beyond gross, but I wouldn't know what was happening for those few blissful moments of unconsciousness.

"Maggie?" Mrs. McGuire repeated. "Are you all right? I'd like to speak with you, if that's okay."

Did she not get that I was in the bathroom for a reason? Probably one that required privacy? Kellan had a similar disregard for personal space. He'd marched right into the bathroom at the cabin and seen me naked as the day I was born, thereby inciting all kinds of inappropriate desire in me when I realized he found me attractive just as I was. Curvy some places, slight in others. A hodgepodge that definitely didn't match Derek's stripper.

Ah hell, who was I kidding? The inappropriate desire had stirred way before then. Probably right about the first time I'd looked into those dark chocolate eyes.

Chocolate sounded good. I was hungry now. Dammit.

Blowing out a breath, I flushed the toilet—twice—and went to the sink to wash my hands about forty-two times. I felt gross, inside and out. Not at all capable of talking to Kellan's mom.

Not in this lifetime or any other.

"Just one second," I called as she knocked one more time. I was probably worrying the poor woman.

God, did she know about me and Kellan? Had he told her about us?

Though that would require him acknowledging there *was* an us. I couldn't deny that his message yesterday had made me hopeful for a good five minutes before I realized I was a dolt.

It was a realization I had often these days. The last time had been an hour ago when I pulled my hoodie over as much of my face as possible and stopped into Bailey Drugs to purchase three pregnancy tests. I would've driven to the next town over if I hadn't been so desperate to find out and only had a short time before work to visit the store.

Of course, the new employee behind the counter just happened to be Derek's second cousin twice removed, and he'd recognized me right away. His eyes had popped wide at the sight of the pregnancy tests too, but he hadn't said anything.

So yeah, curse. It was truly the only explanation.

Reluctantly, I pulled open the door. And jumped back as Mrs. McGuire barreled inside and slammed it behind her. Then she frowned. "I heard retching."

Thinking about curses would just be redundant at this point.

"Yes, I have a bit of a bug." One with two arms and legs and an endless demand for sweet pickles.

Mrs. McGuire just stared.

I poured on the charm. "I'd hug you, but germs and all. It's so wonderful to see you. Such a pleasure. How are you?"

"A bug, is it?" She crossed her arms over her chest, her sturdy mom purse sliding down her arm. "Now I understand why he wanted me to check on you. That rascal."

"He who? What?" I grasped my spinning head. I had no idea if the dizziness was from nerves or another symptom deciding to attack me while I was at my lowest. "You don't mean—"

"Kellan. My son. Oh, I was so happy to hear about you two. Now go on, don't feel like you two kids have to hide anything from me just because you aren't married yet. How far along are you? He mentioned meeting on New Year's, but did it happen that night?"

Before I could even process what she'd said, she launched herself at me and started rubbing my belly as if I was Santa with his big bowl of jelly.

I groaned and jerked back against the sink, holding up a hand to ward her off. "I don't want to toss my cookies again. It's better if I don't move. Or you move any part of me."

Then the rest of what she'd said kicked in. "Kellan told you about us?"

Just as I was about to say what exactly I thought about that, sense kicked in. Not to mention Mrs. McGuire had once been very important to me. I still cared about her.

Treading gently was the order of the day even if I was extremely seasick and her son was a giant dickhead.

She nodded vigorously. "Yes. He asked if I remembered you. I told him of course I do, and I would even if we didn't see each other around town now and then. We were good friends once, weren't we?"

The hope in her deep dark eyes, so much like her son's, made my stomach lurch for a whole new reason. Her hair was a cloud of snow white instead of dark and crazy like Kellan's, but glimpsing those eyes was like seeing a ghost.

One who had spooked me good enough to leave something of himself behind.

"Yes," I said quietly. It was all I could manage.

"He's worried about you, and he asked if I would check on you here. He was playing coy with me, but now I understand why." The smile that wreathed her pretty face made me fumble for the sink behind me. I needed to hold on to something sturdy so I didn't hit the ground. "What did he say when you told him about the baby?"

I shifted to face the dingy window above the sink and turned on the water to splash my hot cheeks. Dripping, I stared at myself. I didn't have an answer.

How could I lie to her? How could I tell her the truth?

We'd had a crazy one-night hookup and hadn't spoken for two weeks, then we'd hooked up again for another wild weekend of sex. And laughing and music and sitting out in the sun and falling in love.

At least I'd fallen. He must care for me a bit if he'd bothered to send his mother to check on me. Cold comfort, however, when he'd basically ripped out my heart and stomped on it. His out-of-the-blue text had only poured more gasoline on the wound.

Especially when I'd been half convinced his message had just been a prelude to requesting my presence at his home for more sex. I was like a booty call delivery service, and my box was the merchandise.

Wrapping paper is free.

Worst of all? I couldn't help wanting said sex, even now. I blamed hormones. I blamed the curse. Hell, I probably would've blamed the planets or the tides if given half a chance.

Mrs. McGuire cleared her throat, obviously waiting for my reply.

God, I didn't want to put his mother in the middle or force her to take sides. There was no side. I loved him because I was a dumbass romantic, and he cared about me enough to have his mother ensure my well-being and to send two-word messages to absolve his guilt. Possibly also enough to text to see if my pussy could make another roundtrip flight for the weekend.

The rest—yeah, I wasn't dealing with that just yet. Not until I'd had a chance to take those three tests and verify exactly how screwed I was.

Swallowing hard, I turned to face her. "I don't know if I'm

pregnant," I said softly, though that wasn't at all what I'd intended to say. "I may just have a bug. I've prayed and prayed for exactly that."

It wasn't easy to deal with the pain and confusion that scrolled across her face. "But why? If Kellan loves you and I'm assuming you love him—"

"Wait. Why would you think Kellan loves me? Just because he asked you to come here?"

A knock sounded on the door and I shot the intruder a cross glance they couldn't see. "Just a minute, please!"

Distinct muttering sounded through the wood. "Not a conference room, you know."

I flipped the closed door the middle finger and glanced back at Kellan's mother, who had lapsed into silence. Whether it was because of what I'd said or my crude display or both, I didn't know. I had bigger fish to fry.

Ugh. No food analogies right now.

"He told me." She adjusted her hold on her purse and gave the door another quick look. "Perhaps we should go somewhere else to chat? Somewhere more private?" She brightened. "I know, you can come to my house. I don't live far from here."

"He told you what?" Forgetting my edict about staying still, I rushed forward to grip her arms. "Tell me the exact words. Please. Don't leave anything out."

"Dear, are you all right?" She reached up to touch my forehead and gasped. "You're burning up."

"It's called raging fear. It'll pass. Please, Mrs. McGuire. If you could just tell me exactly what Kellan said to you, it would really make me feel better."

"He called to ask me to check on you. After he asked if I remembered you, he told me you'd met on New Year's and that he was in love with you. Probably."

"Probably?" I screeched, unintentionally shaking her. "I'm carrying the jerk's baby and he said probably?"

The knock at the door turned into a pounding. "Margaret, we're going to need you to leave the bathroom. Now. Paying customers are lining up to use it."

Oh God, that was my boss, Rick. Just what I needed. I couldn't lose this job. Not when money was more important to me than ever.

My baby was what mattered, not his or her freaking jackass of a father.

I stepped back, cupping a hand over my mouth. Without another look at Mrs. McGuire's shocked expression, I yanked open the door and did a doubletake at the massive line. At the front was my boss.

All those women had to use the bathroom at once? Yeah, right. More like they wanted to hear my life explode, since I hadn't exactly been circumspect. But it was hard not to shout when your world was on the verge of destruction and the guy who'd gleefully skipped right up to the edge at your side *probably* loved you.

Probably.

God, if I ever saw him again, I was going to legit kick his ass.

I shoved my way through the throng of customers, pushing my way around the counter to grab my purse and coat from the back. I pulled on my jacket, slung my purse over my shoulder, and escaped out the back exit, stopping just outside the door to gaze up at the sky. Snow pelted my overheated face, mingling with the tears I couldn't hold back anymore.

What was I going to do?

As if the universe wasn't having enough of a laugh at me, a new song started playing in the pizza shop. Thanks to the external speaker right above where I was standing, Wilder Mind's "Fool for You" filled the alley. Kellan's voice rasped over my skin, making me shiver inside my coat as I wrapped my arms around myself.

It wasn't half as good as having him hold me, but I'd just have to get used to self-love.

I must've been the biggest idiot ever not to realize he was a singer. His low, husky voice was made for songs like this. His rasp turned into his signature growl, the one that made my panties wet in practically a single note.

Me and how many others? How many other women listened to his music and asked him to sign their breasts? It was bad enough I couldn't scour that picture of Kellan at the show out of my brain. That wasn't even mentioning the photo of his bandmate, the one who'd been *in flagrante delicto* next to his drum kit.

That was Kellan's life. From everything I'd read online, Wilder Mind was just beginning their career. They were about to launch a second single, which some reports said was a love song about a chick and others said was basically a breakup anthem. They were headed for the big time, and their current antics were just the opening act.

His world didn't make sense to me. I couldn't relate. But I would try my hardest to understand if Kellan would just let me in.

Fat chance there.

God, he'd never even sang or played for me while I was awake. Somehow that seemed like the biggest betrayal of all. It was as if he'd locked away that part of himself and pretended to be someone else.

You criticized him for looking like a rockstar, remember? You told him flat out you didn't like him that way.

I huffed out a breath and dropped my arms to my sides. All right, fine. Maybe I'd contributed to Kellan thinking he needed to lie. Unwittingly, I had played a role too.

Now we were apart—again—and nothing seemed any better for the distance. It seemed a million times worse.

"Maggie, honey." The door thudded shut behind Mrs. McGuire. "It isn't good for you to get so upset."

"Kind of a lost cause at this point," I said without checking my anger, because she was there and he wasn't.

He was in California and he didn't have to handle any of this. This problem was mine to figure out, mine to solve. While he played rockstar and ruminated on *probably* loving me, my entire life had been thrown into chaos.

In my current state, I couldn't even happily dwell on my multiple orgasms at his hands. Now they were basically fruit from the poison tree. For every moment of bliss he'd given me, I had experienced twice as many moments of worry.

If I was pregnant, everything was going to have to change.

College was probably out for me. I got decent grades but with my work schedule, I couldn't study as much as I wished. I was an A and B student, something I'd hoped to improve at the next level as I prepared for law school.

Instead of law school, I'd be lucky if I could take one or two courses a year in between working my ass off to support us and breastfeeding.

My breasts were already huge. With milk in them, I wouldn't need a floatation raft when I went swimming.

My eyes pricked and I bowed my head. God, if I was knocked up, Kellan probably wouldn't want a thing to do with me. That might be for the best—though it sure didn't feel that way—but what about the baby? I'd helped to bring another life into the world and now my child wasn't going to get to know his or her father. Worse, he or she might grow up thinking bad things about him just as Kellan had about his own.

The cycle was repeating again.

Mrs. McGuire stepped closer and stroked my back. That was enough to open the floodgates.

"Why did you love Kellan's father?" I whispered.

Kellan's mother left her hand on my back. "Because he was electric," she said finally, and I had to nod.

I understood that all too well.

"He wasn't looking for a home and family. I don't suppose I was either, but I took to it better than he did."

"You didn't have a choice."

"Sure, I did. You always have a choice, honey. No matter what." She shrugged. "I loved my babies, and he did too in his own way. He loved me too. It just wasn't enough to keep a household going, but he gave me a lifetime of memories." She smiled faintly, shaking the snow off her hair. "He adds to that memory bank when he blows through town. He's a long-haul truck driver now. Still plays guitar now and then. Nothing like our boy though." Pride laced her tone.

"Guitar. Of course." So many of the pieces were fitting into place. I just wished Kellan had told me himself.

He'd started to that night in bed in California, but I was greedy for so much more.

"Kellan always thought he was more like John than he really is. They're so different. Kellan started looking out for Bethy when he was a youngster himself. He guarded her like a pit bull. Made sure she got her afternoon snack and that no one was bothering her at school and helped her with her homework. To be honest, he was more of a parent to his sister than I was in those days. He was so good at it too. His problem isn't that he doesn't care, Maggie." She rubbed the small of my back. "It's that he cares so much that he's afraid to take the risk."

The ache in my throat had grown as I listened to her speak. What she was saying wasn't a revelation. Not really. It was what I'd felt down deep despite the lack of concrete evidence.

My intuition had guided me when it came to Kellan. I simply couldn't have been that wrong about a man twice. I didn't believe it. Just as I didn't truly believe I could fall that quickly for someone who wasn't worthy of my love. Even if he wasn't sure he wanted it.

I blinked as a memory flashed through my mind of us in the shower that last morning. How he'd begun to tell me something until I'd shushed him. I'd been so desperate to keep our protective bubble intact a little while longer.

What if he'd been trying to tell me who he really was?

He played music for a living, and he was so incredibly talented that I couldn't help watching him in all those grainy clips with a lump in my throat. Not because I was miserable. Well, that too.

Mainly because I was proud. He was so gifted, and he deserved to know I felt that way. I couldn't wait to see him perform live and to sing all his songs along with him—and yes, I now knew all the words. I wasn't mad at him for chasing his dreams.

I was hurt he hadn't shared them with me so we could chase them together.

"Maggie? Are you okay?" Mrs. McGuire asked gently.

No, not really. But I was going to be.

I made myself focus on Kellan's mother. "I realize you aren't aware what occurred between us. I was in the process of trying to forget myself when the smell of tomatoes started making me want to hurl." I held up a hand as Mrs. McGuire tried to interject. "Let's just say we had a brief relationship that included some mistruths on his end and him finally coming clean before I left. I flew back from California two weeks ago and his only contact since then was a text claiming he's sorry. Now he's told you he probably loves me, and I can't decide what is more painful—that he has to use a qualifier on his supposed feelings for me or that he feels guilty enough to send you to check on me, but won't make the effort himself."

"Oh sweetheart, I'm sure he will once he can get away. His job is so stressful. He can't just get up and leave."

"No, and I could try to understand that if he would tell me himself. If he would just say how he's feeling or hell, if he's feeling at all. I gotta tell you, that whole *probably* thing isn't easing my concerns. Not when my pants are already getting tighter."

"But didn't you hear what I said? He's scared to care. Scared to reach out. His father hurt him. I'm afraid I did too, unintentionally."

I blew out a breath. I was concerned I'd done the same with my thoughtless comments about his rockstar persona. But he'd started the ball rolling by not being honest about who he was from the get-go. And until he told me why he'd behaved that way, all I could do was guess.

Unfortunately, with my past, none of my guesses were pretty.

"Oh, I heard you," I said softly. "Every single word. I get being scared. I'm about two breaths away from a panic attack myself." I dashed the tears gathering at the corners of my eyes. "I don't think Kellan's a bad person. That doesn't mean he's going to allow himself to be the man he could be. I don't know if he's ready, and I have to be. My baby deserves two parents who love him or her. He or she deserves everything, even if that means I have to be both mommy and daddy."

Mrs. McGuire gazed at me, her throat working. Then she wrapped me in her arms, cupping my head in her hand while I cried on her shoulder like a dummy.

A dummy who was in love with a rockstar who *probably* loved her.

A dummy who was probably pregnant with said rockstar's baby and didn't know if her parents would disown her or worse, because she hadn't even dared to think overmuch about their reaction yet.

I'd been too focused on Kellan. Always Kellan.

I was almost certain if he told me in person that he was sorry, I would believe him. I wanted it to be true so badly that my heart would decide it was. Just like that stupid, traitorous organ had decided it made total sense to fall in love with a stranger in a matter of days.

The same heart that loved him even still.

17

KELLAN

THIS WAS IT.

This trip was supposed to lead me toward winning back Maggie's heart—if I'd ever had it in the first place. If I hadn't, I was going to devise a plan to get her to fall in love with me.

You know, no big deal. Just another day in the salt mines.

Getting ditched at the airport, however, didn't make for an auspicious start.

I opened the unlocked door to my mother's house and walked inside, stomping the snow off my boots. "Hello?"

No answer. Nor had there been one when I called my mom to pick me up at the damn airport. I'd ended up taking a cab and paying out the ass. All I knew was my mother had bailed as my ride after I'd made sure she could come get me so I wouldn't waste any more time getting to Maggie.

It had taken three days to deal with the planned press and studio time on the docket, not to mention to book a flight, and I still had a rehearsal to get back for in two days. We had a big concert on Friday night. Not arena-sized, but big for us.

I couldn't bail. A band might be able to get by without one of its two guitarists for a night, but the lead singer was an entirely different animal. I couldn't ditch my band unless it was life or death. As the lead singer, I had certain responsibilities.

Whether I'd wanted to admit it before or not, I took my responsibilities seriously. Always had and always would. Which made me a lot less like my father than I'd given myself credit for in the past.

Thanks, Lila.

The talk with my manager had helped me screw my head back on straight. Following it up with a chat with my mom had just emphasized what I was already beginning to understand.

I wasn't my father, and I wasn't going to use him as an excuse for shitty behavior any longer.

I'd finally made it back across the country. With every passing hour, my urgency to talk to Maggie increased. No matter how much I'd told myself I wasn't the best man for her, I knew down deep where I was beyond arguments and logic that she was the best person for me. Now I just had to become worthy of her. One way or another.

First I had to figure out where my mom had disappeared to.

Glancing around for a note, I stepped into the living room and nearly groaned. It was as if my longing had made Maggie materialize.

She was asleep on my mother's couch, her long dark hair draped over the arm, her hands curled under her cheek like a child. She was so fucking beautiful. I'd missed her as much as if someone had ripped out a vital appendage and left a hole behind.

Relief surged through me, drowning out every concern and objection I'd had left. My gut couldn't be wrong about her. I'd trusted it before, and I'd trust it now too. My only hope was she could learn to trust me as well.

I dropped my bag and worked on hinging my jaw back in place before I crossed the room. I tried to rein myself in. Really, I did. But God, I had to touch her. I crouched beside her and brushed a hand over the dark silk of her hair as my heartbeat stampeded in my ears.

Her eyes opened, surprise filtering through them, followed by something akin to happiness. What followed behind it? Fury. The blinding kind that had her pushing me backward with both hands on my chest until I actually fell back on the rug so she could pounce. She straddled me, and it was not for sex.

More like she was using her hips to hold me down while she rained blows over my chest and arms and anywhere else she could reach.

"Didn't you do enough already? Didn't you? Now you come back here without warning me, without giving me time to prepare—" She continued hitting me, and for a small girl, her fists freaking hurt. "I asked you a question. Didn't you? Answer me, you bastard!"

I let her get out most of her anger—and boy, she had a lot. It was truly impressive. Once I sensed her weakening, I reached up to grab her arms and gathered them at the small of her back, sitting up so we were nose to nose. Then I did what any guy would who'd just been attacked by the crazy woman he loved.

I kissed her.

She let out a startled *oomph* as I slanted my mouth over hers, so eager for a taste that I didn't try to soften her up for my advances. I should have, because she deserved that and more, but fuck, fighting with her got me even hotter than I was for her to start with. I'd reached my boiling point plus some.

I licked my way between her lips, teasing her tongue with mine. She definitely didn't respond in kind right away. But the flex of her wrists in my hold just made me more determined to remind her what we were together. What we'd been from the very start.

"Red," I murmured, and her eyes flashed open, the blue hazed with rage and lust.

An expression that I knew matched my own.

At least the lust part. The rage? Not so much. Hard to be angry when you're so goddamn grateful you can't breathe.

I had her back in my arms again. Exactly where she belonged.

"I've missed you," I said softly.

Her eyes narrowed. "Probably?"

I rocked my hips, driving my rigid cock between her legs. "No probably here, baby."

"Oh, horny miss me. Got it. Well, thanks, but I have a vibrator that doesn't piss me off half as much as you do."

As soon as I released her wrists, she started to climb off me. So I gripped her thigh to keep her still for another moment.

"I wasn't hard for you when I saw you. I just fucking missed you, okay? But you climb on a guy who's already crazy for you and hey, things happen." I dropped my gaze pointedly to her breasts, swelling against her blue sweater. "Hard nipples, case in point. And you wanted to kill me."

Why I wasn't completely sure. I understood she was pissed at me after my lies. I fully deserved her anger and more. But she seemed ready to fillet my ass and serve it as a garnish for her steak dinner.

"Want," she corrected, halfway off me and half on. "And my nipples get hard from a breeze now, so whatever."

With that kind of a lead-in, I didn't expect her to let out an exasperated sigh. "I'm annoyed as hell at you for about ten different reasons, but I guess I might as well get off while you're here."

Before I could so much as catch my breath, she hauled off her thin sweater, revealing the pink sweetheart bra that barely seemed capable of holding in her tits.

Fuck. Me.

But she didn't keep going. She just pursed her lips and stared down at me, hair all wild around her head, cheeks blazing. Nipples so tight beneath her bra that I was practically quivering. If she so much as moved against me, I was going to lose it.

"Your mother invited me over for dinner tonight and then had to run out for some sudden thing, but she didn't want me to leave. Was this all a set-up? Did she invite me here to meet you?"

I leaned back on my elbows in a vain effort to get some more air into my lungs. Maggie was such a frigging knockout. "I'm guessing that, yes, it was, but not at my direction. I had no idea you were going to be here. I'm happy as hell you are though. I intended to contact you as soon as I was in town. To be honest, I wasn't sure you'd want to see me."

Her forehead wrinkled adorably and she crossed her arms, which only plumped up her breasts even more. "For sex?"

"Can you ask me that question when I'm not looking at the hottest pair of tits I've ever seen? I'm dealing with severe blood diversion here."

Ducking her head, she smiled slightly and my entire world shifted. What had been okay, even living well, two months ago was now just drudgery. I wanted that smile in my life. I wanted to wake up to it every day. Hell, I even liked when she attacked me and took me to task. Nothing would ever be boring with her, and I couldn't think of a solid reason why we shouldn't be together.

Okay, yes, I could. Half a dozen of them, starting with the living on opposite coasts thing and ending with the small fact that I was a musician and she was a college student with multiple jobs and a family and a busy life right where she was. She didn't have room for me in her world, and making room for her in mine would be difficult because of the distance and our conflicting schedules. But I wanted to make it work.

"I deserve an orgasm," she declared, and I nodded without hesitation.

Yes, she did. I'd happily deliver five of them without stopping to breathe.

"I was miserable when I came over for dinner tonight, and the bright spot in my day was spending time with your mom. She's still so sweet to me. Even after everything."

"Of course, she is." I frowned. "Why shouldn't she be?"

"But we'd barely gotten through the door before she showed me all the food she'd made for me and took off, citing this supposed emergency. It wasn't anything for me to worry about and she wanted me to stick around. Then you show up, and you don't expect me to be here. Seems a little suspicious."

"What it seems like is that she's playing matchmaker." I leaned up to ease her bra strap down and kissed the curve of her shoulder. She shuddered as if I'd touched her with a live wire. "We shouldn't let her down."

"What did she tell you about the other night?" She turned her head away, offering me access to her neck, and I nipped her there, basking in her sigh of pleasure as if I'd been deprived for a lifetime.

It felt like twice that long.

"Not much. That you'd talked and you were okay. I could tell there was more she wasn't saying."

"Understatement," Maggie muttered.

"I wanted to come home right away, but there was stuff going on and I couldn't leave immediately. So I started figuring out the soonest I could get back here."

"You're needed there. It's your responsibility." Her mouth trembled. "A responsibility you are determined to fulfill."

At first I thought she was making fun of me, but as I studied her expression, I realized she wasn't. She worried her lower lip between her teeth and averted her gaze, avoiding mine.

"I have responsibilities to my band, yeah. We had press stuff planned and if I bailed, it would throw stuff into chaos. My mom assured me she was okay. You too. If something is wrong—" I didn't finish the statement.

I couldn't. The idea of something being wrong with Maggie was so abhorrent that my throat sealed shut.

Had my mother lied to me? Maggie certainly appeared whole and vital, but something was off with her. I couldn't place what.

You barely know her. Problem number one.

Swallowing audibly, she nodded. "She told me how you asked her to check on me."

The back of my neck heated. I rubbed it and the warmth grew. Jesus, were my ears pink? How embarrassing.

"Yeah, uh, I was thinking about you all the time. I didn't like how we'd left things."

"Hmm."

"As much as I missed you, I kept telling myself it was probably for the best."

"Probably," she said, shaking her head.

"But logic doesn't mean shit. I don't know how we can make it work, and maybe we can't. But if we quit before we even give it a chance—"

"I'm pregnant."

I didn't reply. I wasn't even sure I was still conscious. Why did it seem like I was floating down a tunnel? Was that a white light I saw in the distance?

But she just kept talking without my input.

"Your mom found me in the bathroom of Pizza Uno, barfing my brains out. By then it was dry heaves since I couldn't keep food down. The internet said it's rare to have nausea before six weeks. The internet lied." She let out a half laugh, half sob, rubbing her wrist under her nose. "I tried to tell her it's a bug. I was still hoping, but I had three pregnancy tests in my bag to take later. Of course, I'm sure Derek already thinks it's his, thanks to that nosy Lance at the drugstore, but he hasn't contacted me yet. Thank God."

"There is no chance it's his."

If I'd guessed what I might say first, that wouldn't have been it. But as shocking as it was hearing her say those two words, her mentioning Derek shortly thereafter had shorted out my brain.

My only clear thought was *Mine. Mine. Mine.*

Not just Maggie, but that baby she was carrying. Hers. Ours.

Ours.

She balled up her fists and braced them on her thighs. "So help me God, Kellan, if you accuse me of not knowing who fathered my baby, I'm going to de-ball you right here with my bare hands." She lifted them and I was too impressed by the glint in her eye to laugh at the picture she made. Tiny and fierce, defending herself and her child.

Our child.

"No." I took one of her hands. "I just want to hear you say it's mine. I know it's crazy. Just say it. Please," I added hoarsely.

Her lower lip wobbled. "It's yours."

Fuck, we had a baby, and I didn't even know how it had happened. Scratch that. I knew how, but I didn't know when. Was it at my place in California? No, it couldn't be. It was too soon. Only two-and-a-half weeks. She might not even know yet, never mind be so sick.

But New Year's Eve was over five weeks ago. That was enough time for her to find out, right? Hell if I knew. But she seemed certain, so that had to be it.

"Fuck, the cold car condom." Even as I said it, I hit myself in the forehead with the heel of my hand. "I knew that was a risk, but—"

"But what?" she demanded, clearly on guard for me to say something horrible.

She'd had to worry about my reaction on top of the fear she'd endured alone for days. I hated that she'd had to face it by herself for even one freaking instant.

We'd made the child together. We'd decide the rest together too. Somehow.

"But I didn't care." I gripped her hands and faced her straight-on. No more evasions. "Just like the night I fucked you raw. I didn't know then that you were on the Pill. Didn't ask. It just wasn't important."

Her eyes filled and my gut wrenched as if it was being wrung out between two fists. Hers, mine. Both of us pulling and twisting to figure out what the hell we wanted from this thing. "You don't think I was trying to trap you," she said quietly.

"No. God, no. Why would you? I've been a complete dick to you. I mean, some of that was foreplay, but—"

Her watery laughter stopped me cold.

Swallowing hard, I framed her gorgeous face in my hands. One of her tears spilled over and rolled toward my thumb and I caught it, brushing it away. "I've missed your laugh. Missed you. I don't know what the fuck I'm doing, Red. Not with you, and definitely not with two. But I know I can't let you go."

Her throat worked as she forced back a sob. "You felt guilty about me. That's not a reason to stay with a person. First I wondered if you just wanted me for sex. Now this."

"Christ almighty, I wish I'd only wanted you for sex."

The hurt that flashed across her features made me shut my eyes. "No. I'm not saying any of this right. Wanting more—needing more —out of this, out of us, is new for me. God, Red. Everything is so different with you. I have no idea what my moves should be. If it had just been about fucking you, I could've moved on. It never was, from the moment you accused me of being a possible deviant with a dungeon."

She chuckled again. "I didn't use those exact words."

"Close enough."

"All of this is nice." She pulled her hand back and circled it between us. "But how am I ever supposed to believe you truly want to be with me for real? *Probably* isn't enough, Kellan. Technically it should be. We're so new, and there's so much we don't know about each other. But for God's sake, I don't want to fall alone. And if you didn't fall all the way with me, maybe it's just better if we end this now."

The mere possibility chilled my skin and stalled my heart. Like hell.

"You talked to my mother."

She nodded.

"She must've told you what I said. That I loved you, days ago."

I shouldn't be telling her this way. I just didn't know if my mother already had. I was fighting to hold on to a chance with her, and that was more important than romance or any other shit I didn't have a clue about.

Honesty was the only thing that could salvage us. Truth all the way.

"She told me you loved me, probably." She raised her head, nailing me with that direct gaze that had slayed me from the instant we'd met. "I know I should focus on the fact you're almost there. *Probably*. A guy like you falling for me, small town Maggie Kelly, is fictional enough. I'm sure some people would think I'm asking for too much. It's too soon, and there's time. Except there isn't." She wiped her cheeks. "Not even just because I have a child growing inside me who isn't going to understand that we were horny and got semi-drunk one night—"

"You might've been semi-drunk, but I was stone cold sober." I wound my fingers through hers and brought them to my mouth. "I told you I lied to you, but I didn't tell you why."

"You haven't told me much, including why if you suspected a cold condom might be a risk, you'd take it. Saying it wasn't important in that moment…" She trailed off. "Have you done that in the past?"

"No. Never. I told you that before. I'm careful about protection."

"Except with me."

"Normally I would've used a rubber from a freezing cold glove compartment precisely never. But I've operated from instinct all my life, and this thing with you feels right. It felt right when you helped me make dinner and just inserted yourself into my space like you belonged. Not because of what my name is or because I might be big time famous one day or how many zeroes are in my checkbook."

"I don't care about any of that. And what do you mean you might be famous? You are already. You're so amazing. There's no way you aren't headed for the stars."

"Besides, even if—" Finally hearing her, I paused. "Say what?"

"You heard me. You're incredibly talented, Kellan. Your voice, your skill on the guitar—which you should play more during concerts, by the way—your persona onstage. You have genuine star quality. The kind that can't be duplicated."

"We already have two guitarists," I said vaguely while my mind reeled.

Was she really saying all that? Did she truly mean it?

"Yes, I mean it, and duh, you should know better." She smiled weakly. "By the way, handy time for you to start speaking your thoughts out loud like I do."

Ahh fuck. Figured I'd get chatty now.

"Thank you." I let out an uneven breath. "But all of that isn't the real me. The music is, of course, but the rest… You saw me, Red." I kissed her fingertips and didn't look at her as she sniffled.

I couldn't.

"Just like I saw you. All that bravado and love for your family. Your strength and your kindness and how you were a little bit crazy, just like me. Maybe not in the crushing-a-beer-can-against-the-side-of-your-head way like some of my bandmates, but we fit. You know it too."

She nodded, and relief expanded in my chest like a damn balloon, crowding out the concern and the panic and everything else except the woman I loved.

"I like the man I am when I'm with you." I gripped her hand in both of mine, focusing on the delicate twisted silver flower ring on her thumb. "I don't want to keep you down or stop you from living your dreams. I have some too. Wild ones, the kind most people don't understand. You might not always understand them either, but I believe you'll try. Just like I'll try with yours." I clenched her hand, only realizing I was squeezing too hard when she gasped. I forced myself to relax my hold. "Give me a chance to learn this shit. I'm smart when I apply myself. It should only take roughly fifty years."

"Oh, is that all?" She pulled her crushed hand free and rubbed her eyes. "Wait a second. Glove compartment? The condom I meant for you to use was in my purse."

"That's what you got from my long ass speech? A speech I dare say was romantic-ish as well." I crossed my arms. "Guess I'm not the only one who needs some schooling."

Ignoring me, she rose to grab her fluffy pink bag off the floor by the couch. I was almost glad to see it. If I named that thing Marsha, it could almost serve as the family pet.

Family. Holy fuck. I was really thinking about something permanent with this woman. Good thing too, since baby and all.

But I was the guy who'd grown up watching his father treat the idea of family like a pair of shoes you took on and off for appearance's sake. He'd always been on the move and settling down hadn't been for him. I'd always assumed the same hold true for me. Add in my career choice, and I'd never thought I would be in this situation. Caught between two coasts, and wanting to be on both at the same damn time.

"Oh my God. You took the wrong one." Cupping her hand over her mouth, Maggie turned back to me and held up the piece of foil she'd unearthed from her purse as if it was a trophy. "It was still in the pocket."

"How was I supposed to know where it was? You said in your car."

"I said in my purse!" She frowned. "Didn't I?"

I pulled myself to my feet, not even bothering to try to be discreet as I adjusted my still rock-hard dick. Her fault for being so irresistible and also half naked. "Little late to be wondering. Besides, if the cold was the issue, it doesn't really make much difference."

"Um, not just cold. That condom was Derek's. He carried it around forever before we had sex the first time. I told him to toss the stupid thing because it had to be older than dirt so he threw it in there. I totally forgot." She shook her head, tipping it back to stare at the ceiling. "I got knocked up because my stripper-loving ex is a pack rat. Why is this my life?"

"How was I supposed to know which was the good rubber and which was the bad? Should've thrown it in the garbage." I dropped down on the couch and raked a hand through my hair, holding the back of my head so it didn't spin off my neck.

Every time she mentioned the baby, blackness encroached on the edges of my vision. Perhaps the panic would fade by the time the kid was in college.

Maybe by graduate school.

"Did you miss the part where I forgot it was in there?" Maggie sat beside me and linked her hands between her knees. "You know, we have options. It's not like we have to stay together forever just because of this if it's not what you want."

"Hell no. We aren't aborting my kid." When she shot me a sharp look, I cleared my throat and silently apologized to Lila. I'd worry about protecting my voice later. "Look, I'm all for you making your own choice. I'll support it even if I don't agree. But if you think that's what I want, it isn't. Absolutely fucking not."

"It's not what I want either. I want this baby." Her damp blue eyes glimmered. "No matter how you felt, I'd already decided to keep my child."

"Our child," I managed before I pressed my face into my hands.

So stupid to feel such relief when I didn't have any right to put demands on her. But fuck, my chest was still tight.

She touched my arm and I lifted my head. "My niece is my favorite person. I don't see her enough, but damn, I love that kid. My brother-in-law wanted my sister to have an abortion, because he said they weren't ready for kids. She told him hell no and kicked him out and he beat her black and blue. She survived and obviously so did Rainy. They're both fine. Both so strong." At Maggie's hitch of breath, I met her gaze. "Christ, Red, I might not get this right the first or even the fiftieth time, but I know I love you. Already. Love at first sight, who knew?"

Her broken laughter was a balm to my soul. She tipped her head against mine and curled her fingers into my palm. That show of trust made me grin like a besotted fool.

Maybe I really could do this. Maybe *we* could.

"I know it's all happening too fast, and I know I have the kind of profession that doesn't exactly help with the trustworthy factor. But I won't slip."

She laughed unsteadily. "You bet your ass you won't. Me either."

"I want this. You and me and our baby." I held out my other hand to her, palm up. "For keeps."

18

KELLAN

"Me too." Maggie gripped my other hand, squeezing it before she let go and bumped her shoulder against mine. "And FYI, every little girl dreams of meeting a rockstar. Chicks don't usually write fanfiction about hooking up with a hot accountant and making little pencil babies, you know."

I laughed. "The usual woman isn't like you. At least not the ones I've met lately."

"You thought I'd look down at you for being in music. That I ever could." Her shoulders slumped. "That's my fault. I gave you the impression I only wanted the version of you I met at the cabin."

"You indicated a strong preference, yes."

"Well, I can't pretend I don't love you all beardy and mountain man-ish. But then I saw you online at one of your shows—make that *all* of your shows. I watched every clip I could find." Her flush was the cutest thing I'd ever seen. "So, um, I'm growing to enjoy that side of you as well."

"That so?"

"Yes, it's so."

"You going groupie on me?"

She bristled until she must've realized I was teasing her. She dipped her head so that her hair fell across one eye. "Maybe I want to be laid out on a drum kit too."

My growl made her giggle as I inched closer. "Only if you let me sign your breasts with my tongue."

"Mmm." She wound a strand of my hair around her finger. "That might be able to be arranged."

Silence reigned between us, but it wasn't awkward. I almost hated to break it.

"Part of why I didn't tell you the truth was because I wanted you to want me for me. Just Kellan, no fame attached. The other reason I didn't tell you is because I thought you'd think the worst of me. It was easier to just fall back on the first profession I had when I went to California than to face all your questions. Questions you have every right to ask." I rubbed my thumb over the back of her hand. "I've been with a lot of women. I'm no saint."

"Yeah, well, I've been with one man besides you and he was a jackass. So I figure our track records cancel each other out and we should start fresh from here." She glanced down at her flat stomach. "As fresh as we can, not counting the miniature alien invader."

Swallowing hard, I slid my free hand over her belly and met her gaze. The hope there nearly killed me.

She wanted to believe in us, as did I. So it was up to me to ease her fears and find a way to make this work.

"I'll commute. There are cars and planes," I said, brushing a kiss over her upturned mouth.

"You won't always be able to. I'll come to you too. You do shows all over, right?" She eased back and cocked her head. "When can I watch you?"

Waggling my brows, I glanced pointedly at my lap. "Keep sitting around in that hot as fuck bra while I touch your belly and I'm thinking three minutes or less."

"Wow, really? You're actually getting aroused by my practically nonexistent baby belly?" Her fascination with that possibility made me chuckle. She reached over and gripped my cock through my jeans and my laughter turned into a groan. "Oh yes, you are. God, I'm so horny. I don't know if that's the pregnancy too or if you broke me or if it's due to years of deprivation or what but—"

"Jesus, woman, if you don't sit on my lap, I'm going to do the honors for you."

"Yes, sir." Her breathy response as she straddled me nearly shot me over right then and there.

Luckily she had a benevolent streak and unzipped me in a hurry. She pushed down my boxers and jeans before giving my length a nice, hard squeeze. "I love how big you are. Just the size I need." She rocked against me, pushing her magnificent tits in my face, and I nuzzled them, savoring her satiny skin and her sexy strawberry fragrance. "Like right now."

"Fuck, yes."

I reached behind her to undo her bra and her breasts tumbled free, practically right into my waiting mouth. After I tossed aside her bra, I sucked on her nipple and she threw back her head, exposing the long pale line of her throat.

"This time will be fast. Next time I'll go slower, I promise. I just have to get inside you before I fucking die."

"Oh, yes. It's been fucking years."

I grinned against her cleavage. I'd probably live right in that spot if I could. "Swearing? So naughty of you."

She gripped a handful of my hair and tugged my head back until our eyes were level. "Bad influence," she whispered, licking her lips before she kissed me. Her tongue streaked into my mouth and I gripped her ass through her jeans, grinding her against my dick. Her cries grew wilder and sharper, and I knew she was getting close.

She wasn't the only one.

"On my cock," I said, and she nodded, eyes bright, as I jerked down her zipper. She understood what I wanted. Probably because she wanted the same thing.

"Oh shit. No condoms again." The realization caused my cock to jerk.

Her chuckle was dirty and dark. "No. All the coming inside me that you like."

"Jesus. My lucky fucking life." I cupped her breast in one hand, tweaking her tight nipple with my thumb. "These are more sensitive."

Her lips trembled, all the answer I needed.

"Getting bigger too. Goddamn, woman, you're a miracle." I drew down her jeans and her panties, shoving them off and onto the floor. Then I picked her up and sat her right on my cock, shutting my eyes at the exquisite feel of her glove-tight pussy sliding down my length. Bare. So wet and hot for me already. I locked my hands around her curvy hips and drew her up and down my shaft, forcing my eyes open to watch her face as we fucked. To see the way her lashes fluttered and the flush that bloomed under her skin and how her perfect tits bounced with every stroke. Knowing she was growing rounder because of what we'd made only turned me on more.

I gritted my teeth to temper my thrusts, but going slow was almost impossible. Her body was so giving around mine. She gripped my shoulders, raising and lowering herself, her knees digging into my sides, her hair flying back with her movements.

If I hadn't fallen in love with her before, just seeing her lose herself would've done it.

The familiar seizing up in my spine and tightening in my balls had me fumbling for her hand. Squeezing her fingers, I brought our joined hands between our legs. For a moment, all I could do was stare. The rosy pink lips of her pussy spreading apart to take in my darker flesh, glistening with our arousal, the fringe of dark delicate curls that barely guarded her distended clit. That hard little pearl made me lick my lips, and following my gaze, she moaned.

"Later," I promised, guiding her fingers to the apex of her thighs. "Now I want to watch you make yourself come."

She wasn't shy. Despite some of her hesitation that first night, she'd lost her inhibitions fast. Keeping her gaze trained on mine, she caressed her clit. Arching up like a kitten needing to be petted, she rocked back and forth, increasing the friction between us and the liquid heat dripping down my shaft.

Goddammit, I was about to blow and she hadn't even come yet.

I tilted my hips, changing the angle enough to cause her eyes to widen. Her rubbing sped up, her whimpers increasing. I reached down and pressed her fingers tighter to her clit, helping her over. She shuddered around me, her long hair trailing silkily over my chest as she bowed her head and rode out her climax.

All I could do was clench my jaw and grip her hip in a vain effort to hold on.

"Turn around," I rasped.

Heavy eyes opened and focused on mine. She didn't seem capable of doing what I asked so I did it myself, seating her on my cock with a long groan. She was still swollen and tight from her orgasm, but the new angle tore a moan from her throat.

I braced a hand on her spine and pushed her forward, treating myself to the sexiest view of my life as she clasped and released my dick. She grabbed my knees, using them to lift herself, working me until I couldn't stop from driving deeper and burying myself inside her snug pussy. I reached around her, grasping her hand as I pulled her back against my chest, still pumping upward. Again and again, I entered her and retreated, the sound slick and erotic, her gasps a sweet torment that extended my own.

Twisting our fingers together, I bit her earlobe as she fisted around me and let go one more time, drenching my still thrusting cock.

I couldn't wait another second.

On a shout, I yanked her against me, holding her still as I spurted my release inside her, shoving deeper with every spasm. She dug her nails into my hand and I pressed my face into her hair, brutally aware of each pulse in my dick as I emptied. Even the last flutters of her climax around my shaft were enough to make me keep coming.

Holy frigging shit.

It only took me five minutes to get my breath back. Maybe ten.

"As soon as I can move again," I promised, licking a path between the strands of her hair stuck to her neck. "I'm going to tongue-fuck you so hard that you pass out."

"About time." She wheezed out a breath. "I was wondering when the good stuff would start."

She laughed as I tickled her ribs. "Wise ass."

"You know, you can have that too." She tossed me a saucy look over her shoulder. "Just in case you think the former Kelly virgin wouldn't be down for butt stuff…"

I kissed her hard enough to silence her giggles. Well, for half a minute until they started up again. So I just kept right on kissing her.

It was pretty much my favorite thing to do.

Once I could bear to stop, I righted us so that we were curled on our sides on my mother's couch. Sweaty, sticky, and exhausted.

And I was happier than I'd ever been in my life.

I crossed my arms over her chest, holding her so close she probably couldn't breathe. But she wasn't trying to get away.

"I love you," she murmured, craning her neck to look back at me. Joy flooded me, but she didn't give me a moment to bask. "Fair warning though—if you decide this isn't for you, I will probably put sugar in your gas tank."

I laughed into her hair. "Lucky for me I know that's not going to happen."

"Lucky for you," she echoed. "Do you think the baby will be artistic like you? You know, the singing, the guitar, the paintings."

Shutting my eyes, I kissed the side of her head. "Being excessively skilled in bed is a creative talent too, you know."

"Oh yeah?" She grinned over her shoulder. "I'll remember that if I ever meet anyone like that."

"Did I mention you're a wise ass?" Shaking my head, I let her go long enough to pull up my boxers and jeans.

My mom might walk in anytime, and we probably shouldn't be naked and freshly fucked.

"Smart thinking. Your mom could show up."

Nodding, I helped her put back on her panties and jeans before I hauled off my Wilder Mind shirt and tugged it over her head.

"What are you doing? My sweater's right over there. Near where you threw my bra."

"Too far away. Besides, I like my band's name on your tits."

She glanced down at herself. "Hmm. That is a plus." She traced the band's Celtic knot logo and grinned up at me, her mouth looking soft and used. "Sure you don't want me smelling like you again too?"

"That is a plus," I echoed, drawing her onto my lap and into my arms where she belonged. "I might be able to let you go in a month or so."

"I hope so, since I have to pee."

I mock-groaned against her neck. "You suck even worse at this romance thing than I do."

She twisted to look down at me, her sparkling eyes and flushed cheeks making her impossibly beautiful. "Guess we'll learn together. Just like diapering and three am feedings and sneaking in quickies in between naps."

I snagged a handful of her hair and pulled her face closer. "Gotta learn how to have quickies too."

Her lips met mine on a laugh. "Practice makes perfect."

After a few minutes, she sighed and gave me one last quick kiss. "Nature calls." She pushed up the long sleeves of my shirt and hopped off my lap.

I couldn't resist swatting her ass, and she giggled again as she rushed off to the bathroom.

She made a pretty picture from behind too.

Sitting up, I leaned forward to grab her sexy pink bra. I flipped the strap around my finger. I might bronze the thing. Or buy her one in every color, starting with virginal white. Red would work too—

The front door swung open, and a cacophony of voices filled the house. Deeper male ones mixed with my sister's and my mom's voices. We'd gotten dressed just in time.

I stopped swinging around Maggie's bra, but it was too late.

Mr. Kelly was at the front of the pack, and he'd just seen me flinging his baby girl's lingerie from my pinkie.

"You," he said, his already ruddy face going completely red as he glimpsed what I was playing with.

Naturally I was also missing my shirt. And his daughter's blue sweater was in a heap on the floor.

Our shit streak was clearly continuing.

I jerked to my feet and stuffed Maggie's bra in my back pocket as well as it would fit. Then I held out a hand. "Sir," I said. "Nice to see you again."

He did not move. Neither did my mother, the lanky guy in glasses beside her, or my sister. But Bethy was turning pink from trying not to laugh, and as had always happened since we were kids, when she laughed, so did I. It was a weird chain reaction thing I'd never been able to stop. The little pain in the ass had used that knowledge often to get me into trouble back in the day.

Looked like that hadn't changed either.

Mr. Kelly did not shake my hand. He glanced at the guy over his shoulder. "You see what she's moved on to? I hope you feel guilty, Derek."

Derek? Oh hell no.

That piece of shit was not going to be allowed to stand in my mother's house and smirk at me. I had no idea why he was there— why any of them were, other than my mother—but that bastard was about to seriously regret his mistakes.

"So you're Derek, huh? The one who cheated on Maggie with a stripper. How's that working out for you?"

He pushed up his glasses, probably the nerd equivalent of bringing out a weapon. "How's being the rebound fling working out for you, McGuire?"

That wasn't the truth. Was it?

Perhaps it had started out that way. Derek knew Maggie way better than I did. She still mentioned him a lot, but that made sense. They'd spent years together.

And I wasn't going to let jealousy ruin a good thing. Hell, a *great* one.

I'd be damned if I let him throw shade on what was happening between me and Maggie. I'd asked her to trust me, so I was going to do the same.

"I wouldn't know, because I'm not." I stepped forward, sidestepping Mr. Kelly when he tried to block me from reaching Derek. I didn't want to have to bodily pick up and displace my possible future father-in-law, but I would if necessary. "You know what I am though?"

Derek didn't reply, but that was just fine by me. I had a ready answer anyway.

"I'm the guy who loves the beautiful, smart, fucking amazing woman you weren't smart enough to hold on to. I'm the one who's having a baby with her, and guess what? I'll probably be the guy who marries her too. So whatever reason you have for being here, hit the road because you're not even fit to breathe her air."

"Kellan."

Maggie's voice had me turning toward the hallway. She was dwarfed by my huge shirt, and she'd pulled her hair up on top of her head. Her lips were kiss-swollen, her chin pink from my scruff. Her eyes were swimming, but she was grinning.

"You said probably again."

I moved toward her and lifted her up, not budging when she

squeezed my shoulders and begged with her eyes to be put down. "That one was for you. To give you a chance to say no."

She tilted her head, a lone dark curl falling forward. "If you ask, I won't say no." Her lips curved. "Probably."

"Maggie," Mr. Kelly said from behind us, and she stilled in my arms. "Is what he said true? Are you pregnant by *him*?"

I set her down and she brushed a shaky hand over her hair. "Daddy, I was going to tell you about the baby."

I covered my face with my hand. Jesus, my track record with this man just got worse and worse. It had never occurred to me her pregnancy was still a secret. I'd figured she would have told her family first, right after she'd talked to my mom and taken those tests.

My deduction skills obviously were not my strong suit. Good thing I had a big cock, enthusiastic hips, and skill with a microphone.

"Honestly, Maggie, couldn't you have chosen just about anyone else on God's green earth to procreate with?"

My mother shot toward Mr. Kelly so fast that he stumbled back. "Wait just a minute, Kevin. I understand you've just had a shock, as did I when I found out the news a few days ago. No, she didn't tell me. I walked in on the poor girl throwing up at her job, and she was a worried wreck. You're a fine parent, and you don't want to say things now out of anger you don't mean."

Mr. Kelly frowned and touched Maggie's cheek. "You've been upset and you didn't come to me? Or to your mother?"

"I was going to. I didn't know how to tell you. I was so afraid you and Mom would be disappointed in me. This wasn't part of the plan."

"Oh, honey, plans change."

"They sure do." Maggie took a shaky breath. "I was just getting used to the idea of being pregnant when Kellan showed up tonight. It seemed important I tell him first." She threw back her shoulders. "I was prepared to do this myself. I lost my job at Pizza Uno due to… unfortunate events, but I still have my office job. I'm still graduating in May. If it takes me a little longer to get through the next phase of school, so be it. I'm still young and I have time to do everything." Maggie smiled and cupped her belly. "And I'm going to figure out how to be a parent. I had the most incredible example ever in Mom, and in you, Daddy."

"Oh, sweetheart," Mr. Kelly murmured, enfolding her in his arms. "I'm going to be a grandfather."

"Yes. You are." She sniffled and hugged him tight. "The best ever."

I couldn't breathe past the rock in my throat.

She was so strong. So vital. A million times more amazing than I'd ever believed I deserved.

I was going to spend the rest of my life proving to her I was worthy of her. Of both of them.

"You're going to be a wonderful mother. That baby is so lucky to have you." Mr. Kelly rubbed her back, then shifted to point at me. His eyes narrowed. "If you hurt her or my grandchild, I will pull your limbs from your body, one by one, and leave them out in the street for the animals to feed on. Do you understand me?"

For the oddest reason, I started to laugh. "Now I see where she gets the threats."

He was not amused. Shocker.

I cleared my throat. *Yeah, yeah, Lila, lozenges for the rest of the day.* "I'm going to try my hardest not to hurt her or the baby, I swear. I only want to take care of them."

"Don't try, do." He tipped up Maggie's damp face and wiped away her tears. "I have a shotgun, a shovel, and a passport. Just say the word, baby girl."

"He'll do just fine, Daddy." She sent me a sexy look under her lashes, and I went stone hard even though members from both of our families and the biggest dickhead ever to walk the planet were mere feet away. "I have a good feeling about him."

"Mr. Kelly, what did you invite me over here for?" Derek asked, rocking back and forth as if he was chomping at the bit to leave.

He better go fast or else I was going to wipe the driveway with his smug little head just for fun.

"I didn't invite you. You were the one who showed up at our house, pleading to talk to Maggie. Bad timing on your part to be there when Mrs. McGuire arrived."

"You begged to come over when I told you Maggie was here," my mom said to Derek. "No one invited you. You inserted yourself."

"You mean just like you did, setting up tonight's meeting between Maggie and Kellan, Mom?" Bethy questioned, shaking her head. "If that wasn't enough, then you had to try to make us into a big, happy family by gathering us all in one spot. Pretending your car broke down outside Maggie's house and calling me to come pick you up. Really, Mom?" She clucked her tongue. "Such a matchmaker you are."

"They'd already made the match." My mom smiled. "I just gave them a nudge."

Bethy walked toward me and angled her head to the side to give me an exaggerated glance from head to toe. "Hmm, still looks like my big brother. Still feels like him too, but that speech you just gave sure didn't sound like the guy I used to know. Gotta say I like the changes." She pinched my biceps and grinned. "Stability looks good on you, Kell."

I hugged her, resting my chin on her head while I gazed at Maggie. "You forgot happiness."

"That too. I'm so happy for both of you. And a cousin for Rainy. She's going to be so excited." Bethy moved back and turned toward Maggie. "We've never met, but I've heard a lot about you. You made quite the impression on both my mom and my brother. You must be a good person, since they have excellent judgment."

Maggie smiled and stepped away from her father. "Thank you, Beth. I've heard a lot about you too."

"Welcome to the family, Maggie." Bethy held open her arms and Maggie moved into them, closing her eyes as she let out a giant sigh.

Mr. Kelly arched a brow at me. "If you're expecting a hug—"

"Thanks, Dad." I stepped forward and wrapped my arms around him. He was about as flexible as a board, but the women started to laugh.

I stepped back before he could deck me. If I wasn't mistaken, there might've even been a glint of amusement in his eyes.

Might've. I wasn't about to be carving the Kelly family's turkey anytime soon. But that was okay. I was prepared to work for what I wanted. For as long as it took.

"Maggie," Derek said. "Are you sure about this?"

Maggie unfurled her hair from its bun, twirling it out behind her. "I'm sure. I'm also sure that your dumping me for Trini was the biggest favor you could've ever done for me. How is she anyway?"

Derek blanched. "We broke up."

"I'm sorry to hear that." To Maggie's credit, she really did look sorry.

Either she was a great actress or she was kinder than that jerk deserved.

"I came to your place to see if you might still have feelings for me, but I guess every woman has their rockstar fantasies." Derek smirked.

"Thanks, but no thanks. As you can tell, I've moved on. But you have it all wrong. I had grouchy jerk fantasies. The rockstar thing was an unexpected—and welcome—bonus." Maggie smiled at me, then glanced at my mom. "As was meeting up with Mrs. McGuire again and realizing she was the mother of the man I loved."

"Aww, sweetheart." My mom pulled her into a hug. "You've done my heart good by being with him." My mom shifted her smile from Maggie to me. "You'll be good for each other. I know it."

"We already are." I moved toward Maggie.

We'd spent way too long apart. I was done talking and ready to start getting to know every little thing about my girlfriend.

Maybe someday she'd even be my wife.

"Ahem. Remember this?" Mr. Kelly stepped up behind me and flung something over my shoulder before I had a chance to react.

Maggie's bra hit the floor.

Without blinking, Maggie kicked it aside and looped her arms around my neck. "Think you can spring for two towels at the cabin now?"

"Nah." I tugged her as close as humanly possible. "We'll just share one. Worked out pretty good the first time, don't you think?"

She pretended to consider the question as her lips twitched. "Probably."

19

MAGGIE

September

"YOU KNOW you're not supposed to get overstimulated at this stage of your pregnancy, right? This might be too much excitement for an old preggo chick," Kendra teased, sipping champagne.

We were in the limo on the way to Kellan's big concert at the Allied Center. She wasn't kidding. I'd had to get special clearance from my doctor to fly this close to my due date, and he'd basically said this was it. From here on out, I'd be on one coast until the delivery.

For any other event, I wouldn't have taken the chance. But this was the big time and it meant so much to Kellan for me to be there. Tonight, Wilder Mind was the opening act for one of their idols, Oblivion, and we were doing it up in style for our entrance.

Hell, I did most everything in style now. Even my lingerie had changed to La Perla rather than what was on sale at Walmart.

I still wasn't used to my new life. I didn't know if I ever would be. Going from being a single, struggling college student with two jobs to a pregnant woman with a famous boyfriend with serious money and no need to work if I didn't want to—which I did, absolutely—was like *Twilight Zone* time. My brain and body still hadn't caught up.

My bestie, on the other hand, was all about this new lifestyle. She'd grown up as the only daughter of a widowed police officer father. While she hadn't been poor, she was used to scrimping, especially when it came to her education and working two jobs. Now she was traveling in limos with me and day drinking champagne.

The downside was that I wasn't drinking champagne, since I was oh, eight months pregnant. The other downside was that we were surrounded in said limo by my entire family, as this big concert of Kellan's was a family affair. He'd gotten tickets for all of us, and while I'd had hoped that one or more of my siblings would pass on the opportunity, nope. They had all crowded into our stretch limo and were drinking and laughing and chatting enough to make my head hurt.

Maeve was wearing a hot pink dress that offset her streaked blond hair and flawless skin. She was also busting out of it up top, which meant she had to tug up the bodice every time she laughed. A frequent occurrence since she'd brought her boyfriend du jour, a landscaper named Mark.

She'd asked more than once if she could get a backstage pass, though of course that went without saying. She'd met the band before, but I swore she was a groupie in training.

Lately she'd even started playing the piano again after not touching it for years. I wouldn't be surprised if she decided to join a band or something.

Anything went with my sisters. That one, especially.

In a gorgeous plunging red dress, Regan silently sipped her own champagne and viewed the rest of us with her usual bemused expression. She was solo—a fact that "delighted" her, she claimed.

She wasn't ready to settle down. Unlike *some* of us, a statement made with a pointed glance at me.

I think she secretly assumed I planned to have a passel of Kelly-

McGuire kids rather than go to law school as I planned. I didn't try to disabuse her of the idea. I wasn't sure how I'd make it all happen yet. Not having to worry about money was a big help, since Kellan's career seemed aimed for the stars.

But I wanted to work to achieve my goals. That was how I was raised. Kellan was our child's father, but that didn't mean he was responsible for me too. Not financially. It was bad enough I wasn't working that much now since I was the size of a Humvee and way more cranky about being pushed for speed.

I enjoyed these special occasions, but I was adamant that our kid wasn't going to eat from a platinum spoon. That was why I was living happily in the cabin in Turnbull while Kellan traveled back and forth from the west coast, though he'd insisted on making more than a few updates before I could live there.

Like an upgraded kitchen and heating system, tons of security, and a part-time bodyguard who also drove me places and looked hulking if anyone eyed me sideways. I thought it was more than a little ridiculous, but Kellan's public profile had grown exponentially in recent months. With that came a bit of notoriety for me and his bastard baby, as one kind tabloid had referred to us. After that Kellan's hypothetical marriage talk had become more frequent.

I was just getting through day by day and trying to keep my life as normal as possible. Kellan had to keep up certain appearances, but baby X and I did not have to when we were outside the glare of the public eye.

We didn't know yet if we were having a boy or a girl. We'd decided early on to be surprised, though my impatient boyfriend tried continually to get my doctor to accidentally reveal the gender. I was almost certain Kellan wanted a girl so Rainy would have a playmate. All I wanted was a healthy baby and a uterus that belonged solely to me.

I'd never realized how much of a full body sport pregnancy was until I'd discovered even rolling over was a challenge at this stage. As for sex? The second trimester had been incredible, with many semi-athletic feats I couldn't imagine pulling off now. The third? Let's just say I bought Kellan an industrial size container of Vaseline and told him to have fun.

"You okay over there, Mags?"

I glanced away from my stem glass of apple juice—that I'd been staring into as if it were tea leaves—to meet Liam's concerned gaze. He'd been even more overprotective than usual this entire pregnancy. He seemed convinced Kellan would leave me for some groupie any day now. Lachlan, being his identical twin, had immediately taken the opposite stance and decided Kellan was the best friend he'd ever had. Angus didn't seem to be overly concerned either way, and for that, he was basically my favorite person on the planet.

My family was amazing, but jeez louise, give a grown, on-the-verge-of-exploding-with-child woman some personal space.

"She's fine," Kendra answered before I could, slipping her arm through mine. "She's just thinking about how she's going to roll on top of that rockstar stud of hers tonight while he's all sweaty from his amazing show and—"

"Oh my God, Ken!" I smacked her thigh, unintentionally pushing her already nearly obscene black minidress higher. "Shows how little you know. I'm more for side access at this point."

"Margaret," my mother chided, reminding me succinctly of her presence. God forbid I forget for one eensy second that I was surrounded by *The Partridge Family*, crazy Irish 2000s edition. "Not in front of your father."

"Or in front of me either, thanks very much." Liam brooded into his beer, but not before I saw his gaze linger entirely too long on my best friend.

Specifically, her long, bare legs, displayed to maximum perfection in her four-inch heels.

But I wasn't jealous, not even a little. So what if I had on mud brown Crocs under my floor-length royal blue muu-muu? In a few weeks, I'd also have a hopefully healthy baby and a vacated uterus.

Yes, I was focused on the uterus. So sue me.

By the time we pulled up to the venue and were herded into our special VIP box near stage right, I had decided three very important things. One, I wasn't fond of crowds when they impeded my ability to quickly reach a bathroom. Two, as soon as I wasn't pregnant anymore, I was going to go out wearing only a bikini—whether or not I was headed to the beach—just to feel air moving over my bare skin. Third, I had to pee. Really, really badly.

Have I mentioned this place was packed with people?

Beside me, Kendra laid a hand on my arm. "Wiggle much? Stop moving. You're distracting me from scoping out all the hot men. I told you I came here to get laid tonight."

On my other side, Liam coughed. Where Kendra went lately, Liam seemed to follow. I didn't know why. Nor did I know why my brother kept looking at Ken like she was a large, juicy steak. They'd been frenemies since we were kids. All of a sudden, the vibes I was getting from Liam's side were something different.

Ken, however, barely seemed to know he was alive. If he'd fallen over dead at my feet, I think she would've stepped over him and called for a clean-up in the VIP box.

"Hello, preggo bladder. I have to pee."

"Now? The other opening act will be starting soon. The Thrashers are my favorite band ever, you know that." I gave her a hard stare and she patted her updo. "Did I say that? Second favorite band ever. There, that sounds better."

"Why, planning on doing one of them? Did you manage to fit condoms in that matchbox of yours?" Liam cast a derisive glance at Kendra's tiny red clutch.

"Oh, you better believe it. After this one," she pointed at me, "I practically insist on a double layer of latex. Not taking any chances."

I crossed my arms over my enormous belly. "Thank you, sweet godmother of my child who has ears and can hear you quite clearly."

"Sorry, kiddo." Kendra patted my stomach and glanced at her bangle watch. "All right, let's go now before the Thrashers start. Though we're cutting it awfully close."

"Maybe you can hookup on the way to the bathroom," I offered, only half joking.

When Kendra was on a sex mission, she was a sight to behold.

"Hmm, maybe."

"If your boyfriend comes out here, I'll tell him you're helping Ken have sex."

Since I was more focused on the fact that Kendra was leading me to safety—aka the bathroom—I barely paid Liam any mind. "Okay, great, thanks," I called over my shoulder.

My thoughtful boyfriend had gotten us seats in the section nearest the bathroom. The only problem was I'd vastly underestimated the size of the crowd. My head swam just from trying to see through the sea of bodies. The bathroom doorway might as well have been an oasis in the middle of the Sahara, and I was approximately two miles away. Evidently everyone in the arena had decided to use the first opening act's performance time to get their pee on.

And my baby was doing a tap dance on my bladder.

"Are you sure you can't hold it?" Kendra asked, urging me forward with her hand on the small of my back as the house lights dimmed and the crowd began to cheer. Loudly. Kellan had told me the first act's portion would only be like three songs, basically just a teaser before Wilder Mind came on.

We'd have to have made it to the front of the line before the end of the Thrashers set, right?

Please God, yes.

"I'm thirty-five weeks pregnant," I shouted over the guitar licks coming from the stage. "I'm holding it right now by not peeing on your damn foot."

"What?" Kendra shouted back.

I gave her the finger.

We shuffled forward about an inch per song. I rubbed the ache in the small of my back, shifting to alleviate the pressure. All I wanted to do was sit down. I'd even chance it by lowering my keister onto the bathroom seat. I needed to rest that badly. Not to mention I was—

"Oof," I muttered, gripping my lower belly. "That wasn't…" I trailed off, since Kendra wasn't listening to me and couldn't have heard me even if she tried.

Was that a contraction? I'd had Braxton-Hicks during the flight to California on Donovan Lewis's jet. Donovan owned Kellan's record company and seemed to be a pretty cool guy. He was also ridiculously rich—hence why almost everyone called him Lord Lewis under their breath—so he'd arranged for the special flight for me and my ginormous family.

I rubbed my lower back with one hand and my belly with the other as the line slowly inched forward. We could hear the band from here, but we weren't quite able to view the stage. We could see the crowd going crazy, dancing and waving their arms and shouting the lyrics to songs I didn't know. I was trying to broaden my musical knowledge because of Kell but I still tended to like the Luscious Lovahboys the best, much to my boyfriend's chagrin. Wilder Mind was up there too of course, but that was a given. I might've even gotten Kellan to sing to me a time or two during intimate acts. Really intimate, when different vibrations were a very good thing. No one growled quite like him.

God, not even thoughts about my sexy guy were enough to distract me from the clenching in my lower back and belly. My entire midsection felt like it was seizing up, and sweat dotted my brow. Discreetly, I tried to wipe it away only to feel more appear right away. It was a warm day and there were tons of bodies all crammed together in a small space, but we were standing right near a vent. Not that it was helping.

"You okay?" Kendra peered at me as the line moved forward and I sagged against the wall.

I shook my head as another odd sensation went through my belly. More Braxton-Hicks, maybe? I needed to talk to my mom. The pressure in my abdomen was growing and I wasn't certain I just had to pee any longer.

"It's too early," I said under my breath, and she frowned, not understanding me.

The crowd yelled as she leaned closer, and I caught a fragment of what was being said in the main bowl of the arena. The Thrashers were already finishing up their set, and we were still what felt like miles from the bathroom.

"You're all red. Here, let me rub your back." She moved behind me and tried to find the right spot to make me feel better.

Since that would've taken about sixteen hands and a miracle from on high, her fumbling touches weren't cutting it.

"Stop it. No. *Ow.* Go away." I flapped my hands at her and she lifted her brows.

I didn't ever talk to her like that unless she was being super annoying and I had PMS. That clearly was not the case here.

"You're acting weird," she shouted back.

I swallowed, shutting my eyes. Now I was starting to feel queasy too. Had to be nerves. There were so many people around us, all pressing too close, and the only thing I wanted was my mother. She'd know what the heck was happening inside me. I sure didn't.

"Do you want me to call Kellan?" Kendra yelled beside my ear.

"He's about to go on stage," I replied loudly, nudging her back. "He can't come out here and hold my hand."

"Fine, then I will." Kendra gripped my hand and stared me down with her no-nonsense dark eyes. "What do you need?"

"A damn toilet and some air and maybe some water." If I could keep any down.

"Maybe I should tell your mom to come out here. Or your dad. Or Li—"

I wagged my finger in her face. "Do not even finish that statement. I can't give birth with my overprotective brother and father trying to keep my vagina on lockdown." I waved my hand in front of my face. "Too late now."

Another wave of pain went through me, and my face must've gone white or red or who knows what because Kendra took one more glance at me and whipped out her phone.

"Do not call Kellan," I said, snatching her cell. "He can't leave the stage right now."

She snatched it back and leaned closer so I could hear her. "I wasn't texting him. I was texting your brother. I'd text one of the others but this is a new phone and Liam's number is the only one I have right now."

I angled back to stare at her. "Why do you only have Liam's number in your phone?"

She released an exasperated sigh. "There's no time for this. I'm getting your family or a voodoo doctor or someone, anyone, out here to help you."

The growl that left me was entirely involuntary. Kendra just continued typing, her fingers flying fast enough to make me dizzy.

"I'm fine," I insisted through gritted teeth. "I just need to damn pee!"

A woman a few feet ahead of us motioned us forward. "Here, ma'am, take my spot."

"I'm not a ma'am, I'm only twenty-three!" But I didn't hesitate to step in front of her, muttering my thanks.

"Wow," Kendra said. "She's done lost it. I'm sorry, ma'am," she said pointedly to the other woman. "Think the demon's coming out."

"I understand. I had four." The woman held up four fingers to go with her shouting and I grimaced.

I needed a chair, a cold washcloth, and some Xanax. Stat.

"Ken," I mumbled pitifully, raising my voice when she didn't appear to hear me. "Ken!"

"What, what? I'm here." She resumed rubbing my back again, and this time it didn't feel like she was a gnome with gnarled hands intent on bringing me pain. I leaned against her, shutting my eyes as heat swept over me again, drenching me in sweat from head to toe.

"Something's happening. I don't know what. I'm freaking out." Tears sprung into my eyes and I reached for her hand. "Don't leave me."

"I'm not. I won't. You're just probably in labor."

Kendra's ridiculously calm voice did not ease my fears. In fact, it enraged me. Sure, *she* could be calm. She didn't have someone about to forcibly push his or her way out of a microscopic opening so not meant for that.

So maybe it *was* meant for that, actually, but hello, design flaw. If you have to squeeze out a watermelon, make it a watermelon-sized hole. I was convinced mine was smaller than average. I probably shouldn't be having kids. I wondered if I could halt the process now.

No? Guess not.

I peered up at Kendra as new tears filled my eyes. "I've decided not to have this baby. It hurts. Oh God, it hurts."

She gripped me by my upper arms and propelled me forward. "Just pee first," she said against my ear. "Then we'll see how you feel. Liam is on his way. There was a commotion in your aisle and he's having trouble getting out."

"What commotion?" Oh shoot, was that the last minute soundcheck I could hear? The Thrashers were off stage now. I was about to miss Kellan's performance and I still hadn't made it to the bathroom. "I'm going back to my seat," I decided, pushing my way out of the line.

If I was going to be in hell from the boobs down anyway, I might as well get to scream for Kellan until I passed out.

Which might be happening soon.

I'd taken two steps—more like two waddles—when Kendra grabbed hold of me from behind and muscled me back toward the line. "You need to pee. You've waited this long," she said. "You'll drown."

"I want to see Kellan," I wailed.

About three-fourths of the line craned their necks to see who was scream-crying now, though for a different reason than most.

Two teenagers broke free from the pack and held up a signed poster of Bryan, the drummer. He was wearing leather pants in the shot and had signed in Day-Glo green ink right over his crotch. "Kellan's super hot, but Bry is our favorite," they said in unison.

Later, I would probably feel bad for my response. Then again, maybe not.

I punched through their poster and left them shrieking in my wake as I charged toward the front of the line, mumbling apologies and possibly prayers as I went.

"Crazy pregnant lady coming through," Kendra called, chasing after me.

The first notes of "Fool for You" soared through the arena and I started crying for real. I could not believe I'd traveled all this way and endured great personal trials only to have it end here, mere yards from a row of communal toilets.

"Shh, baby girl, they'll have it all on YouTube," Kendra soothed.

I cried harder. That was my consolation? That JimmySucksYou in row two might upload some sucktastic footage with grainy vocals and I could watch it from the comfort of my hospital bed while I writhed in agony?

A melee broke out behind us with people scrambling and shouting out expletives, and I turned in time to see Liam jockeying for position in the line.

"You okay?" he asked, hurtling himself at me and nearly knocking me over like a giant pin felled by a wrecking ball. That I remained standing was a testament to my motherly instinct.

Kendra grappled for one arm and he seized the other, then they both pulled me forward. "Dry her eyes," he commanded Kendra on my other side, who gave him the middle finger without lifting her hand.

It was impressive, really.

"I can dry my own eyes," I said. "I just want them wet right now. Is that okay with you?" I fully realized he probably couldn't hear me over the extremely noisy crowd. I did not care.

"Get her nose too," Liam added.

"Do I look like I carry tissues?"

"In your bra, maybe?" Liam dropped his gaze to Kendra's chest. Since he had to lean over me to speak to my best friend, I saw it all. And was flabbergasted.

"Oh, hell no," Kendra said, swinging her tiny clutch with clear intent to do him harm.

I so did not blame her.

"Jesus, K, that's not what I meant. You're frigging perfect everywhere and you know it."

K? Now he had a cute nickname for my bestie? What the hell was going on?

"Oh sure. Try to cover up your lame remarks now. Too little, too late, Kelly."

I pushed up my arms between them and let out an ear-splitting screech. "Can you not do this right now?"

"Sorry." Both looked away.

That might've appeased me, if the fire-clenching dragon currently shredding my abdomen with its claws had not been wreaking havoc once again. I groaned, gripping my stomach, and threw back my head as lights popped on above me. Seriously bright lights that made everyone yell out in confusion and nearly blinded me from their intensity.

"Straighten her up! Get her shoulders back! They're about to turn on the cameras!"

I had no idea what my older brother was shouting about. I was seeing spots, doubled over, nauseated, in pain, sweating, and five seconds away from either peeing on myself or having a panic attack when the crowd started to scream and the song changed. "Fool for You" had ended and now they were playing something else, but it wasn't either of their other two singles, "Felicity" or "I Can't Sleep."

Not that I could focus on what song those particular chords belonged to or even what my hot as hades boyfriend was shouting to the audience. Liquid was dripping down my legs, proving that one should never assume a day cannot get worse, because oh, yes, it surely could.

"Fix her hair," Liam shouted, and they both started patting the sides of my head as if they were beauticians gone mad. I couldn't even stop them, since I was now weeping tears of joy.

I hadn't just peed on myself. My water had broken. Oh God.

Someone with a handheld camera pushed their way up to me, getting right in my face, and I didn't yell. Somehow I could now make out the song that Kellan was singing for me—*to* me—though I wasn't where I should be to hear it. The song was one of the ones we'd watched on New Year's Eve, "Will You Marry Me?" by the Luscious Lovahboys. And I was laughing and crying as people swarmed around us and Kendra and Liam tried to fix my makeup.

All the while, the camera recorded everything, probably showing it to the crowd on one of those big screens.

I hoped JimmySucksYou was still recording. I'd definitely need to see this later, even if I wanted to die over my appearance.

But who cared about smeared makeup and messy hair and muu-muus? I was in labor and I was going to get married.

Maybe. If I lived through giving birth.

The cameraman smiled at me and flipped out his mini screen to show me Kellan on his knees onstage, singing his heart out to the song I knew he hated. More tears flowed down my face, and I swallowed my sobs until it sounded as if I was choking.

Hey, no one ever accused me of being sexy.

Then the song ended and Kellan said a whole bunch of sweet words about how his girlfriend was here, and we were having a baby, and it had been a surprise but the best surprise ever. I was sniffling so much I barely noticed him look straight at the camera.

"I love you, Maggie, my Red Riding Hood. Will you marry me and drive me crazy for the rest of my life?"

The cameraman swung the camera toward me and Liam slapped something near my throat that was either a tranquilizer patch or a microphone. "Yes, I'll marry you," I yelled, and the audience screamed and cheered wildly, including most everyone in line in front of and behind me. "Oh, and by the way, I think I'm in labor!" I added, and Kellan went stark white, his grin freezing on his face.

The shouts turned deafening and I glanced at Kendra, who was screaming and crying and jumping right along with everyone else. At her side stood my stoically smiling older brother.

Out of the corner of my eye, I could see the rest of my family, all wearing smiles as they tried to reach me. It was probably the sweetest moment of my life.

Until Kellan's eyes wheeled and he took a dive off the stage, right into the first row.

"He fainted!" a woman shouted behind me.

One thing was for sure—our life together would never be boring.

EPILOGUE

KELLAN

New Year's Eve

"I did not faint. I had low blood sugar."

Maggie adjusted the blanket around our son in his rocking bassinet then sat on the couch, crossing her jean-clad legs. This year she was not wearing only a towel as we watched that infernal New Year's show. Far from it. She had on jeans, a hoodie, and fingerless gloves and was still moaning about being cold.

I'd fetched us both a beer and she'd taken one sip before deciding to travel down memory lane. I was merely setting the record straight.

She shifted, drawing my attention to the painting I'd done of her at seven months pregnant that hung on the wall above her head. Just looking at her bare belly, full and round with our child, made me rigid. Even if Maggie in the flesh was currently smirking at me.

Ah hell, who was I kidding? Everything about the woman had me wrapped.

"Sure you did, sweetie."

I gave her serious side-eye but she wasn't looking at me. She was focused on the screen. As if it wasn't bad enough that I had serious stylistic differences with the Luscious Lovahboys, now the mere sight of them reminded me of singing that crappy song for her, only to have the spotlight pan to her empty seat in the VIP area.

Luckily Maggie's entire family had known what was going down and Liam's quick actions had managed to avert a total shitshow. It had all ended up pretty sweet, if I noticed such things. It was just rather shocking to be notified on stage your girlfriend was in labor, that was all.

"You could've announced the news with more care." I crossed my arms. "I don't hold that against you though."

"Aww, thanks, sweetie."

"I am holding your excessive use of lovey-dovey terms during this conversation against you, however. Whatever happened to Wolf?"

Maggie toed the bassinet with her foot to keep it rocking. "Since we named the baby Wolf, it doesn't seem quite right to shout it out during sex anymore, you know?"

"That was your idea to name him Wolfgang not mine. Gotta say it's a pretty badass name."

Wolfgang Redstone—the second part had been my decision, and Maggie still hadn't forgiven me for 'ruining' Wolf with such a stuffy sounding middle name, whether it was for her or not—had been born after eleven hours of hard labor. He'd started coming, then just stopped and chilled for a while until he felt like getting the process moving again. By the time he'd decided to make his actual entrance, I'd revived enough to be pacing at Maggie's bedside. Then I'd taken up circling the waiting room after she kicked me out. My whole band had been there too to cheer us on and possibly to scoop me up off the floor if I hit the ground again.

Low blood sugar was a tricky thing. I still felt the effects sometimes when I looked at our absolutely beautiful, perfect son, with his red curls, chubby pink cheeks, and sky blue eyes. And I definitely felt it when I glanced up and realized Maggie was looking at me in that certain type of way I hadn't seen in forever.

Not since second trimester or thereabouts. I wasn't counting or anything, excluding my Google calendar app that told me how many days it had been since I'd last had sex.

I barely even cared. So what if my fiancée looked absolutely smokin' hot, even while all covered up in her sweatshirt and gloves? Paradoxically, the way we'd met made me fetishize her in layers. I saw her all bundled up and my dick tried to escape my damn pants.

"Admit it," she teased. "You're hoping he ends up with a guitar in his hand just like Daddy."

I stretched my arm along the back of the sofa and toyed with the ends of her long dark hair. "Right now, I'm thinking about getting something else in my hand."

She lowered her lashes and scooted away.

I bit off a sigh. That whole screaming "Wolf" during sex thing wasn't a consideration in our lives at the moment.

After our son's birth, he had to stay in the hospital for a few weeks because he was born premature. He'd had to gain some weight and show the doctors he had good strong lungs—something that I'd known was a certainty since hey, my kid. We'd both been run ragged spending long hours at the hospital, and then after we'd finally gotten him home and were able to tuck him in his own bed, I'd been needed back in California for final touches on the album releasing in early spring. We'd also had press and shows and all the things that kept me on the other coast, far away from my family.

Among them the fact that our keyboardist had been acting seriously odd for months. Back in the day I'd felt like I knew Myles better than anyone. Now I wasn't so sure. He'd been acting especially weird since "Felicity" dropped, and I didn't know if he'd stayed in

California for the holidays or gone back to Baltimore with his supposed best friend or what.

Something was up with the dude, big time. I just hoped it didn't upset the already tenuous balance in the band.

Bryan, fucking any chick that moved. AJ and Cooper, alternating between fistfights and drunken hookups with random girls and writing kickass songs together. And then there was Jake, just doing his thing. Focusing on the music. Imagine that.

Myles was the wild card right now, and I didn't want to dwell on any of it. Not while I was spending my first holiday season with my brand-new family.

Maggie had been cool about all of it, from the band squabbles to rehearsal changes and penciled-in shows. She said she understood, and she'd brought out Wolf to sit in on some jam sessions once she'd fitted him with his own tiny pair of well-cushioned earphones. She'd also given me one hell of a Christmas present when she told me she'd gotten into UCLA and was starting in January. That meant no more bicoastal living, at least for now.

We were finally going to be under the same roof, all three of us. The way it should be.

The proper clearances from her doctor as far as having sex had finally come through a couple of weeks ago, but since she'd made no move in that direction, I hadn't either. I was no expert on pregnancy yet even I knew sometimes it took time for a woman to be interested again. That was fine. We could take as long as she needed.

Besides, I had something else to bring up tonight. Something important.

Luscious Lovahboys started the second song of their set, an ode to making love, and I rolled my eyes as Maggie inched forward on the couch. "Seriously? You know we're number two behind them and you're still all up in their business? They're all that's standing between Wilder Mind and a damn number one record."

And I wasn't the slightest bit bitter about that.

"Actually," Maggie said, rising, "I'd rather be all up in *your* business." She put the fingers of her gloves in her mouth and pulled them off, letting them fly before she tugged her hoodie over her head and dropped it behind her.

Underneath, she was not wearing a turtleneck as I'd assumed. Try a sexy purple teddy with more cutouts and lace than a horny guy who hadn't had sex with his girl for almost six months could stand.

"That low blood sugar thing is kicking in again," I muttered, making her giggle as she undid the button and zipper on her jeans. She bent over with her ass facing me to shimmy out of them, and I couldn't resist.

I grabbed her waist and pulled her kicking and screeching with laughter onto my lap, but we both went still when the baby started to fuss. Then I dumped her on her side on the couch and rose to check on our son.

"Hey, buddy, it's okay. Mama's fine." I crouched beside the bassinette and stroked his downy hair until he settled. "See?"

Maggie sat up and flicked her hair out of her face. "I see who comes first with you, McGuire. Even the prospect of hot, dirty fucking isn't as interesting to you as our boy." She grinned. "That's my rockstar daddy."

"Don't listen to your mama's foul mouth." I pretended to cover Wolf's tiny ears as he blew spit bubbles at me.

"Oh, I can get much fouler. Want me to tell you how wet my pus—"

"We should go into the bedroom," I interrupted.

"Why?"

"Do you want our son to end up in therapy in fifteen years?" I tickled Wolf's belly before returning to the sofa. "Things like this can scar a child."

She laughed, shaking her head. "Yes, so detrimental to him that his parents can't keep their hands off each other. You're such an adorable grouch."

"Adorable? Seriously? You're gonna pay for that one, Red." I tugged her jeans down her legs before flipping her underneath me on the couch. She squealed with laughter as I tickled her ribs, but after a minute or so, we both fell silent.

We were literally in the exact same position we'd been in one year before. Except now everything was so different.

So incredible.

"Happy New Year, Maggie." I trailed my finger over her lips. "An entire year. Can you believe it?"

"No. It feels like I've known you my entire life." Her mouth curved under my finger. "I have sort of known you for most of it, by proxy anyway. You know, since I loved your mom and you loved on my sister."

I grunted and she laughed again, tipping back her head and exposing her throat. I bit her right over her pulse, drawing that delicate bit of skin between my teeth. With my other hand, I cupped her breast and relished her moan. "God, I've missed being inside you."

"That so?"

"Absolutely." Gripping her wrists, I tugged her arms above her head, stretching her out beneath me so her glorious breasts strained against her teddy. "You're the most beautiful woman I've ever seen. I'm going to fuck you so hard you see the fucking Big Dipper."

Trembling beneath me, mirth in her big blue eyes, she batted her lashes. "Oh, baby, I already have. Sucked on it too."

I choked on my laugher. "Goddamn, I love you. What are you doing April fifteenth?"

"Besides paying my taxes? And lighting a candle for the day I was excommunicated from church?"

My shoulders shook as I tried to hold back my laughter. "You weren't really excommunicated."

"Tell that to Father Wilkins of Our Holy Mother Church of The Four Corners. He still can't look me in the eye to this day."

Her seriousness made me snort. "Babe, I don't believe for a second you did anything that bad. You still hardly ever even swear."

"How about streaking through the lower church on a dare from Kendra?"

"What?"

She sighed. Heavily. "We used to play Truth or Dare all the time. I came out on the wrong end that day. Hey, that's a great idea."

"What?"

"I should play Truth or Dare with Ken so she has to tell me the truth about what's up with her and my brother."

"Which one? You have like five."

She kneed me entirely too close to my mini mandolin. "Only three, as you very well know. There's some serious tension brewing between her and Liam. It's been there ever since they came to collect me from your place in California." She rolled her eyes. "Maybe they joined the mile-high club?" As soon as she said it, she shook her head. "Ugh no. Not them. Anyone but them. They've hated each other for years. Total opposites."

"You hated me when we first met." I nudged my cock against the satin panel between her thighs. "You see how that turned out."

"I didn't really hate you. You just intimidated me. So big and pseudo-mean, when underneath you're soft and squishy like brownie mix."

"Why do I love you again?"

She licked her lips, raising her brows.

I grinned. "Yeah. You do have your special gifts."

"As for the fifteenth, hmm, nothing. Why?" She wiggled beneath me. "Let me guess. Huge show? Oh God, who are you opening for now? Oblivion again? No, wait. Even bigger. The Killers? 30 Seconds to Mars? Mumford & Sons?"

I stared down at her, amazed at how she'd worked on expanding her musical knowledge for me. "What if I said Luscious Lovahboys, your favorite band ever?"

She made a face. "False. I was only watching them tonight to give you better memories to associate with their music other than fainting onstage because you were such a cute, panicked daddy-to-be." The tip of her tongue peeked out between her teeth. "Like wild, hard, deep fucking."

"Hell yeah. I like the sound of that. Even if you are trying to distract me from your love of my competition."

"Is it working?"

Growling, I buried my face in the crook of her shoulder. "Let's get married April fifteenth, smart ass."

A tremor went through her, but she didn't try to break free of my hold on her wrists. "Why then?"

I lifted my head. "So you have better memories to associate with that day than doing taxes?"

"Now who's a smart ass, huh?" She slid out of my hold and reached down to pinch my butt. "Good thing I'm so stupidly in love with you I can't see straight."

I couldn't stop my grin. "Yeah, good thing. And ditto."

"I'll marry you then on one condition."

My heart started to roar in my ears just as it had when I'd stood on that stage and watched the spotlight bounce over her empty chair. Then again as the camera had found her in the hall outside the bathroom. Most of all, when I'd heard our son's first cry, because I'd sneaked back into Maggie's hospital room. Nothing could've kept me away from them in that moment.

Or any of the ones that came after.

"What's that?"

"I want you to sing for me." She leaned up to kiss me so gently I couldn't help chasing her lips as she moved back. "*To* me."

When I started to hum one of the songs on our new album, she grinned. "Love that one, but can I make a request?"

I groaned in mock distress. "Again with the Luscious Lovahboys?"

"Nah. I was thinking more like 'I'm in Love with a Serial Killer.'"

I threw back my head and laughed.

FOR MORE STEAMY TARYN QUINN READS TURN THE PAGE...

UNWRAPPED

When plotting to finally lose your virginity, it was important to keep your eye on the prize.

In this case, the one between her legs.

A relationship? Not necessary. But someone she trusted was a must.

Caitlyn Sachs blew out a breath and gazed around the kitchen in her mom's small place. Relationships were tricky business, as evidenced by her mother and her sisters' issues with their significant others. It was hard to find a decent guy, one who wouldn't feed you a line and then vanish when you turned your back. At least that was all she'd seen while growing up.

At almost twenty-five, Cait's record was virtually spotless. Sure, she'd gotten her heart dented a few times, but she'd managed to avoid the trainwreck relationships her friends and family had been sucked into.

And that still-happened-to-be-a-virgin thing? Merely a technicality, because she'd certainly done her share of messing around. She'd done almost everything but the deed itself.

Multiple times.

But hell, she was tired of having the expectation of her first time looming ahead. She knew it would probably be shitty, so she needed to get on to having good sex. Finally. Her irrational fear of an unplanned pregnancy was getting old. She'd gone on birth control as soon as she'd made the decision to have sex, and she'd insist on condoms too.

See, she was thinking practically.

"Marnie, settle those kids down. I can't think with all this racket," Mrs. Sachs said, bracing the hand that held her spatula on her hip.

"Jeez, Mama, what do you want me to do? Stuff something in their mouths?"

"Maybe. If it'll quiet this place down, then yes."

Cait braced her head on her hand and tried not to breathe in the scent of burnt onions and too much perfume.

She could be out Christmas shopping instead of dealing with the insanity of home. Home meant her younger sisters and their babies and her frustrated mother.

Cait understood frustration. Just not the same kind. Hers was all situationally based.

She sighed. Eh, she didn't feel like shopping right now. Too much on her mind. But she could be getting a manicure. Maybe even seeing a movie with one of her best friends, assuming she could drag Tristan away from his desk or Matthew away from the game on TV. But no, she'd come home to do her duty, though at the moment she would've preferred to be anywhere else.

They were her guys. Her center in all ways. And maybe after this weekend, one of them would be that much more.

Perhaps one of them would be her lover, at least temporarily.

It wasn't like she could choose between Matt and Tristan. She loved them both equally. Plus they were hot as hell. That the three of them lived together in the loft above Tristan Design, their graphic design business, only made it that much easier to coordinate. Slide in, slide out, cross the hall, and shut the door.

This weekend, she'd make her proposal. Whether that proposal would be well received was anyone's guess, but she suspected that was part of why she felt so antsy tonight.

She needed to speak up before she chickened out.

Another reason she'd chosen to sleep with Tristan or Matt. This would be on her terms. She could control the parameters, say when it began and when it ended. They'd never push her.

In the meantime, she had to push herself and get home. She had a deflowering to arrange. Though in her case it wasn't deflowering so much as a...deadheading. She grinned. Yeah, that worked. She'd be snapping off a worn-out worry she'd carried around way too long.

She rose to her feet as her mother and her sister Marnie started arguing about how they'd fit a nursery into an already crowded three-bedroom apartment. Before she could leave, her baby sister, Valerie, rushed through the back door into the kitchen, her golden hair hidden by her hooded sweatshirt. Under her arm she carried the basketball that seemed to be her constant companion. Keeping her eyes straight ahead, she jogged through without stopping.

"Val?" Cait hurried forward to grip her elbow. Out of all of them, Val was her favorite. At fourteen, Val was a straight-A student and already on the varsity basketball team. "Where's the fire?"

"Gotta study," she said, not meeting Cait's gaze.

"Midterms week, huh? One reason Christmas sucks." Smiling, Cait rubbed her shoulder. "Grades still good?" she asked, raising her voice above her mother and Marnie's argument. Thank God her other sister Ginny had finally herded Marnie's two kids and her own two into the living room. "Should we expect another perfect report card?"

Val yanked back her sweatshirt, revealing the sunny twin ponytails she usually hid under hoods and ball caps. "Grades are fine."

Cait frowned. Normally Val was a chatterbox, but tonight she seemed unwilling to say much at all. Strange. Maybe the family drama was getting to her. "You know, you could always come stay with me at the loft for a couple of days," she said in an undertone. "You could get more studying done."

"No, thanks." Val gave her big sister a weak smile. "I just lock myself in my room."

"But you share a room with Ginny. How can you get any privacy?"

Val gave her an odd look. "Why would I need privacy? All I ever do is schoolwork and play basketball."

That was a good thing at least. Val was so smart and pretty and athletic. God, she didn't have to settle. And she wouldn't, if her older sister had anything to say about it.

"Basketball going okay? I'll be at the game on Sunday. Can't wait to watch you guys destroy the Thundercats." She grinned and waited for Val to grin back.

She didn't.

"I'm not going to be playing Sunday," she whispered.

"*What?* Why?"

"I got suspended from the team."

Cait sucked in a breath and tried not to panic. "How come? What happened?"

"It's no big deal. I'll be able to play again after Christmas."

"No big deal?" Basketball was Val's life. Or it had been. "Games like this are what get the scouts interested. Even this early in your high school career, you need to start thinking about scholarships. You're one of the best guards in the state. Believe me, colleges are already watching your performances."

"It's no big deal," Val said again, brushing off Cait's hand. "I've gotta study. See ya later."

"Val—" Cait called as her sister tore out of the room, long ponytails flying.

She released a breath and forced herself not to run after her sister. Val was in ninth grade, and that was a tough year for even the most well-adjusted kids.

Somehow she'd get Val through whatever difficulty had led to her suspension. If Val wouldn't tell Cait what was going on, she would call her coach directly. No matter what, she'd be there for her and get her back on the right path.

Cait glanced at her sister and her mother, who'd now moved their spat to the small pantry off the kitchen. Apparently that would be the location of the nursery.

Cait grabbed the box of breakables her mother had packed up for her and headed for the back door. Time to go.

On the way out of her mom's parking lot, her cell chirped. She checked the readout and dutifully stopped the car, a smile already forming. "Hey, you."

"Hey." Tristan's warm voice flowed over the line. "Where are you?"

The sounds of a scuffle ensued, complete with colorful curses. "Yeah, where are you? And wherever it is, can you bring back food?" Matt chimed in, coaxing forth a laugh.

"You have a car. Go get your own takeout. What do I look like, your maid?"

"How about French maid? I can see you in one of those little black-and-white outfits. With one of those lacy things on your hair and a really short skirt --"

"Her skirts are already plenty short," Tristan put in after yet another scuffle. "We thought you'd be around for dinner."

"I headed out to my mom's. Didn't Matt tell you?"

"You know how he is. Half-witted."

"If he didn't spend all his time playing video games, he might eventually make it to a full three quarters," she replied, knowing Matt would have some smart comment.

"Watch the insults," Matt interjected. "Or else I'm going to torch all your clothes and fill up your closet with slut gear."

She grinned and tried to ignore the typical flutter in her stomach at that word. *Slut.* If she knew anything, it was that Matt and Tris would never hurt her—with names or otherwise. "You again. Don't you have anything to do but spy on personal phone calls?"

"Dickweed put you on speakerphone."

"I feel the love." She laughed. "Try not to go at each other too badly before I get home, 'kay?"

"We'll try to control ourselves." Tristan's dry tone made her laugh again. "So how's the fam?"

"They're fine." She wet her dry lips. "Um, I got some of Abe's stuff done. Well, I started thinking about it anyway."

"Thinking's a definite plus. So you're leaving us on our own tonight?"

She glanced out the windshield as icy flakes started to drift down from the dark gray sky. Nightfall came so early this time of year, and she really wasn't a fan of driving around in snow. But she needed just a little more time.

"Not the whole night. I'll be around in a while. Probably by ten." Her growling stomach provided a handy excuse. "I'm going to go grab some food, but then I'd like to talk to you. If you have time."

"I always have time for you. Have some right now, actually."

"Oh sure, food. Right." Matt let out a pitiful moan. "Leave us here to starve."

She ignored Matt. "Nah, later's good. Anytime this weekend works. It's not urgent."

Her hymen might say otherwise, but she'd chosen not to heed its silent screams. Since she'd waited this long, she could wait another few hours or even a day or two to have the big talk with her boys.

"Whatever works for you. I'm ready, willing, and able."

Just like that, her mind zoomed into the gutter. She had no doubt at all how able Tristan was. Or little, anyway, since she couldn't know for sure until she'd gotten him naked. But if imagination counted, she'd already slept with him a dozen times. Probably more.

"Thanks. I'll see you in a bit. You boys be good."

"Always. See ya."

"Bad's better," Matt said just before she clicked off with a smile.

They were insane, both of them. Matt more so, but Tristan had his own streak of crazy. And she loved them so damn much.

After she'd roamed around the mall and run out of ways to stall, she headed back to the loft. It was nearly nine when she walked into the big open communal office area—currently devoid of her partners —that served as the headquarters of Tristan Design.

Three big desks formed a spaced-out L, making it easy for her to toss balled-up paper at Matt across the aisle. That Tris got annoyed at the paper waste increased her enjoyment. He was militant about keeping office expenses down. Anything else, spending-wise, was fair game. His wardrobe in particular. The guy had a suit for every damn day of the week. But when it came to equipment and supplies, he watched Cait and Matt like a hawk.

Not that they took him seriously. A couple of bats of her blue eyes and he was putty in her hands.

She grinned and set down the box from her mom's on the counter of the kitchenette in back where they ate most of their lunches and just as many of their dinners. They worked late a lot, especially at this time of year. Everyone wanted to get their spring ad campaigns finalized before the end-of-the-year holidays, so Cait and Tris were designing their asses off. Matt, as their de facto tech guy-slash-accountant-slash-web designer, kept everything running smoothly.

Tomorrow she'd start the new series of ads they were designing for one of their biggest clients, Abe Donnelly of Donnelly Clothiers. She couldn't wait. Abe always pushed her for the most cutting-edge layouts, and she relished rising to the challenge.

She glanced at her watch. Though it was still early, her friends weren't anywhere in sight. Weird. So much for hoping to talk to Tristan tonight. The plan had been to mention her ideas for Abe's project; then maybe if her nerve held, she'd segue into the discussion she hoped to have with him and Matt about other, more carnal matters.

She'd told them she wouldn't be back until closer to ten, true, but she'd overestimated her ability to waste time driving around as the snow worsened. Of course if she hadn't rushed out of her mom's house, she wouldn't have had that problem.

Her chest constricted, and she frowned. Yep, right on cue. She always got a case of the guilties after escaping back to her ordered, happy life.

She should've stayed longer. Her family drove her wacky sometimes, but she loved them. *All* of them. And it was almost Christmas. The kids were bouncing off the walls over Santa. At least the ones old enough to have a clue who Santa was, anyway.

Next time she'd stick around. Better yet, maybe she'd knock off work early tomorrow night and go take the kids to the movies. Give her sisters and her mom a night off.

She yanked open the fridge door and poked her head in. Soda? Or better yet, something with kick? She grabbed a beer and uncapped it, sighing as the cold brew slid down her throat.

While she drank, she rummaged through the packages of snacks on the counter. Pretzels, meh. No diet food near Christmas. Why bother? She grinned and eyed an unopened bright orange bag. Cheese puffs were a much better option.

Tucking them under her arm, she stepped into the back hallway that led upstairs. All quiet. Even the stray kitty Tristan liked to feed wasn't curled up in the box he'd set up for him to stay in on cold nights. Maybe Tris hadn't been able to round him up tonight.

She smiled. It was always so cute to hear Tristan calling, "Hey, cat!" as he walked around outside with a handful of treats.

Cait ascended the spiral staircase, then stopped at the top to listen. For what, she wasn't sure. The guys probably weren't home. Maybe they'd gone out to grab a pizza. Or maybe one of them had had a last-minute date. It was Friday, after all. And they were sexy single guys.

Too single. Too sexy.

She wrinkled her nose. Not that she cared that they dated eagerly and often. Their hookup with her—whichever one of them turned out to be willing to aid in her virginity search-and-destroy mission—would be a one-time thing. Then all would return to normal.

Hey, if she got an orgasm or two out of the deal, she'd consider the maneuver a rousing success.

She strolled down the hall that branched off into three sections. Matt's was first, hers in the middle. But instead of heading straight for her set of rooms, she hesitated.

It was too quiet. Unnaturally so.

A line of sweat trickled down between her shoulder blades. Slowly, she unwound her scarf. She'd forgotten to take off her outer clothes. No wonder she was hot. She had no reason to be nervous in her own house.

Did she?

Then she heard a heavy scraping sound, like furniture being moved, and she pressed her back to the wall. Oh God. She'd known something was wrong. The lights were off, so who the hell would be moving furniture? Maybe someone had broken in and overpowered the guys. They could be tied up even now or worse. Maybe the serial killer was rolling their bodies up in the rug in Tristan's living room.

She shoved her fist into her mouth to keep from making a noise. The smart thing to do would be to run downstairs and get help. Maybe the police would arrive in time.

A groan ripped through the air, disturbing the silence so fully that the sound echoed. And it sure didn't seem like pain. Well, not regular pain. She'd heard that particular sound before when guys—

Again. A long, low sound of pleasure.

She bit down on her knuckles, forgetting the cheese puffs she held under her arm. The bag clattered to the floor, but whoever was boinking in the bedroom couldn't hear. Not when they were now screwing so loudly that the bed was moving.

Tristan's bed.

That had been the noise she'd heard. They were going at it so hard that the frame kept slamming against the wall.

Creak. Creak. A pause. *Slam.*

Her stomach twisted, hard. The beer suddenly tasted rancid on her tongue.

Why should she be jealous? Stupid. Tris was a talented lover. Of course women wanted him. Matt too. Women wanted Matt, she amended, only half-aware that her feet were carrying her closer to the bedroom instead of away.

The door to Tristan's section was shut. Though this level had been split equally into three distinct areas, the doors that separated them from one another were usually only closed when someone had a girlfriend or boyfriend over. Even then Matt in particular could be counted on to leave the door cracked, as if he got off on the idea of making his roommates listen to his bedroom antics. He was noisy as hell in bed, grunting and yelling with the best of them.

Honestly, she envied him. She sure hadn't ever experienced anything to elicit sounds like he regularly made. Moans, sure. But grunts wrested from the depth of her soul?

That would be a no.

She stopped, her throat convulsing at the new groans reverberating down the hall. That wasn't Tristan.

No way.

Matthew was in Tristan's apartment, but why? Did they have a girl in there? Were they having a threesome?

Shit.

They'd never told her they did stuff like that, but single guys in their late twenties were apt to do any damn thing.

More than ever, her virginity felt like a giant weight pressing down on her chest. And other overstimulated parts of her body.

If they were having a threesome, why hadn't they asked her? She was their frigging best friend. The one who cleaned them up and dumped them into bed when they'd had too much fun on Saturday night, the one who picked out presents for Matt's mom because he hated to and sent out office Christmas cards because Tristan's handwriting looked like a mass murderer's.

They were a trio, and as such, if they'd progressed to ménages, it only made sense that she be the third spoke of their sexfest.

She rubbed her knuckles against her hip and inhaled deeply. Wait, what? What in God's name was she thinking? She didn't want to have a threesome.

With them or anyone. Ordinary twosome sex was vexing enough.

Fisting her hands, Cait continued on until she reached Tris's door. She pushed it open as quietly as possible and stepped inside the darkened living room. Silence prevailed but only briefly. Then the bed banging erupted again, more violently than before. The moans that sliced through the night mixed and mingled, though each was distinct and completely recognizable.

Jerks.

Their earlier conversation flashed through her mind, tinged heavily with a sense of betrayal she couldn't repress. She never liked being left out, but this brought that feeling home with a vengeance. Just when she'd made a decision to take a definitive step toward embracing her sexuality, they had to reenact some kind of tawdry movie mere feet away from her own bed.

"Try not to go at each other too badly before I get home, 'kay?"

"We'll try to control ourselves."

Lie of the century right there. Control themselves? Not hardly.

Tristan *and* Matt were in that room. In the three years they'd lived together, she'd heard them more often than she could count, and she knew she was hearing them now.

"So you're leaving us on our own tonight?"

Man, they'd jumped all over her absence, hadn't they? She was thrilled she'd helped them get lucky.

Her heartbeat quickened as the groans hit a crescendo. The lump in her throat became a rock, keeping out the oxygen she couldn't gulp in fast enough.

Still she kept moving toward Tristan's bedroom. Crazy or not, she had to know who was in there with them. The woman must be the quiet type.

Cait would just ease open the door, peek in, get the scoop, and back out with no one the wiser. They'd never know.

But the door was already open, just a little. Just enough for her to see the action on the bed and the two figures going at it.

Two.

Only two.

The one beneath fisted his hands in the sheets, sheets that were already more off the bed than on. A strong grip was all that could anchor him in place with the force of the thrusts into his ass. Each one sent the frame clattering against the wall. Probably leaving scuff marks. Probably tearing strips out of the floor.

They'd spent hours varnishing that hardwood, lovingly restoring it after the previous owners' lackluster care. Now it would be ruined.

Everything had been ruined. *Everything.*

"Fucking hell, I'm coming."

Tristan's exclamation sent her careening back into her body, ripping away thoughts of the floor, of life as she'd known it before she walked out the door that night. In its place was something entirely different, a new reality she couldn't quite focus on as her eyes struggled to behold what her mind couldn't—*wouldn't*—comprehend.

"Me too. Shit."

She clutched her beer, her heart rampaging so hard she feared she'd pass out. Her nipples puckered, and her vision blurred. Their long, muscled, perspiration-sheened bodies doubled. Even so she was incapable of looking away from the erotic tableau spread out in front of her.

Tristan reared back to tear off the condom, then gripped his long, erect cock—maybe she still had double vision, because he couldn't be *that* big—and pumped it over Matt's flexing back until long streams of cum shot off like a fountain. Tristan groaned and tipped his head forward, working his erection for every drop.

She breathed through her mouth, stunned and aroused beyond belief. And she was confused. So freaking confused. But she couldn't turn away, and she couldn't shut off the longing knifing through her lower belly.

It took all her will not to fling herself over the threshold and beg Tris to take her the way he'd seen fit to take their best friend. Hard. Untamed.

That was what she craved.

She didn't want Tristan to treat her as if she were a delicate, breakable doll, his innocent Caity Bait, the name he'd christened her with in college because she'd been younger than everyone else and too tempting for the older guys.

She needed to be possessed in the way he'd possessed Matt. Ached to be caught beneath that spray of cum. Except she wanted it on her breasts, where she could use her fingers to mop it up. Then she'd taste him, let the flavor of his release explode on her tongue. Drink up every bit of him and ask for more.

To keep from moaning herself, she took a quick swallow of beer. It still tasted off. Not like it had tasted even minutes ago.

Matt stroked his own cock now, fast and rough. Any instant now, he'd go off too.

She'd never seen two men together before. Never realized she wanted to. Especially *her* men. But God, it was so hot. So unbelievable.

Matt shifted slightly, giving her a better view of the show. And then he came with a wild cry, his spurts disappearing into the tangled sheets, making her clench with unfulfilled want.

Cait gasped and took a step backward. Her knees locked, making further movement impossible. Jesus, what was her problem? She could process what she'd seen later, after she was safely in her own bedroom, far from the pants and shudders that had arousal pooling in her panties.

But she'd only managed a step when Matt shifted his head as he fought to catch his breath. His eyes met hers for one long, charged moment.

"Holy shit," he whispered.

Tristan laughed, but he didn't respond to Matt's curse, probably figuring it had to do with his spectacular finish.

Not quite.

Matt looked as shocked as she felt. Gobsmacked, actually. He started to get up, but Tristan bent, still holding his cock, and licked a trail up between Matt's shoulder blades. Matt fisted his hands in the sheets again and closed his eyes as aftershocks racked his body.

Tristan licked for a while, careful to clean up every remnant of the mess he'd made. Matt barely whimpered, but she could tell from his rigid stance over the bed he would be ready to go again in no time.

If she hadn't been there, he would probably already be rolling over and taking hold of Tris's cock, bringing the still-stiff length to his lips and swallowing the salty tang of the release she yearned to taste.

A hot wave of urgency swept over her. She quivered, her tight nipples pressing against the bodice of her wool dress. She couldn't watch this anymore. Not unless she intended to become part of the scene and not just a voyeur.

Not that they'd invited her.

The party she'd crashed was clearly just for two, and she'd already overstayed her welcome.

Though she stumbled, she managed to turn and get the hell out of there.

Would you like to read more?
tarynquinn.com

FILTHY SCROOGE

KAY

"If you don't get out on that dance floor, I'm going to kick your ass."

"I'm going, I'm going." I tugged at my short red velvet skirt. Mel had convinced me to schlep all the way to Brooklyn to go to this club, the least I could do was get my dance on. I missed it. Working seventy hour weeks had killed any extracurricular activities in my life. Starting my own company was worth it, dammit.

There'd been a time when a club had been my favorite outlet. I could lose myself in the colors, the music, the anonymity of it all. This place—Purgatory—lived up to its name in every way. It was in between in all ways that mattered. Depending on the day, the center of the huge building could be a dance club or concert venue. Outside was a sidewalk cafe with a garden straight out of England.

I could let the wilder side of me free.

I didn't have to be Kandy Kane here, with all that sugary name implied. Most of the time I loved it. Hell, I made my career around my name.

Here, I was just Kay.

I didn't have to make decisions or give orders.

I could feel a man's hands on my skin without the promise of anything more.

The lights flared, then dimmed. A wash of purple and red swirled over the crowd turning everyone the same hue—cool and hot at the same time. The lights and the dancers pulsed as the low beat of the song ebbed and flowed.

I felt an answering echo in my lower belly.

Bad sign.

"There she is."

I threw a narrow-eyed-glare at my best friend and assistant. She knew me far too well. "One dance."

Her glossy red lips lifted at one corner before she wrapped her lips around her straw. "Sure. I'll be here, drinking my courage."

"And you expect me to just go on out there?"

"Yes. Go let loose."

I flicked my heavily curled hair over my shoulder and took a deep breath. It was just like riding a bike.

I glided into the crush of people. Instinct took over as the music infused into the marrow of my bones. There was no expectation. No one knew me. So I let go. The watery undertones of the song urged my hips into soft, fluid circles. This was exactly what I needed. As usual, Mel had been right.

I found my spot in the center of the crush of people. I ignored the bump of strangers, and the dancers who thought they were far more talented than they were. I let my gaze drift to the whirling lights above me as the tension in my shoulders melted away.

My body became one with the underlying beat of the song. The heartbeat. I could find it in any piece of music. A Christmas carol, a hymn, a rap song, a country tune—it didn't matter. There was always heart to a good song.

Once I found it, everything else fell into place.

I slipped my fingers into my hair and let the dreamy music take me away. Clubs often extended the song with remixes and I chased the rhythm. My breath raced as the song built up and spun out.

Eyes were on me.

I ignored them.

Right now, I didn't want small talk, or someone grinding on my ass.

I just wanted this. The only release I could find.

The song changed to a big hit that had been reduced to a shadow of its original flavor. One that I didn't want to dance to. I raised my arms to shimmy my way through the crowd when a large hand slid along my waist. The pads of a man's fingers skimmed along the raised hem of my shirt.

Being in a club meant hands on you whether you wanted them or not. I'd broken my share of fingers when I wasn't in the mood. I lowered my hand to do just that when the guy invaded my space.

Strong thighs aligned with mine as he pushed me back toward the center of the floor.

My eyes flashed wide, met eyes the color of blue flame. An intense, unflinching stare. There was no guesswork, no teasing—just pure heat. His fingers slid around to the small of my back. His hips moved in time to my own.

He didn't hold me tight. Just enough to keep me close.

I tipped my head, curiosity riding me harder than annoyance. I shouldn't have allowed it. He was too big, too overwhelming to be the kind of man I normally danced with. I preferred fun and smiles. No harm, no foul kind of guys who didn't give me trouble when the dancing was over.

Not like this man.

His broad shoulders were encased in a fitted black shirt with another collared shirt under it in the same jet color. In fact, he was dressed in black from head to toe.

He stroked his thumb under my chin to bring my attention back up to his eyes. He didn't speak. Not that either of us could be heard over the music, but he didn't even bother with the pretense.

Just those ridiculous blue eyes burning into mine.

The song faded into one that I loved. Watery strings with a staccato lyric to start before the drums and crashing tones filled the space. His hand grew bolder, coasted down my back to my ass, and his knee slid between my thighs.

Our gazes didn't waver.

Our bodies melted together in a sexual dance that should have been far too provocative for strangers. My heart raced and a wash of heat rushed from my thighs up to my sex. I couldn't remember the last time I'd had such a heady reaction to anyone, let alone a man who didn't know my name any more than I did his.

Did he do this often? I knew I sure as hell didn't.

I swallowed down a sudden flood of panic. I glanced around us. No one was paying attention to us.

His thumb was at my chin again, dragging my gaze back to his.

"Right here," he mouthed.

I swallowed and tried to step back. He brought his hand to my hip and caught my hand with his other, lacing our fingers. His skin was smooth with a ridge of calluses along his palm. The beat of the song was harder, darker than the previous ones played.

I moved into him this time.

Maybe I didn't want the link broken. Just for a few more moments.

The tingle along my thighs grew with each brush of his. The roll of his hips in time to the song changed the simple buzz to a surge. My nipples throbbed and my thighs were soaked under my skirt. Arousal slammed into me. Panic licked along my lower spine and activated my flight response.

Dancing was one thing. More?

No, that wasn't me.

I twisted away and pushed my way through the dancers. The

murmur of pissed off people doubled. The next song was a Britany remix that had the room pulsing again.

My heart crashed in my ears as I finally broke free from the dance floor.

Don't do it. Don't turn around.

But I couldn't help myself. I glanced back to see if my mystery man was following, but he was not.

He'd probably moved on to the next girl.

So stupid. He'd probably lost interest the moment I'd pulled back like a frightened virgin.

Worldly. Yeah, that was me.

I might know how to find my inner dancing queen, but the vixen half of me had yet to figure out how to play.

I placed my hand over my midriff. Everything was still buzzing and fluttering madly. I tugged my shirt down, then smoothed my skirt. Disappointment crashed into self-preservation.

Besides, there was no way I could test the waters with someone like that. I was better off with Jason. He was one of my temps at work. He'd been asking me out for the last three weeks. He was sweet and would undoubtedly take his time—and surely let me take mine.

I'd been putting him off because he was my employee, but the season was officially over tomorrow. At least the Christmas season, which pretty much floated most of my business for the year. Maybe if he asked me again, I'd have to just say yes for once.

Eyes the color of blue flame flashed into my head. Intense eyes. Hooded eyes with slashing cheekbones, giving his face arresting angles.

A man like that didn't seem nice. He'd take and demand.

Damn if that didn't give me a serious pause.

No. I shook my head firmly—not for me. The Jasons of the world were more my speed. My fingernails dug into my palms. I couldn't even pull Jason's face up at the moment. Kind brown eyes...maybe? Or were they hazel?

I straightened my shoulders and headed for the bar.

Those damn blue eyes were sticking. I had little doubt they'd follow me into my dreams tonight. Time to find Mel and get the hell out of here. I had a huge day ahead of me tomorrow anyway.

I could trust work.

I understood work.

Just one more day to get through.

Want more?
Lincoln is deliciously dirty.
C'mon, you know you want more…
www.tarynquinn.com

ROCKSTARS YOU SAY?

We also have two other pennames out there. Turn the page for a preview of our LOST IN OBLIVION series under our Cari Quinn & Taryn Elliott names.

Rocked is the one that started us on this journey. A lot longer, and bursting with characters who have become near and dear to us.

If you'd like to learn more head on over to rockerreads.com and find out all about us!

ROCKED

Harper Pruitt hauled another tray out of her seven-tiered food cart. Lunch was the big meal when it came to a rock tour. The roadies and technicians would be working right up until the 7:30 p.m. curtain time, so they needed to fuel up now. Then she and her staff would break it down and start all over for the musicians and their guests.

Already the first wave was lined up in the doorway to the make-shift cafeteria. Pop-up tents, two dozen banquet tables, and a whirring portable air conditioner gave a brief reprieve to the outrageous heat of Alpharetta, Georgia. Honestly, how was anyone supposed to think clearly when the air was thick enough to chew?

"C'mon, Harper. It doesn't need to be perfect. We're just going to demolish it anyway."

"You will wait until I'm ready, Randy Pruitt." Her brother, a third generation roadie, was always first in line for food. He might be whip-skinny, but he could pack it away.

She snapped the last of the trays over cold packs she'd designed after much of their first week had been spent cleaning up after the rapidly melting ice. No matter how hard that air conditioning unit chugged, it was still hot as hell with seventy plus bodies in the room.

She might be low man on the cooking staff, but she had standards, dammit. She made the best lunch these idiots would ever taste. Refusing to believe that everything was wasted on the tour animals that called themselves roadies, she ignored the shuffling feet and groans behind her.

Any man or woman that didn't want a broken finger knew better than to rush her. She knew how to handle the burly, the grouchy, and most definitely the too friendly.

Setting out the last tray—rolls and bread—she stepped back a good four feet, put her hands together in a mock prayer, and bowed. "You may begin."

And boy did they. Within eight minutes her pretty display looked more like a sad deli counter. The bed of lettuce leaves she'd used were scattered like discarded pages from a TV writer's room during sweeps week. All but the chicken salad had been scraped clean.

She hauled the tray out of its housing. What the heck did they have against her chicken? Unless it was slathered in jar mayo or mustard, a lot of these guys turned their noses up. Each day she tried to sneak in a little something new, believing that even roadies deserved culture—but alas, they proved her wrong again and again.

She waved at her brother as he jammed ham and turkey into a roll —his third sandwich, thank you very much—and crammed it into his mouth on the way out the door. Randy was still young enough to be excited about the prospect of sweating over the lighting rig that had to be set up.

It was the last leg of this particular tour. She'd graduated from culinary school and hopped on a plane the next day to work this job.

She had six weeks to prove herself to Meg and Danny so they'd hire her on full time.

"All set, Harper?"

She blinked out of her thoughts and smiled at Mel, one of her cleanup staff. "Yeah, you can start loading up."

The clang of metal trays and crinkle of white paper table covers was part of her everyday symphony. Roll it out, roll it up, rinse and repeat. Crap, she was only six days into the tour and already she was tired of tuna salad and cold cuts.

Not good.

"Excuse me?"

"Sorry, we're all done for the lunch rush, but you can come ba—" She stopped mid-turn, her eyes stuck on one of the most impressive male chests she'd ever seen. And seriously, she'd seen a lot of nice ones over the years. But sweet Pete.

Wide, firm pecs filled out a vintage Journey t-shirt with little room to spare. In fact, the faded scarab logo had little tears in it from the stretch to accommodate his toned muscles. That had to be some seriously amazing man flesh under there.

She forced her gaze up, and up, and wow.

He smiled, and a dimple dug into his left cheek. The slash of white teeth and the dent was bad enough but man...the eyes. Green. Middle-of-the-forest green, earthy, and cool—the kind that contact commercials promised with their too beautiful to be real colors.

They had to be fake.

Who had green eyes with flecks of sunlit gold in the center? Not real people, that's who. Or...

"Anything protein will do. I just finished up a workout, and I could sure use some fuel before soundcheck."

Or rock stars. Of course he was a musician. While there were a few men on staff that bumped her hotter-than-hell-meter into taking notice, the first one to put her meter into the red had to be off limits.

"I really don't have anything left." She caught one tray out of the corner of her eye. "Well, I have some chicken salad left, but…"

"That's perfect. Chicken salad is perfect." He crossed one arm over his drool-worthy chest and gripped his triceps, rubbing absently. A wide tattoo stretched across his left forearm in bold, black letters that looked like they'd been through an earthquake with a teasing red devil tail wound through the letters. Oblivion.

Holy hot.

Nope.

No looking, Harper Lee.

Man, his bicep really bulged beautifully. And on the arm he gripped a flash of more black and red ink teased beneath the edges of his t-shirt sleeve. A sleeve that was seriously working hard at not ripping. That just wasn't right. She forced her eyes up to his face and that dimple was back, deeper than ever.

Crap. Now he was going to think she was interested. Damn, double damn, and triple crap. She snatched the ice cream scooper out of her apron and snagged one of the paper salad boats stacked up beside the plates.

"Another scoop if that's okay."

She tried to ignore the deep tone of his voice. She was such a sucker for baritones. "You don't even know how it tastes."

He leaned down into her space, and she bit back a groan. He smelled like cedar chips and something fresh. The ocean? She took a giant step back. "Whoa there."

Unrepentant, he picked up a fork and scooped out some. "See, tastes…"

He stopped chewing, and she winced. She'd made her own dressing, sprinkling in some balsamic for a kick to make it just a little less boring. The tender breast chunks had sucked up the vinegar. Definitely not a traditional chicken salad.

"What is this?"

She pulled the paper boat closer to her chest. "I think I might have some turkey——"

"No, seriously. That's awesome." He took her scooper out of her limp fingers and put another two helpings on his paper boat. Then he reached around her for a few of the last few tomatoes on the veggie tray.

"Awesome?"

"Wow." He shoveled another forkful into his mouth, those sharp, perfect teeth slicing through a tomato with ease. "I usually have to choke down whatever protein I can find with a Coke, but this is awesome. Can you make me this every day?"

"That would get pretty boring."

"Have you tasted this?" He turned his fork out to her.

"I made it. I taste everything before I put it out."

He shrugged. "More for me." He transferred the boat, a wad of napkins, his fork, and his phone all to one hand. Long fingers handled the entire bundle with ease. He held out his right hand. "I'm Deacon by the way."

Oh, hell no. He had tingles written all over him. There was no way she could shake his hand and keep up the cool, calm, and collected deal. Especially when his hand looked like it could swallow hers and have room for two more. He was ridiculously big. Like wow-you-must-play-basketball tall. God, why did she have to be so tactile? She couldn't walk through a store without touching everything. And Deacon had plenty of real estate to touch.

Harper Lee, catch a clue.

She smiled up at him and then wiggled her black latex clad fingers. Dodged that one.

He gave her that lopsided smile again, and the dimple deepened. Instead of being put out, he simply shuffled his food back to his empty hand, tucked his phone into his pocket, and resumed eating. "This really is great."

The burst of pleasure that hummed through her middle made her swallow a groan.

Simmer down. He's just flirting.

"Thanks. Glad someone likes it."

Deacon glanced down at the tray. "Obviously people don't know a good thing."

Resisting the call of a warm glow, she stacked the now empty veggie trays.

"What's your name? I can tell you right now you're going to see a lot of me. I'm pretty much a black hole when it comes to food."

Sidestepping the question, she picked up another tray. "I've been on the tour for almost a week now, and this is the first time we've seen each other."

"That's because my band just met up with the tour last night. We're opening for Rebel Rage."

Ding, ding. Musician confirmed.

She'd known it, but man, it really was too bad. She didn't date musicians. Heck, she didn't even interact with them. They were way too into themselves and this first job really needed to be drama free so she could concentrate on establishing herself.

"That's great." She flashed him her professional smile. "Welcome to the tour."

"You're really not going to give me your name?"

It *really* was too bad. Because that voice would sound delicious all low and close in her ear. "I'm just the help. You don't need to know my name."

"Maybe some musicians are like that, but not me. Six months ago I was waiting tables and hustling pool for gas money."

Don't be endearing. Seriously. That just wasn't fair. Not to mention the quick flash of him stretched out over a pool table was way too easy to picture. She did not need that lodged in her brain. Those long fingers making a cage for the cue stick?

Stop it!

"Boss's orders. We're to be seen and not heard." She scooped one last serving of the chicken salad, slid it onto his rapidly disappearing pile, and then loaded the tray on her cart. "Have a good show, sir."

"Deacon," he reminded her.

Harper hunched up her shoulders and nearly ran across the lunch room and out into the brutal humidity. The wheels of her cart rumbled and popped over the uneven pavement. She careened around the crew trucks to the huge, silver and white Food Riot trailer.

"Hey, where's the fire, honey girl?" Mitch Hale slapped one meaty hand on her runaway cart.

Harper tripped a few more steps before she halted the forward momentum on the cart that weighed about the same as she did. She swiped her forearm over her sweaty forehead and then tugged her purple checked bandanna back down. "Sorry."

"It's too hot to be running around."

She stepped away from the cart to smooth her hand down Mitch's huge arm and then leaned into his solid chest for a moment. He was three hundred plus pounds of Hawaiian teddy bear, and he had gotten her this job. He also happened to be her father's oldest friend and her uncle for all intents and purposes.

He tugged on her ponytail. "What's doin?"

She nuzzled her nose into his t-shirt, taking in his ever-present coconut scent before stepping back again. "Just cleaning up from the road crew."

Mitch swayed lightly from side to side. You could take the man out of the ocean, but you couldn't take the ocean out of the man. "My team's heading in for the second wave. Johnny's got a wild hair for barbecue chicken before the show."

She was beginning to get the feeling Johnny Cage got a wild hair every other day. The singer for Rebel Rage liked to keep the food staff on their toes. Most musicians liked a light meal before going on stage, especially on the summer tours, but the guys of Rebel Rage had cast iron stomachs.

She wondered what kind of food Deacon liked.

What the hell, Pruitt? One little compliment and you forget all the rules? Weak.

She cracked her neck and returned to her cart. "I don't remember that being on the prep sheet today."

"Nope, we got the news at noon."

Harper cringed. Getting barbecue together in a few hours wasn't easy. And she was pretty sure the guys from Rebel Rage expected the real deal and not barbecue sauce slathered on grilled chicken.

She muscled the cart up the ramp and into Food Riot's truck. Meg and Danny had transformed the inside of a big rig into a kitchen on the road. The smoker was set on the pavement at the opening of the back of the truck. Pineapple and cedar clouded the air, dragging another memory of Deacon into her subconscious.

Wow.

Seriously. She needed to get a head check. Obviously her self-imposed drought had been too long. Harper had wanted to concentrate on her final projects without the distraction of the opposite sex. Of course, interning at a restaurant as well as a full roster of classes made that easy.

Now she had way too much time on her hands. Maybe once she got to work with the lead chefs she'd have more to do.

"Pruitt!"

"Yeah!" she called back as she tucked her cart into its locking slot. Dishwashers started unloading the trays, dishes, and plastic into the super washer they'd dubbed Kong.

"I need you on deck," Meg called. "I'm doing a super quick chili and need you dicing onions."

It was a little late to be putting chili together. The main tent ate in less than two hours.

Meg must have noticed her quizzical look. "You've been bitching that you want to help out with main dishes, so fucking help. I'll need you in the dining room too."

"Right. Of course." Harper snagged a chef's knife from the magnetic strip. About damn time.

Want more?
You know you do…
www.rockerreads.com

LOST IN OBLIVION
A ROCKSTAR ROMANCE SERIES

SEDUCED

Music kept them going. Now it might tear them apart… Guitarist Nick Crandall has one focus in his life—Oblivion, the band he started with his closest friends, lead singer Simon Kagan and bassist Deacon McCoy. After losing their drummer to rehab, they take on two members, one of them female. A YouTube video gone viral later, Oblivion is heading to the top faster than they ever dreamed. If the band doesn't break up—and hearts don't get broken—before they manage to sign their first recording contract.

ROCKED

Music saved him, but now it's keeping him from the only woman he craves... Hot nights with a naughty, inventive rockstar are one thing, but more isn't on the playlist. Until Deacon's dream with his best friends starts turning into a nightmare, and Harper begins to see the real man behind the façade. Except Harper has her own dreams to chase, even if what she's started with Deacon might be the most important one of all.

ROCK, RATTLE & ROLL

Loving in fast forward... A beachfront cottage, hours of alone time, and plenty of skin on skin action is just what the rockstar ordered. Until the future once again comes much quicker than Deacon and Harper expected, threatening to crumble not only their perfect honeymoon but also their brand new marriage.

TWISTED

Sometimes the knight in shining armor needs to be saved himself... Being the rhythm guitarist in one of the country's hottest bands with his best friend Jazz is Gray Duffy's dream come true. Now that they're making music together, the time is right for Jazz to make a move toward the man she loves. If the secret he's keeping doesn't destroy them—and their band.

UNTWISTED

Falling in love was easy...figuring out the rhythm of being a couple, not so much. Now that they've pressed play, life is going way too fast for Gray Duffy and Jazz Edwards. A super hot video has boosted their band Oblivion's popularity even higher, and suddenly Gray and Jazz are the reigning prince and princess of rock. But as their private wedding ceremony in their treasured place approaches, they realize they can't go forward without facing their roots.

DESTROYED

Only one woman has ever refused him...and she's the only one he wants. Now that he's beyond successful with Oblivion, lead singer Simon Kagan is enjoying his all-access pass to the groupie train. But from the moment he met Margo Reece, he knew the classy, buttoned-up violinist was different. After an amazing night in the studio, he's finally connected with someone on a deeper level—only to have her walk away without a backward glance. Except maybe Margo is ready to take a walk on the wild side...or even fall in love with the one man she was never supposed to. If it's not already too late.

CONSUMED

Is it better to burn out or fade away... Oblivion lead singer Simon Kagan is used to being in the spotlight, but not because of the epic ending to Oblivion's last show. That unforgettable night rocked the band in more ways than one, and now the journey back seems almost impossible. The only bright spot is

Margo. As long as she never realizes the man she fell for no longer exists, maybe he won't lose everything that matters due to just one all-consuming night.

SHATTERED

He's shattered…and she's the only woman who can help him pick up the pieces. Nick Crandall has everything he ever thought he wanted, but it doesn't stop his dream from shattering, right before his eyes.Until the person he least expects pulls him back from the brink. Ripper Records exec Lila Shawcross isn't about to let a hot-headed, hard-bodied lead guitarist wreck her orderly existence or dilute her focus from managing the band. Except Nick is determined to possess her…and what Nick wants, Nick gets.

FUSED

They're shattered…and he's the only one who can fuse them back together. From the pinnacle of success to the depths of despair, Oblivion has been through it all. Nick Crandall is the only one who can begin to put the pieces back together after the most catastrophic night of his life. And that includes making a stand to win back the woman he needs. His only choice is to fight hard and dirty for what—and who—he loves.

OWNED

Music kept them going. Now it's torn them apart… Guitarist Nick Crandall lost the most important thing in his life—his band—just as he was falling in love. A year after going on hiatus, Oblivion is returning to the studio and he's about to ask the woman he loves to marry him. Simon has spent the past year trying to find his way back to the thing that sustained him in his darkest hours, then grew to be his biggest demon. With Margo's help, he's ready to admit it's showtime. It's do or die, one more time.

Lost In Oblivion

the Series

SEDUCED (intro)

ROCKED (book #1)

ROCK, RATTLE & ROLL (book #1.5)

TWISTED (book #2)

UNTWISTED (book #2.5)

DESTROYED (book #3)

CONSUMED (book #3.5)

SHATTERED (book #4)

FUSED (book #4.5)

OWNED (book #5)

OUTTAKES

extras for people that just can't get enough of the Oblivion peeps

COMMITTED (book #3.7)

GIFTED (book #4.2)

MERRY OBLIVION (book #5.2)

IF YOU'D LIKE MORE INFORMATION ABOUT THE SERIES & EXTRAS, PLEASE VISIT ROCKERREADS.COM.

Taryn Quinn is the redheaded stepchild of *USA Today* bestselling authors Cari Quinn & Taryn Elliott. We have been writing together for a lifetime–wait, no it's really been only a handful of years, but we have a lot of fun. Sometimes we write stories that don't quite fit into our regular catalog.

Do you like shorter and dirtier reads?

Anything goes with this penname.

- Sexy—check.
- Erotic—check.
- Sweet—usually mixed in with the sexy…so, yeah—check.
- RomCom—check.
- Dark—oh, yeah…check.
- Paranormal—check.

Did we mention that we like all the genres?

So, c'mon in. Light some candles, pour a glass of wine…maybe even put on some sexy music.

For more information about us…

tarynquinn.com
tq@tarynquinn.com

www.ingramcontent.com/pod-product-compliance
Lightning Source LLC
Chambersburg PA
CBHW061947170626
46813CB00006B/2563